THE LIAR'S CODE

AN ANDREA KELLNER MYSTERY

DANA KILLION

Obscura Press

1

What a dumbass move. Did this guy really think no one would notice a cockroach sandwich?

I stared out the window of the cab, watching the Chicago cityscape flash by, torn between revulsion and stunned confusion over how customers of The Chicken Shack hadn't run away in droves. The local chain was six small joints on the South and West Sides that specialized in fried bird, and its owner, Orlando Gaetano, was scheduled to appear this morning at the Cook County Circuit Court. Allegedly, Gaetano was too cheap to put in proper hygiene protocols to keep the crunchy critters at bay but somehow found enough cash to stuff an envelope for the safety inspector every quarter.

It didn't matter how fat those envelopes were, eventually, roaches dropping from the ceiling into your mashed potatoes and gravy was something you couldn't brush aside as a one-off. In a normal city, the health inspector would have shut this food-poisoning incubator down long ago, but in Chicago, greased palms were not only the first line of defense but the shield of authenticity.

I'd been covering the latest legal maneuvers in the case for

Link-Media ever since a whistleblower inside the Department of Public Health spilled the beans. Over the past ten years, the chain had seen numerous small fines thrown their way. From where I stood, those fines seemed to be nothing more than a slap on the wrist now and then to keep the obviousness of the scheme hidden, but Gaetano's attempts at making himself out to be a reformed business owner never lasted beyond a payroll cycle or two, according to the employee rumor mill.

It was an incredibly shortsighted business decision, as the odds were high that eventually word was going to get out and customers would start voting with their wallets, or a serious pathogen would be traced back to the joint if it caused a major illness or a death. And those were far more painful legal and financial issues than small fines. Apparently, this guy was a bigger gambler than I was. And someone inside had taken it upon himself to right the wrong—or mete out some payback, perhaps.

Repeated safety violations were nothing to sneeze at, but the real story, in my mind, wasn't the conditions at the restaurant but the bribery. How had he pulled that off? Granted, the residents of Chicago needed to know that spending their hard-earned cash at The Chicken Shack might come with a stomach pump or explosive diarrhea, and I was happy to splash that all over Link-Media's home page, but bribery of a city official was a notch up on the *big-story* pyramid.

If the outcome was simply another wrist slap, I knew that three months after this ordeal, Gaetano would re-open under new management with a new name and try to pull this shit again. If I could forever associate him with the nickname Cockroach King, it would taint anything else the man tried to do in the food service industry, regardless of new signage, and hopefully prevent a few cases of listeria in the process.

The health inspector was the weak link in this story. If he

was taking payola from one loser, he was likely taking dough from others as well. So as I neared the courthouse, the questions in my mind were: Who else was playing the game? Were there any other inspectors on the take, and did it go any higher in the department? In other words, what did this guy's supervisor know or not know? And was he involved?

I jumped out of the taxi at Washington and Dearborn and headed into Daley Plaza, where a gaggle of attorneys and plaintiffs stood in small groups chatting, scrolling their phones, or just getting fresh air before hours spent indoors waiting for their turn at bat. The skies were clear and the temperature perfect. September in Chicago was about as good as it got, and I looked longingly at an open bench.

As I strolled toward the building, not wanting to rush the weather experience, I caught sight of my dear friend Cai about fifteen feet ahead of me involved in an animated conversation on her cell.

A legal bulldog working for one of Chicago's big five firms, she could spar with the best of them, and she knew the Daley Center as well as she knew her own apartment.

"Hey, are you out here avoiding a client?"

She turned at the sound of my voice and smiled. Her long dark hair was pulled back in a clip, and she wore one of her many "You're damn right I'm an attorney!" tailored suits.

"Hi! That call was with someone I wish I could avoid," she said. "He's a massive pain in the ass. One of those clients who thinks because he has been a CEO and watched a lot of legal dramas on TV, he knows what the hell he's talking about. I would dump him in a heartbeat if he weren't a neighbor of one of the partners."

"In other words, you're going to be bitchy until the damn case is done."

"Bitchy? Me? Never." She gave me a disarming smile.

I loved Cai's utter intolerance of fools. Although always the consummate professional, Cai knocked back any man predisposed to thinking Asian women were the meek, retiring types. Inevitably there would be a "come to Jesus" moment the minute they tried to manipulate her. Her sweet smile could quickly morph into fangs when some guy was being a jerk.

"It just means I'm going to need to spend a lot of time with you. Someone has to remind me that the world can be rational. Are you free tonight? A night on the terrace at Nico sounds divine. Or is Michael monopolizing your time this evening?"

"I'm all yours. Meet you there at seven?"

"Works for me. But I'm starting to think Michael and I should work out some shared-custody arrangement. Or will I have to ask my secretary to schedule you a month out, as I'm forced to with my married friends?"

She narrowed her eyes and gave me her infamous attorney glare. The one she used liberally when she thought a defendant was full of shit.

I had been dating Detective Michael Hewitt for just over a year, and Cai had started dropping little annoyance bombs into our conversations now that there were additional demands on my time. I knew she liked the guy, but these jabs were coming far too often not to be noticed. My relationship with Michael was complicated enough—our jobs, our romantic history—and tension with Cai over it wasn't a pleasant thought.

"Shouldn't you be heading inside?" I asked. "I assume you're not standing in Daley Plaza just to enjoy the weather."

"In theory. Today is a role-reversal day. I'm testifying in this really messy divorce." She let out an exasperated sigh and shot her eyes toward the nearest cluster of folks out of caution. "I handle some of the legal work for the wife's business, and her jackass of a husband, who also happens to be an attorney, is questioning her business valuation in their divorce. He wants to grill the forensic accountant, the bookkeeper, the office manager. And he wants to grill me. Basically, I think he's another one of those dipshits who wants to bankrupt her through legal fees just for spite."

"Should I assume the husband is representing himself?"

"But of course." She laughed. "Big surprise, right? The arrogant ones are always the worst."

"There is nothing pleasant about divorce, but when the plaintiff and the attorney are the same, as the saying goes, someone has a fool for a client," I added.

"Anyway, our judge has been delayed, so I'm hanging outside waiting for the update, or to be told I can take my toys and go home. What about you?"

"I'm scoping out a preliminary hearing. That guy I told you about, the one who owns the chicken joint and has been paying off the health inspector. Not that I wanted to think about insects for breakfast, but I think the inspector might be a bigger story, so I'm going to suffer through a discussion on rodent and insect droppings to see if I can get any read on whether there are others involved."

"Don't let it ruin your appetite for dinner," she said, shifting her bag higher on her shoulder and glancing at her phone.

The sound of a car laying on its horn, long and loud, made us both jump, and we turned in unison toward the blare. Just fifteen feet away, a black Escalade with tinted windows was blocking the entrance to the alley that led to staff parking. Probably some foolish suburban limo driver being lazy as he waited to pick up his client. The Lexus sedan behind him was none too happy, hitting his horn again.

Clearly, the driver of the SUV didn't understand downtown Chicago etiquette or he would have inched forward just enough to let the sedan pass without abandoning the prime double-park spot. When the Escalade made no effort to move, the Lexus hit his horn hard and didn't let up.

"I think we might be in for a little road rage if this SUV doesn't get his ass out of that spot in the next half second," Cai said, amused. Weather and bad driving were the topics of at least fifty percent of all Chicago conversations, with local sports or politics filling the rest.

The loud screech of the horn was now drawing the annoyed stares of others in the Plaza as the sound reverberated off the glass and steel high-rises surrounding us. A light beep here and there was par for the course in downtown living, but pushing the horn and holding it for longer than five seconds wasn't part of our social contract.

"Is the driver even in the Escalade, or did he park and run?" I said.

Just then the door to the Lexis opened, and a tall thin man exited the vehicle and began an angry march toward the SUV. His jaw was set, and I could tell by the look on his face that he had a few choice words in mind. If it were a few degrees cooler, steam would have been forming on his wire-rimmed glasses.

"Looks like my guy has finally arrived," Cai said. "That's Bradford Reynolds, the judge in my client's case. Good. If he can get this jerk to let him into the parking garage, I should be ready to roll in a few minutes."

Abruptly, the front doors of the SUV swung open, and two men dressed all in black, rubber Halloween masks over their faces and guns drawn, approached the judge. Cai and I stared in stunned silence as Reynolds stopped in the street, arms raised, a look of terror on his face.

"Go ahead, take the car. Keys are inside. I don't have any cash on me. Just take the car," he said, his voice holding just a hint of waver.

The men stared each other down. People around us were

beginning to notice and scuttle away. My eyes locked on the guns, I slowly slipped my hand into the outer pocket of my bag and wrapped my finger around the plastic case of my phone. Shielding my activity as much as I could, I dialed 911 and raised my phone while Cai grabbed my arm and started pulling me back.

"What's your emergency?" said the voice on the other end of the line.

A shot rang out before I could respond, then another, and another, and Reynolds slumped to the ground. Screams filled the air around us, and my heart drummed in my chest. I watched, frozen in place, as the shooter jumped back into his SUV and his partner into the Lexus, speeding off, tires squealing as Cai and I stared at the blood pooling around the man on the ground.

Cai and I ran to the judge as the vehicles pulled away, crouching down at the victim's side. I grabbed a cardigan out of my bag and stuffed it futilely into the gaping wound in the man's chest, then updated the 911 operator while Cai checked for a pulse. She shook her head while we stared at each other in silent disbelief.

A small group of people began to hover around us. "Is he dead?" "Did you see that?" "Right here in Daley fucking Plaza!" The voices of shock. Already a police siren wailed in the distance.

"Good riddance."

I turned toward the icy voice behind me that had uttered the hate-filled comment, seeing a middle-aged white man with gray wavy hair and an ill-fitting suit buttoned over his enormous stomach. He stared at the judge dead on the ground, his face in a snarl, while another guy beside him nodded in agreement.

"The son of a bitch deserves what he got," he continued. "His kind don't deserve to make judgment."

2

EMTs and police cruisers screeched to a stop, lights flashing and sirens blaring minutes after the shots rang out, parking just beyond where the two vehicles had initially stopped. Cai and I remained crouched, helpless alongside Judge Reynolds's body, not wanting to leave him, as professionals with medical equipment and a stretcher reached us.

Although it seemed obvious that the man was dead, I still held pressure on his chest with shaky hands, not knowing what else to do, as dark red stained his crisp white dress shirt and blood pooled on the blacktop in an ever-growing puddle. His wire-rimmed glasses had been thrown as he tumbled to the ground, landing next to his head, and one brown leather loafer had slipped from his foot in the fall.

Cai's eyes were riveted on me, her mouth agape, her phone ringing repeatedly, still in her hand, seemingly unaware of its draw. I didn't know how well she knew the man or whether their only association was her current case. The judge worked in the domestic relations division, and she handled corporate law. I assumed they would've had little reason to interact professionally outside of their current case.

The shock in her eyes was a reality I knew only too well. Seeing someone killed before your eyes, particularly someone you knew, is something never forgotten, and Cai would live with the rawness of this memory for quite some time.

As the EMTs organized their gear and stepped toward the victim, the crowd of onlookers increased, drawn to the chaos. I could hear snips of speculation about what had happened as it filtered through the medical chatter. Two police officers pushed back the crowd and established the perimeter while Cai and I remained glued to our spots.

Another officer knelt next to me. "You can let the pros take it from here," he said gently.

I lifted my bloody hands, but I couldn't pull my eyes away from the stillness of Reynolds's face, watching for any slight eye movement or facial twitch that would tell me the man wasn't really dead.

The officer led us toward a police vehicle, where an EMT poured water on my hands and handed me a towel.

"Can you tell me what happened here?" the officer asked.

I glanced at his badge, which read Acevedo, and then at his probing green eyes. He stood, classic cop stance, feet spread, thumbs hooked into his belt, looking from me to Cai.

Cai still seemed unable to find her voice.

"The victim is a judge named Reynolds," I said, my pulse pounding with adrenaline. Stress sweat dampened the back of my neck, and I clenched my hands into fists, trying unsuccessfully to still them.

"Bradford Reynolds," Cai added, coming out of her fog. "He works in the domestic relations court system. I was supposed to see him today."

The officer winced slightly, and I assumed he thought Cai was a plaintiff in a divorce case.

"It wasn't her divorce," I said. "My friend is an attorney, corporate law, and she was here to give testimony. Apparently, the judge was delayed, and we were standing out here on the sidewalk talking when the incident occurred."

I wasn't sure why I was telling him about the case or why we were standing outside, but the unimportant details spilled out anyway.

"There was a vehicle," I continued. "An SUV, blocking the parking entrance when the judge drove up. He honked a few times, but the car didn't budge, so Judge Reynolds got out to have a word with the driver. Before he got within ten feet of the car, two men got out and just shot him."

The basics of the story tumbled out of me, partly from shock, partly from my professional background kicking in. Minutes mattered, and the quicker the cop got a handle on what happened, the quicker he could get the right people doing their jobs.

The officer turned and motioned to one of his colleagues. When his partner arrived, he continued with his questions, both men watching us intently.

"What happened after they shot him?" Acevedo asked.

"One guy got back into the SUV, the other jumped in the judge's Lexus, and they both sped off, north on Dearborn and then a left on Washington, I think," I said, looking toward Cai for reinforcement.

A familiar face appeared next to the men. Michael. The officers nodded in recognition. He looked quizzically from me to Cai before giving me a small smile, his eyes speaking in a way his words couldn't. We were always cautious about revealing our relationship outside of the safe bubble of Cai and Michael's partner, Karl Janek.

"Did these men say anything before they fired? Was there an exchange?" Michael asked.

His eyes were soft, watching me for signs of distress, and I could see worry etched on his face. Knew he wanted to pull me close and make sure I was really okay.

"Not a word, at least not from the shooters. The judge saw the gun immediately," I responded. "Told them to take the car, that he didn't have any cash. They just stood there and shot anyway."

"And did you get a look at these guys? Can you describe them?" The second officer was now joining in, jotting down notes while he asked the standard questions.

"That's another strange thing. They wore masks. Rubber Halloween types," Cai answered, her shock waning. "Not sure what characters they were supposed to be, but you know what I'm talking about, right?"

The cops looked at each other, saying nothing, using the unspoken language of cop eyes to do the work for them.

"They were two guys of medium build and average height," I added, my former prosecutor background finding its way to the surface. "They wore gloves and masks and dark clothing. Black long-sleeved T-shirts, black pants, no logos. There was no skin showing to identify race and nothing unusual about their bodies. I know it's not helpful, but that's what we saw. It seems pretty obvious that these guys planned to attack the judge. Or if not the judge himself, perhaps another judicial employee. I believe this parking lot is reserved for judicial staff, judges primarily."

Michael's eyes drilled into me, and I didn't need to know the cop code for what that look meant. He knew I was already racing ahead of the facts, projecting possibilities for consideration, wondering what was behind it all. And I knew him well enough to know he was doing the same.

"But why take the car? If they just wanted to kill the guy, they didn't need to jack the Lexus too," one cop said.

"Tell me about the vehicles," the other officer prompted while Michael remained silent, his mind active with potential scenarios.

"The shooters drove a black Escalade," I said. "Tinted windows. So, it was tough to see if anyone was in the vehicle at first. I assumed it was a limo service waiting on his fare. I'm no car expert, but it was a fairly recent model. No obvious scrapes or dings or stickers. As I said, the judge drove Lexus, a sedan, silver, an LS model, I think. If there were any markings, I didn't see them."

"Did you catch the license plates?" Michael asked.

I thought for a moment, then shook my head. "Illinois plates, but now that I think about it, I don't think they were livery plates. Maybe an Uber? I didn't catch anything else. Cai, did you?"

I watched as she racked her brain for a moment. "I also thought it was probably a limo service. They double-park all the time, but I can't be certain about the plates. I was more focused on..."

She trailed off as the clang of the ambulance door closing jolted us, pulling our attention back to the victim. We watched solemnly as the vehicle flipped on its siren and lights and pulled away from the curb.

Officers in the forensic team had cordoned off two lanes of traffic and much of the immediate sidewalk and were now tagging spots for further analysis. Location markers dotted the blacktop. A shell casing. A footprint. What appeared to be tire marks. All were being photographed and bagged and prepped for analysis back at the forensics lab.

I glanced around, looking for security cameras that might have captured the incident, noting them on posts at the entrance to the alley, and knew there were others, given the significance of the government building.

"Okay, we'll need your contact information," Officer Acevedo said.

Cai and I fished out business cards, handing them to the officer.

Acevedo looked at me, then shrugged at Michael. "She's a reporter. That's one way to hop into a story. I guess I know what you're doing after we leave." He rolled his eyes and flashed the card at Michael, who gave me a small grin.

"Gotta use the opportunities as they present themselves," I said out of habit, feeling the instinct to protest the vulture side of my profession.

The two officers left us, moving toward the rest of the team, who were now questioning bystanders. With any luck, a license plate number would come out of the canvassing or the recorded video footage.

"Are you guys okay?" Michael asked, looking from me to Cai, who still seemed unsteady. I'd been in a version of this place before, had seen death occur before my eyes, had nearly been a victim myself. It wasn't easy and would never be okay. Cai, however, lived in a world where the worst of the crime she'd experienced was audacious embezzlement. Although insidious and evil, white-collar crime lacked the gut punch of a bloody body, and I knew that this would have repercussions on her psyche.

"I think I'm still in shock," she said. "It's not quite sinking in that this really happened right in front of me to someone I knew."

"How well did you know him?" I asked.

"Well, I suppose I knew *of* him would be more accurate. We worked in completely different areas of the law, so I never appeared in his court. But the judicial community is small.

Everyone knows of everyone through reputation or functions or minor city political associations. To be an African American judge in any city, even one the size of Chicago, brings some level of extra attention, so he was well known. I'd spoken to him at a conference once or twice, but that's it. His reputation is for being firm but fair. I understand his wife died of cancer last year. Not sure if they had kids..."

Her words trailed off again, and we were left wondering whose world would be shattered today with the news.

"Are we free to go?" Cai asked. "My client is probably wandering the halls frantically, thinking I've abandoned her. She's the emotional type, and she's probably left me a dozen phone messages."

"Got to get back to my client" was Cai spitting out the professional line, but I suspected she wanted to run as far away as she could get from the images now burned into her brain. Shut it off for now so that she could process her emotions later.

"Yes, you can go," Michael said. "Reach out if you remember anything else."

"Touch base with me later about dinner," I said. "If you're not feeling up to it, I understand. This kind of emotional stuff can sneak up on you."

I gave her a hug, and Michael and I watched silently as she walked toward the building.

"Are you okay?" he asked.

I shrugged. There were no words that could explain the emotions that swirled inside me after witnessing a violent end to someone's life, and I wanted his arms around me. Stealing a glance at the officers nearby, I smiled but couldn't lean against his chest. Not now, regardless of how much we both wanted that.

The deeper we got, the harder it was becoming to insulate our romantic relationship from our professional lives. Michael's partner, Karl Janek, knew, of course, and we downplayed any rumors that popped up, but there would be a reckoning at some point unless one of us made a sudden career change or the relationship fizzled out.

Coming out of a marriage tainted with infidelity, my trust in the male species, as well as the institution itself, was still shaky. I didn't know if I'd ever be ready to recommit to marriage, or fully to Michael, for that matter. I didn't want to date anyone else, and I was deeply in like with the man, but the fear of losing myself to love was overpowering, holding me back from the commitment Michael seemed ready to make. How he could be so certain? Had he simply had more time to package up the baggage of his own divorce, or had he not fully processed the lingering emotional side effects?

"I should get back to work," Michael said, reaching over and running a finger along the side of my hand. "Call me later, okay?"

I said I would, then watched him walk away, still feeling his touch and feeling myself flush with confusion.

Shaking it off, I moved toward the courthouse, expecting to find the building had been locked down over the incident. Pulling my phone out of my bag for a status check-in with the clerk on my case, I saw the man who'd made the disparaging remarks about Judge Reynolds. He was leaning against one of the pillars, a raggedy briefcase resting at his feet.

His jacket was open, and he'd loosened his tie, but the smirky grin was still plastered on his face as he took a call.

The words he'd uttered standing behind me came back, as did his tone, while I watched him tug on the collar of his shirt.

His kind.

I rushed into the Link-Media office, adrenaline still coursing in my veins, having accomplished nothing I had intended to this morning. But I had a new story. The killing of a domestic relations judge right outside the courthouse in broad daylight. It had locked the building down and cancelled all the proceedings that were scheduled for the day. The Chicken Shack's owner would have a brief reprieve from uncomfortable questions while the calendar was reworked, not that it would prevent the inevitable. But who needed him when I now had a front-row ticket to the story of the day?

Staff stood huddled in front of a bank of televisions watching the coverage of Judge Reynolds's murder as I entered the space. Heads turned toward me as I traversed the large loft, faces wearing that strange journalistic mix of envy and curiosity when forced to watch the car wreck from the sidelines.

Brynn Campbell, one of the junior reporters who did double duty as my research assistant, came straight toward me, her eyes full of questions as she followed me into my office, a venti coffee in hand, as usual.

After tossing my bag on the desk, I threw open my laptop.

My mind was racing through the incident, fearing I'd forget a small but crucial detail. Needing to capture the intricacies of what I'd seen and heard while it was all still raw and fresh, I played it all back in my mind. My thoughts ricocheted from the fear in Judge Reynolds's voice, to the explosion of the gun, to the image of his body as it collapsed on the pavement. I could feel my shoulders tighten again and my breath clench in shallow bursts as I relived it.

"Were you there?" Brynn asked as she hurried into the room. Sliding her athletic frame into the chair across the desk, she watched me expectantly, awaiting the download.

"Hold on. Andrea, what happened to your shirt? Is that blood?"

I looked down at my rolled cuff, where a red stain the size of a silver dollar marred the light gray silk. I shuddered again at the memory of the blast, the image of Judge Reynolds as I knelt over his lifeless body and tried futilely to stem the tide of blood from his chest.

"So it is." I stared at the crimson spot, feeling my body recoil again as the jolt of the shot piercing the air filled my memory. I'd taken a small piece of his life, his essence, with me.

I let out a breath and looked up from my sleeve. "I never made it inside the courthouse. Before the session started, I was outside talking to Cai. Judge Reynolds was shot right in front of us. He wasn't more than fifteen feet away."

"That's his blood? Tell me what happened!" Her innocent brown eyes were wide with alarm. Barely out of college, she did not yet view the world through the jaded eyes of a journalist. Neither did I, but I was twelve years her senior and better at masking it.

"I'm still not entirely sure what happened," I said, hearing my voice waver, still grappling with the reality of what I had seen and the deliberateness of the killing. "It looked like the shooters had planned a carjacking and didn't care how it went down. Blasted the judge in the chest when he tried to confront them."

Images flashed again like a slide show. Reynolds standing outside his car. The gun raised, pointing at his chest. The puddle of deep red blood spreading around the body.

"Hey, you with me? Can I get you something? All the color just drained out of your face."

I shook my head. "Even when you see it happen, it's hard to wrap your head around what you saw. Doesn't seem real. As if your own eyes are gaslighting you."

"Did the judge try to fight them off or something?"

"No, not even close. He threw up his hands and said to take the car as soon as he saw the gun."

"Are you thinking this is about something more than a car?" Brynn asked, sensing my unease, her intuition kicking in.

"Well, the shooters wore masks," I began. "You know those rubber types that look like past presidents or famous people."

I grabbed a pencil and made a half-assed attempt to sketch the features embedded in rubber before they faded.

"Sounds like that movie *The Town.* Do you remember it? The one where the bank robbers dressed as nuns."

"That's exactly what it was like," I said, my mind searching back for the storyline. "The shooters were two men in a dark SUV. Tinted windows. They blocked the entrance to the parking garage so the judge couldn't pull in. Got out of the vehicle and flat-out fired when he approached them, then drove away with his car."

"The first press pass is playing this as just two guys with anger management issues. Sounds more like an ambush."

"I agree. But honestly, I don't know if they were targeting Reynolds specifically or if this was just horrendous timing and he was the unlucky victim. He was a judge with the domestic relations court division, but I don't know if that's relevant," I said, wondering about Reynolds's own family and the heartache that was hitting them today. "The shooters didn't say anything at all. It seemed so deliberate."

I was grabbing at my gut for answers. Searching for possible motives. Masks. The direct, calculated attack. It just didn't scream carjacking to me, but I also didn't have any other explanation.

"Maybe someone was mad about their alimony payment. But that would be a hell of a way to decide a divorce case."

Brynn threw out the obvious, although extreme, first thought: anger over a judicial ruling.

"Divorce is horrible, but that seems a bit over the top, even for one of the tough cases. And this was an organized hit. If someone gets dead in a divorce, it's usually a spouse or a lover, not the judge. I saw the whole thing happen, and I couldn't tell if the judge was a target or if these guys were simply determined to pick off the next unlucky person who drove up. That garage is for judicial staff only, so maybe they figured it was an easy way to heist an expensive car." It sounded preposterous, even to me. My gut told me this was about something else, but I was too close, too wrapped in my own experience of it to frame out my questions right now.

"Also seems like an extreme way to jack a car," she said, pondering the motive. "The sentence for murder is a hell of a lot worse than auto theft."

"True, in theory, but since these guys had guns, carjacking holds a penalty of up to fifteen years. A murder rap would depend on whether someone convicted them of first-or second-degree murder. Skilled legal wrangling might convince a jury that the shooting wasn't premeditated, although the disguises would argue against that. If so, they could get off with a sentence of under twenty. Since they pulled this off in Daley Plaza in front of witnesses, it would be a ballsy argument, but you can be sure any decent attorney would have to try."

"Do you have any other plausible scenarios for why they shot this particular guy?"

"My mind is a little mushy right now, but if he was targeted, that opens up a whole new set of possibilities. Knowing nothing about the man, it's tough to go there. I mean, the guy was a judge. His background would almost have to be squeaky clean."

I paused, letting my mind rumble.

"What?" Brynn asked. "I see that look. You have another idea?"

"Well, I was just thinking about your reference to that movie. The guys who wore masks in the film were bank robbers. Reliance Bank is across the street. Maybe the SUV was just parked there because it was convenient and they had an inside team in the bank? Maybe the SUV guys were the getaway car, and the judge got in the way."

"So they panicked and shot him? And then the judge's car could be used, too?"

"A gift with purchase. May as well nab it and send it to the chop shop for a few more dollars or use it for a vehicle switch after the robbery. Serves a purpose either way."

"Did you see anything else funky going on to support that? It's not Halloween for another six weeks, so I expect masked men would stand out."

"Not a damn thing." I shook my head. My eyes swung back to my computer screen for a moment. Was there something I had seen and not yet made a connection to? "Maybe it will come to me later. Observational skills lose a little strength in the middle of something like this. Anyway, the courthouse went on lockdown, and the restaurant hearing is being rescheduled. I'm going to write up what I've got on the judge's killing now and get a draft in to Art before regrouping."

Brynn left, and I did a quick scroll through Twitter to see what coverage of the incident had already been released, then hit the keyboard. My fingers flew, chronicling details and observations as the images flooded back. For now, there was no order, no chronology. I simply let my memory release onto the screen.

A half an hour later, thoughts organized, I walked into managing director Art Borkowski's office with a draft, ignoring the curious faces of those around me who were dying to hear details.

I had inherited Link-Media eighteen months earlier, after my estranged husband had been killed, but my interests and skills were better suited to staying on the reporter side. Coming out of a storied career at the *Chicago Tribune*, Borkowski handled the day-to-day decision-making and editorial approval. It was an odd dynamic as the two of us sorted through who had the last word, but after an initial rough start, we were bumbling through.

"Here's a first pass," I said, shoving two pages of copy under his nose, not needing to explain further.

He grabbed my document without looking up from the stack of papers in front of him. Despite our structure as an all-digital news organization, Borkowski couldn't seem to rid himself of the paper habit. Old school worked for him. I'd made a few attempts to bring him into the twenty-first century, even pointing out the money spent on printer cartridges as part of my argument, but to no avail. This old dog did not like new tricks.

"We have an angle no one has," I said. "I mean, my hands were stuffed into the man's chest. I think there's a lot more to come on the case, but this gives us a good edge."

I needed to explain none of this, yet the banality tumbled out of my mouth, an effort to sound objectively journalistic, I supposed. Or maybe it was my own trauma processing what had happened.

He scanned my copy over the top of his tortoise-shell reading glasses.

"Just the right amount of gore and human drama," he said, nodding. "This works. Okay, you had convenient timing, Kellner, but what's not being told? What's next?"

"Not clear yet. Cops are going with carjacking. I didn't see anything that would suggest otherwise. Of course, I'll keep on it, but it's not obvious yet."

"The masks put a question on that, don't you think?"

"Agreed. But at this point, the only thing I can say with certainty is that they planned this. Whether Reynolds specifically meant something to them or any car that fell into the trap would do, I can't say."

He redlined a few lines of text and handed back the sheet.

"Get this on the site and do your tweety thing, since that's apparently what serves as the delivery vehicle of choice these days." His tone was a mix of disgust and confusion whenever the reality of social media was foisted upon him. "My father would turn over in his grave if he knew what had happened to his beloved newspaper industry." He shook his head and shooed me out with another flick of his hand.

I held back my eye roll until out of Borkowski's sight, made my corrections to the piece, and posted. Then stared at the bloodstain on my blouse that I could not unsee. I shuddered again and then forced my eyes back to the screen to check the coverage the competition was posting before pulling out my notes on the health inspector.

Nestor Morales was a twenty-year veteran with the Public Health Department. That was a lot of rodent droppings to see in one lifetime, a lot of stinky garbage, and a lot of grease traps. I wondered how much the city paid for this thankless, but necessary, job. Like most city positions, you were lucky if it was an almost-decent middle-class living, provided your personal situation didn't have any extenuating factors.

Was Morales acting out of greed or hardship? It probably didn't matter as far as the legal case was concerned. A bribe was a bribe, but if his involvement could be proven, hardship might pull a few heartstrings with the right jury.

It also brought my thoughts back to Judge Reynolds and my eyes to the blood, his blood, I had taken with me. Did something lurk in his background? Money was a powerful motivator.

4

———

The pungent aroma of garlic and hot grease permeated the windows of my Audi as I sat, waiting for Mateo Ortiz to show his face. According to a Chicken Shack employee I had been pestering, Ortiz had been a prep cook there for five years but was now working for the Chef Boyardee of Italian restaurants, Pasta Perfect. The current employee had been reluctant to talk, but eventually, I'd annoyed her enough that she'd passed on Mateo's name to get me to leave her alone. This employee claimed Ortiz had been fired under sketchy circumstances, and sketchy circumstances were a reporter's dream scenario.

Lifting a travel mug of Earl Grey to my mouth, I took a sip, contemplating the revolving door of employment that was food service and how this bribery scenario might play out. How many employees had passed through the hamster wheel that was this one restaurant chain? Surely someone had stories to tell about their boss.

And did someone have stories to tell about the inspector, too? If there was a payola relationship between Morales and Gaetano, it was easy to assume there could be others who had been offered an inspector special. Straight-up greed and the story was basically told. If this was nothing more than a couple hundred bucks here and there, it wasn't front-page material. But throw a challenging personal financial situation into the mix, and that could mean the inspector needed more cash than one small restaurant chain could provide—and therefore more participants. Or maybe his boss was involved, too? Getting his own cut. Maybe even steering the ship with Chicago's version of "You pat my back, I'll pat yours." That made it company-sanctioned graft. A side hustle. I knew I was reaching, but this was Chicago, after all, with a deep pay-to-play history that extended even further back than the Al Capone gangster years. And a city that birthed corrupt aldermen like rabbits.

I'd been parked on the street on the west side of the restaurant where Ortiz now worked for almost forty-five minutes and still had seen no sign of the guy. Rather than making me hungry, the odors were souring my stomach. I flipped on the A/C even though it was only 75 degrees, just to get the stench out before my hair smelled like sautéed peppers.

It was nearly four o'clock and too early for the early bird special crowd, but the staff would be well into prep for the upcoming dinner rush. A handful of late-model cars were jammed into the tight space behind the building next to the dumpster, leaving what precious parking there was open for paying customers. I stared through my windshield at pedestrians' faces, assuming the guy would be on foot. Like most Chicago neighborhoods, street parking here in Little Village was a fraught affair full of confusing permits, an hour spent circling the block for an open spot, and short time limits on the commercial streets, so driving to work was annoying, at best.

My source claimed Ortiz worked the dinner shift Monday, Wednesday, and Friday, but I had yet to match anyone to the photo I'd seen on his Facebook page. Unless he had snuck in the back entrance or called in sick, my target was eluding me. As I waited, I scrolled my phone out of boredom one more time, calculating how much longer I should sit here before pushing off the task for another day.

My Twitter feed buzzed with commentary on the judge's death. Most of it was banal or inane. Scanning for any tidbits that seemed inflammatory or overly personal, I looked for postings that might spark a hint of the man's backstory, perhaps by a disgruntled neighbor or former friend inclined to weigh in.

My article was gaining eyeballs, but so much of the story felt untold. Several texts to Michael confirmed that CPD had not yet identified the SUV, nor had they found the judge's Lexus. Not surprising. It was probably already at a chop shop in Indiana. What I couldn't let go of was why kill the guy? He had offered up the keys. Willingly handed them a seventy-thousand-dollar car without a fight, so why shoot the man? He wasn't some fool trying to play tough guy over a hunk of metal. Knocking him to the ground with the butt of the gun would have been just as effective. Killing him made no sense if this was just about the car.

A CTA bus squeaked to a stop across the street. After the bus continued its route, I watched a man cross over toward the lot. Mid-thirties. Stocky. Hispanic.

I plopped my tea back in the cupholder, grabbed my bag, and beelined for the guy.

"Excuse me. Are you Mateo Ortiz?"

He stopped, giving me a confused look. "Yeah, who are you?"

"My name is Andrea Kellner. I'm a journalist with Link-Media," I said, handing him my card. "I understand you used to work at The Chicken Shack, the one over on Cermak."

He perused my offering before responding. "So? Who hasn't? What about it?"

"You're making it sound like it's a revolving door. Why is

that?" I watched his face as he sized me up, seeing the reaction I'd grown familiar with. *What the hell do you want?*

"Because it's food service," he said, as if it were the dumbest question he'd ever been asked. "Because the pay is crap. Because they treat people like shit. Duh! You've been living in Lincoln Park too long, lady, if you need someone to explain that to you." He looked me up and down, taking in my leather shoes and silk blouse.

I ignored the dig. "Well, the way you said it, I thought maybe there was a bigger problem at The Chicken Shack compared to other restaurants. Did I misread your comment?"

"Everybody I know can tell you about half a dozen jobs they've had that were no different. More if the place hires undocumented workers. Come on, you know this. Everyone knows how it works. If you're thinking this is some big exposé, reporter lady, let me tell you, no one cares. People just want their damn food, and they want it cheap. They don't care that the guy scrubbing their dishes is living on seven bucks an hour. Or that some guy named José has to get to work at five a.m. to meet the delivery truck. Or that four other people are still working at two o'clock in the morning, bagging trash and cleaning out grease traps."

"But they care that their food is safe to eat."

He looked at me, then shot his eyes to the ground, shaking his head. "So that's what this is about. You want to talk about the King of the Chickens?" He laughed and kicked at a plastic bottle top at his feet. "Good luck with that. I gotta go to work."

"King of the Chickens? Is that a name you've given him, or is that what everyone calls him behind his back?"

"That's just my little pet name for him. *Depravado*, or sleazebag to you white folks, is what everyone calls him."

"You do mean Orlando Gaetano, right? The owner? I hear he fired you. Is that why you call him a sleazebag?"

"Hold it, lady. I didn't do anything to get myself fired. Gaetano just makes shit up when he doesn't like the look of your face anymore. Doesn't matter how long you been there or how good you are at your job. The minute you do something horrible, like asking for a raise one too many times, he cans your ass."

"You were fired because you asked for a raise?"

"Like I said, he's a cheap son of a bitch, and the last thing he wants is anyone around with an opinion or a mouth. Open yours and you're gone. You put up with his shit and stay quiet, or you're out on your ass. There will always be some other fool desperate for a job, or with a sketchy job history, or just so damn broke they'll take anything. Most of us aren't working in this industry because we have a lot of options. Gaetano knows it and takes advantage. And anyone who needs to suffer through that environment is on a short leash. The store managers are just mini versions of this goon, doing his bidding. Right before I got canned, one of my coworkers, Sebastian, demanded overtime pay for the sixty-hour workweeks he was putting in. Threatened to report Gaetano. Surprise, surprise, a week later the assistant manager 'accidentally' splashed hot grease on the guy's arm." A scowl of contempt washed over his face. "That was just a warning."

Based on the narrative playing out in the bribery case, I wouldn't have expected Gaetano to be a model businessman, but an intentional burn was another thing. And if he was willing to infect his customers with disease-carrying insects, what else might he be doing to shave expenses to line his own pockets?

"That's extreme." On its face, I wasn't sure I bought the grease-burn-as-threat story, but I tucked it away. "How do I get a hold of your friend Sebastian?"

He looked up at the sky and shook his head with a sigh. "I'll see if he wants to talk. He works the lunch shift at a place in the

Loop these days. More than anyone, he knows what Gaetano is really like and still has the scars to prove it."

"Gaetano sounds like a total ass," I said. "I assume employee relations weren't the only area where he played fast and loose with the law." Ortiz's hatred of the man was crystal clear, but would he take it a step further and help me out? "While you worked at The Chicken Shack, did you ever see health inspectors on-site?"

He looked at me and clenched his jaw, calculating my motives, I assumed, and his risk.

"So that's what this is about. You're looking for dirt on the inspections. You're hassling the wrong guy. Nothing good will come out of it, not for me. I got fired from one job for opening my mouth. Do you think employers like it when staff bad-mouth owners?" He nodded his head toward the restaurant. "I don't need them thinking I'm some troublemaker. I'm still on probation, and the quickest path to ending this job too would be my name in print trashing my former boss."

He shook his head and stepped toward the door.

"What if we talk off the record?"

He stopped.

"I won't use your name or any information that might compromise your identity. If this guy is as bad as you seem to think he is, shouldn't people know about that?"

He turned. "I don't know. Look, I'm not going to shed a tear if King of the Chickens gets dumped with an enormous pile of chickenshit, but there are a lot of good people who depend on those jobs, even if he is a corrupt tyrant. What happens to them if the boss man goes down?"

We looked at each other for a moment. I couldn't argue with his concern for his former coworkers, but how long would it be until someone died of food poisoning? A slap on the wrist wasn't going to turn Gaetano into a changed man.

"I'm going to be late for work. I gotta go." Ortiz turned toward the building.

"I understand your concern," I said to his back. "But one way or another, there will be consequences that affect the business, and therefore the employees," I added. "It might not hit them now, but it will eventually. What if someone dies from food poisoning?"

He turned, grimacing at my drama ploy, but I had his attention.

"If something horrible happens, those jobs will be gone," I said. "What isn't clear yet is how big of a problem this is. I want to know how long this has been going on. Is there more than one inspector involved? What if other restaurants, places Gaetano isn't involved in, have been paying off inspectors too? I understand your hesitation. You're concerned about the people you know who are forced to work in these awful conditions because of circumstances. What I would ask you to consider is how you're going to feel if we learn customers are being seriously sickened, or if someone dies, and you had knowledge that could have prevented it."

5

"Are you okay?"

Cai was sitting on the outdoor patio at Nico Osteria when I arrived, ice melting in a glass of amber liquid on the table in front of her. Still in her work clothes, she'd removed her jacket and pulled out the clip that held back her long dark hair. Her eyes were closed, and I wasn't sure if she was blocking the late-day sun or squeezing in a mini meditation. Her lids popped open as I pulled out a chair, and she looked up at me lazily.

"It's a shame that we only have another six weeks of this weather before being pushed back into dry, overheated rooms and fuzzy sweaters." She smiled, but without her normal spark.

"Seriously, Cai, how are you?" I tapped her glass. "If you're drinking scotch, I know that this wasn't one of your smoothest days."

On the surface, Cai's emotional body armor often appeared impenetrable. It was one reason she was so damn good at her job. The arrogant, corporate bulls she typically had as clients would never tolerate frailty, real or perceived, in an attorney. But we were practically sisters. I saw the cracks and knew when her interior world was on shaky ground.

"I keep replaying the tape," she said, leaning her elbows on the table, her eyes searching mine. "I keep seeing him fall. Seeing his last breath. All that blood. I keep running scenarios where I could have done something to change the outcome. I know I couldn't have stopped what happened, but my brain goes there."

"Of course it does. You knew the man, and that makes it all the harder. It's a normal reaction, at least from anyone who possesses empathy. There was nothing either of us could have done other than get shot ourselves," I said, laying a hand on her arm, glad I'd had time to change out of my bloodstained blouse. She didn't need a graphic reminder of what had happened earlier. "Try not to beat yourself up. Easier said than done, I know, and very clichéd, but it's true."

My thoughts flashed back to the night my former husband, Erik, had been killed in front of me. I still heard the gunshot ring out. Still felt the blood drain from me as I played back the moment his body went limp. I couldn't stop my mind from cycling through those memories any more than Cai could stop hers right now. The feelings of conflict and guilt and horror were still with me, even though we'd been mid-divorce at the time. Shock still infiltrated my thoughts despite the amount of time that had passed.

She nodded and lifted her glass to her mouth. I flagged our server and ordered a Nebbiolo and two different crudo plates for us to nibble on while we decompressed and enjoyed the early fall weather, along with half of Chicago, it seemed. The triangle of streets around neighboring Mariano Park housed a mini restaurant row in Chicago's Gold Coast, sporting half a dozen eating establishments and a constant parade of bodies looking for food porn or engaging in sidewalk social life.

"Did you get any work done today?" I asked. "Given the security situation, they pushed back my preliminary hearing. I assume your testimony was moved as well."

Knowing Cai, she'd marched back to her office and busied her mind with a legal brief, trying to minimize any emotional impact of the shooting. But trauma popped through, like it or not, conveniently timed or not. Even the most engaging of paperwork would not keep her from experiencing after-effects, even if they didn't fully hit her until much later.

"Yes. Lucky me, I get to reshuffle my calendar again after they assign a new judge so they can take another go at this ridiculousness." She scowled. "This divorce case is getting completely out of hand. This will be my fourth rescheduling with these people. All it takes is a front-row seat to a couple of these bad ones, and you'll swear off marriage as an institution. Hard to imagine why anyone does it. Oh, sorry. Present company excluded."

"No need to remind me of my marital history. The world must be full of hopeless romantics, because the habit doesn't seem to stop. You never go into the relationship thinking you're going to become a statistic, yet the odds are pretty depressing." Thoughts of my marriage, thoughts of Michael's increasing desire to move in together, and fears of being hurt again all cycled through my mind.

"Maybe we're just not meant to be monogamous for a lifetime? Maybe the whole concept needs to be rethought and the legal process, too? I don't see why prenups aren't mandatory or why the marital contract can't be chunked out in five-year terms."

Cai's love life required a scorecard. It was a first date here, two months there, or who-was-that-again source of entertainment for her. She'd kick the guy to the curb whenever boredom set in or the poor slob dared to put demands on her time. At least, that's what she claimed. My view was that she simply hadn't met her equal. Occasionally, I envied her no-strings-attached views of dating, but the guy-of-the-week wasn't part of my makeup. Although, the current flavor of the day had hung in for a few weeks so far. Maybe the tide was turning.

"So romantic of you." I raised my glass in a toast. "Tell me about this case again. Why exactly are you involved? I'm not sure I was following when you told me earlier."

"Good question. The bottom line is my client is married to a psychopath. And a psychopath attorney at that."

"Those aren't the same things?" I laughed. Attorney jokes were always the favorite of attorneys, even when they knew them to be based in truth.

"Haha. I'm not sure making fun of your former profession, and your best friend, is a good life strategy right now." She lifted her eyebrows in feigned disgust before flashing a smile. "Trust me, this is the kind of guy who's responsible for at least seventy percent of the bad lawyer jokes. You've seen the type. He's one of those screaming, yelling, everyone's-wrong-but-me guys that give our profession a bad name."

"They're also the type that grossly overestimates their skill," I added. "Maybe we should just call them narcissistic bullies and be done with it."

"Yep, this guy is a walking billboard for the dangers of narcissism. He's found reason to oppose everything. None of her chosen experts are good enough. He thinks the discovery documents were fabricated. He's gotten one judge to recuse himself from the case over false claims of conflict. If I were a judge, I wouldn't want this man in my courtroom, either. The only reason I'm still in the mix is that there isn't anyone else he can squeeze. He's disputing the articles of incorporation, for God's sake. Trust me, I'd kick the whole thing to the curb if I could. And if she thought she could get away with it, my client would take a flamethrower to his Lamborghini. This man is sick. I don't know how she tolerated eighteen years of him. Thankfully, I'm on the fringes of this mess."

The case sounded awful and the man even worse, proving once again that marriage could be as complicated as an unsolvable riddle. Toxic narcissism and lawyering was the worst possible combination, yet the power position of attorney often attracted the type like honey.

"Makes for an awful lot of billable hours, however," I said.

"I don't want to earn my money that way. But I suspect she's surpassed the price of a really great car and is moving into suburban home territory by now with her overall billing."

"What part of the dispute requires your involvement?"

"I got dragged into this because I set up the legal structure for her salons and have helped her with her expansion plans. She owns five locations at this point, has franchised two more, and wants to continue down that path. We pulled in a forensic accountant to value the business, of course, but Mr. Jerk claims we're all part of some grand conspiracy to undervalue her assets to disadvantage him. It's bullshit, of course, and I have no idea what new light my testimony will bring to substantiate his claim, but he wants to go there, so I have to show up and pretend to play nice."

"To what end? I assume she's the one that filed for divorce. Is this revenge gone wild?"

"Personally, I think this is his version of torture. As you surmised, he's representing himself, which means his expenses are just time and energy. My client, on the other hand, is paying through the nose for ridiculous and excessive legal requests."

"Is he trying to break her financially?" I asked, nibbling on a piece of yellowtail.

"That, or to wear her down so much that she says the hell with it and gives him anything he wants just to be rid of the man for good. It's a power struggle for this guy, nothing more. He needs to win any way he can. Thank God they don't have kids or he'd be in her life forever. With Reynolds dead, her time frame is now shot to hell. I feel sorry for whoever the new judge is. Getting up to speed is going to be an ordeal. There are libraries with fewer pages of reading material than this case."

"Maybe it's a diversion?" I said, thinking back to a fraud case I remembered from a few years ago. "Scream so much here that she won't look over there at his financials?"

Could Reynolds's carjacking be a distraction?

6

———————

Junk. Junk. And more junk. I scrolled through the emails that had arrived overnight, looking for subject lines that suggested content that wasn't a random, poorly directed marketing attempt. I was hoping Ortiz, the prep cook, had softened his stance and reached out, but my wishful thinking wasn't handing over any gifts just yet.

Although he hadn't been willing to say much yesterday, the cringe he gave me when I ratcheted up the guilt trip told me I'd put a minor crack in his shell. Maybe his conscience would get the better of him over the next few days. If not, I had at least primed the pump for a future conversation and another layer of guilt.

What Ortiz had delivered was the allegation of an intentional retaliatory burn. If true, that spoke volumes about the ruthlessness of management, and perhaps Sebastian was pissed off enough to talk.

What I needed was someone in the Health Department to lay out for me the operational standards and how tightly the inspectors were leashed. I raised my head above my computer screen, hoping to catch Brynn's eye, then motioned her over.

"What's up?" she asked, unfolding herself into the chair on the opposite side of my desk.

Brynn was my secret weapon. A name, a data point, a statistic—there was little she couldn't pull out of hiding, given the time. She was also snarky as hell. The occasional staff meeting tête-à-têtes between her and Borkowski were so amusing that there was rarely an empty seat in the room as the encounters had become must-see events.

"I need research on the processes used in the Health Department. Food inspections specifically. I want to understand the scope of individual inspectors' responsibility, and how they're assigned. Reporting structure. Whatever you can get."

"Is this about the chicken story? I know you don't find it as funny as I do, but come on, there is a little poetic justice in there, right?" An amused smile spread across her face, and she pushed up the sleeves of her Oxford shirt.

"No, I'm not amused. It's horrifying that so many people regularly eat all that greasy, deep-fried, artery-clogging crap, let alone risk listeria infections on top of it. And since you seem to find Cheetos a major food group, why is this funny to you?"

Brynn's diet was a constant source of confused horror to me. If it didn't come from the junk food aisle or a fast-food joint, she didn't eat it. The closest thing to a fruit or a vegetable I could remember seeing her eat was ketchup.

"I just keep picturing some poor schmuck digging into his sandwich, not realizing part of that crunch is fried bug. There is a certain element of karma to that, don't you think?"

I shuddered at the image once again.

"I'm not sure which is more damaging, crunchy critters topping off the meal or the meal itself. And to answer that, we'd need to get into a conversation about nutrition, the overall health of the American people, and a medical system focused on peddling pills. So, perhaps we should table, pun intended, that conversation."

She looked at me with a smirk, enjoying my disgust with the subject matter. Processed snack foods were not leaving her diet anytime soon, and Brussels sprouts were not leaving mine. It was one of our agree-to-disagree topics.

"What I'd like you to find out is whether they routinely assign the same inspector to the same restaurants, or do the inspectors rotate? I'm curious about their territory. How many locations they're responsible for, et cetera. The lawsuit is focused solely on The Chicken Shack, its owner, and the one inspector, but I'm wondering if there might be other restaurants pulling the same scam with this guy's help, or maybe other inspectors are involved who haven't been caught yet."

"In other words, is this just one rotten apple, or is more of the barrel rotten, too?"

"Cute. But you're not going to try to use that as your argument not to eat fresh fruit, are you?" My mom voice was poking through, the one I normally only used on my sister, Lane. Brynn smiled and shrugged, taking no heed and probably wishing she had a Snickers. "This could also be a situation where the inspector's boss was taking a cut, too," I added. "If so, you might want to reconsider some of your dining choices or you could be the one munching on fried insects."

One restaurant spreading disease would not change Brynn's food choices, but maybe she'd reconsider hole-in-the-wall indie joints with what-you-don't-know-can't-hurt-you mottos when she needed to get her fix. She rolled her eyes, then gave me a wink as she left.

A flash on the TV screen in the corner of my office caught my eye, and I turned up the volume. The annoying young twit from Channel 32 was mustering up a stern look and flicking back her hair outside the courthouse. She regurgitated the briefest of details on the judge's shooting without adding a shred of new information, as usual. This chick had not been hired for her intellect. Carjacking. End of story. She'd at least mentioned the shooters had been masked, but her tone was more about creating a layer of fear in the public rather than educating. Although I had no information to the contrary, the explanation just wasn't sitting well. They hadn't needed to kill Reynolds to get his car. So why had they? I couldn't shake the thought.

I switched off the twit-wit, grabbed my phone, and called my contact in the Public Affairs Office at CPD. Sensitive to protocol, she never gave me more than the official police department talking points, but we had developed an informal code of long pauses and strategically placed emphasis that occasionally told me I was on the right track.

"Hey, Janet. It's Andrea."

"I've been expecting your number to show up on caller ID. You waited a whole day to check in on the Reynolds murder. I'm impressed."

"Well, since I had my hands in the man's bloody chest, I've had plenty of material to work with."

"Sorry. That sounded callous, didn't it? I've spent too much time in the emotional void of Copland. I just assume everyone is an unfeeling prick." She chuckled. "Hey, don't quote me!"

"I know better. You'd never take my calls again if I did."

I didn't know if the rumor mill at CPD had sent any rumblings about me and Michael in Janet's direction, but every time I spoke to her, I was expecting, "Is it true?" As if I needed another reminder of how foolish it was to be involved with a cop.

"You doing okay?" she asked. "Beyond the obvious unpleasantness of blood and gore, of course."

Unpleasantness? I guess that was one way to minimize a lost life. Geez, even the administrative staff was jaded.

"Yeah, sure. Not my first rodeo," I said. It wasn't worth the energy to say any more than that. "Look, I'm following up on a tip I got. Did you guys get any calls yesterday about activity at Reliance Bank? The one on Dearborn across from Daley Plaza?"

She didn't need to know the only tip was my imagination. If it got me something, a minor stretch of the truth was worthwhile.

"Reliance Bank? That would be news to me. Someone tying this to Reynolds?" she asked.

When I didn't elaborate: "Hold on." And I could hear the click of keys on the other end of the phone.

"Nothing showing up, but if it was some dumbass annoyance call, I wouldn't hear about it."

"Anything in the recent past at Reliance? No foiled robbery attempts or incidents that journalists didn't think important enough?"

"Last time they got hit was two years ago when someone tried to jack the money truck. Unsuccessfully, I might add. I think your 'tipster' probably has it wrong, or just got confused. Happens a lot when there's a commotion. People speculate. Everybody wants their fifteen minutes."

"Yeah, you're probably right. Thanks for checking. And you better call me first if there's anything new on the Reynolds case."

"You keep trying, but this isn't a 'first dibs' office. I gotta talk to all you people. But if there's going to be an announcement, hint, hint, I'll give you a heads-up so you can make sure your calendar is clear."

"Fair enough. But I'm not going to promise I won't keep trying to wiggle in ahead of the pack."

"I expect it." She laughed. "Luckily, your tenaciousness

rarely crosses over to obnoxious, but if it does, I do have a naughty list, and you don't want to be on that."

I leaned back in my chair after the call. My thought that yesterday's confrontation might be tied to a heist attempt wasn't yielding any fruit, but that still didn't rule out these guys being the getaway car for another crime. Maybe they panicked when a wrench was thrown into the works. They could have aborted early before their robbery intent was clear.

The other possibility was that Judge Reynolds had been the target of a direct hit and stealing the car was simply icing on the cake. The ugly words from the man at the scene came back to me. *His kind.*

I glanced at the clock. It was nearly nine, which meant my two favorite cops were likely sitting down for coffee. I sent Michael a text, grabbed my bag, and headed out the door.

I saw Janek's chiseled face in the back corner as I walked in. He lifted his brows when he saw me, then said something to Michael. The guys were tucked into their regular corner booth at their coffee shop of choice. An old-school diner in the Loop where their cups were never empty and their meals always on the house. It was home away from home for these two whnever a case didn't require them to be out of range when the mood or the stomach called.

My eyes lingered on the back of Michael's neck as I got close, feeling the urge to nibble on one of his favorite spots. Instead, I behaved myself and slid into the booth next to him, letting my gaze do the talking. Janek cleared his throat loudly, and Michael shot me one of his "not in front of dad" smiles.

"Going for the low-fat meal, I see," I said, leaning over to look at the plates mounded with fried potatoes, eggs swimming in grease, and corned beef hash buried in ketchup. Not a fruit or healthy vegetable to be found. Michael scooped up a forkful of potatoes dripping with oily brown liquid and offered it to me. I rolled my eyes and shook my head while Janek snorted a laugh. If they'd had more notice, they probably would have pranked me with thick slabs of Spam topped with Doritos and fake spray cheese just to watch the look on my face as they ate.

I flagged over the server and ordered tea.

"So, what brings you over here? Just miss my smiling face?" Michael said, his eyes full of things unsaid.

"Of course. You don't think I came for the food, do you?"

Janek sighed heavily on the other side of the table. "Would you two cut it out? I'm trying to eat here."

Janek was one of the few people aware that our professional relationship was also a hot and heavy personal one, but that didn't mean he wanted to be reminded of it, and a quick kiss, despite the urge, was out of bounds.

"Have you found Judge Reynolds's car yet?" I asked, easing into the subject.

"Please, that car is in fifty pieces and being scattered around the country as we speak," Janek said, barely stopping to take a breath between bites of corned beef.

"You don't really think this was a simple carjacking, do you?" I asked.

"Here we go," Michael said. "Lois Lane is off on some new conspiracy storyline. What now? You may as well put it out on the table. There is some wild-ass theory bopping around that beautiful brain of yours. You may as well spill it before our breakfast gets cold."

His tone was playful, but sometimes I couldn't tell whether I was amusing him or annoying him.

"I'm just trying to figure out why they killed the guy. The judge wasn't armed. He was annoyed, but not threatening, and the minute he saw the gun, his hands were up. He offered them the car. All they had to do was jump in and drive away, if that's what they wanted. So why didn't they? I just don't see a logical reason, based on what I saw, for them to shoot."

"First off, you have to stop assuming criminals are logical," Janek added, wiping ketchup off his lower lip. "Second, sometimes these guys answer everything with a gun. It's how all disputes are settled in their world."

"So, if this wasn't a carjacking, which is what you seem to suggest," Michael said, "what exactly is your theory?"

I had known these men long enough and shown sound enough instincts that they no longer brushed me off immediately, but it was still a delicate game. I dangled a theory. They refused to confirm. I read between the lines based on how vehemently they said nothing and learned a lot from how quickly they grimaced.

"I'm wondering about a backstory. Maybe this is some jerk with a grudge. A case that didn't go his way. Something racially motivated, maybe," I said, thinking about the "his kind" comment.

"I hear you, but the guy was a divorce judge. Everybody hates them," Janek said. "Not as much as divorce attorneys, but it's built into the job. That doesn't mean someone's gonna knock the guy off just because they don't like the visitation schedule they got." Janek shrugged as if the idea was ridiculous. "And suggesting that sporting dark suits and rubber masks is the latest Klan costume is rather nutty."

"Racists don't need an outfit to be racists, and I'm not saying they killed Reynolds because of his ethnicity, but it feels like a hit. The shooters played it out like it was something right out of a movie plot, masks and all. It may look like a carjacking on the surface, but I'm wondering if this guy was targeted, and if so, why?"

7

———————

aley Plaza hummed with men and women in dark suits and bulging leather briefcases in hand, scurrying toward the courthouse entrance, lost in their phones or in their heads, practicing their opening arguments. Their civilian companions, on the other hand, shuffled, worry on their faces over their upcoming court appearances. Looking at the surrounding normalcy, it was hard to fathom that only yesterday a man had been murdered here. That life, for some, had not been affected.

I scanned the perimeter, my adrenaline elevated, and I instinctively watched for dark SUVs and Halloween masks and wondered how many security cameras had recorded yesterday's incident.

The spot on the street where Judge Reynolds had lost his life was still cordoned off, and my chest tightened at the sight of the stain on the pavement. Without thinking, I found myself walking back to the curb, back to the spot the murder had taken place. Would anyone lay flowers at this spot or memorialize his passing here? Or would his dried blood become the debris of city life, something to be washed away by the street sweepers the next time they passed?

I pulled my eyes from the stain up toward the steel-and-glass structure behind me and shuddered, wondering if any of the judge's staff had witnessed his death from the windows. Pushing the thought out of my mind, I headed toward the building.

The judge's administrative staff was likely shell-shocked this morning, wondering what to do next and how to process the loss of someone they worked with so closely. There would be a whole host of in-process proceedings that were now disrupted. Likely, the entire domestic relations court would be in some level of disarray as other judges became responsible for pending cases and dealt with the shock and grief of losing a colleague.

Despite Janek's dismissive reaction to my questions, I couldn't let go of the thought that Reynolds's death had been a hit—a dispute, an angry defendant, or even something in his personal life. His administrative office was my first stop. I knew enough people in the court system and how things operated to make my way into the building. But would anyone talk to me?

I passed through security and went straight to the third floor, where I followed the narrow hallway. The administrative staff was tucked away in the judicial maze out of sight of litigants or devastated family members, but close enough to the action that attorneys and judges could get to the office quickly.

Tiana Williams was the clerk who ran Judge Reynolds's schedule and the person most likely to have insight into his personal life. I sensed the emotional disarray as soon as I entered the cluttered space. Instead of staff concentrating on their computers or being buried in the avalanche of paperwork that was still a crucial part of the court process, small groups of people huddled, whispering, hugging, shock etched in their eyes and in their shaky hands. Those forced to hover over their keyboards by some necessary deadline or because distraction kept them from crumbling at the loss looked stricken. Confused and grieving, their faces were ashen, and tissues sat nearby.

I stepped up to the first desk and asked if I could speak with Ms. Williams. The woman nodded and called over to her coworker, flipping a hand in my direction. Tiana was round in the right places with cheeks red and blotchy, made even more obvious by her white hair.

"My name is Andrea Kellner," I said when she approached. "I'm with Link-Media. I was wondering if I could speak to you for a moment about Judge Reynolds."

"I'm sorry, I can't talk to the media. You'll have to go through the division administrator," she said, her voice breaking, then she sniffed and dabbed at her nose. Her eyes were bloodshot pools, and she clutched a soggy wad of tissues in her hand.

I looked at her hard. "I was there," I said softly. "I was there when it happened. My friend and I are the ones that called 911 and stayed with him."

Her mouth trembled as she stared back, fresh tears spilling onto her cheeks. Making no attempt to stifle them, she nodded. "Let's go to the conference room."

As her coworkers watched, I followed her to a bland beige room outfitted with a table, a gaggle of chairs, a big whiteboard, and the ubiquitous fluorescent lighting that made everyone look like they were about to retch.

"Please, have a seat. I'm sorry. Can you tell me your name again? My mind isn't working very well today. We're all so stunned. Not much work is getting done, but we all seem to need to be here anyway."

She sat clutching her shaking hands on the table in front of her.

"I understand. It helps not to be alone during a tragedy. I'm Andrea Kellner. I'm with Link-Media." I laid a business card in front of her.

She nodded and dabbed at her nose. "You said you were there. Did you see it all happen?" Her face seemed frozen in fear, as if she'd rather not know any more than she already did.

"I'm afraid so. The shooter's vehicle was blocking access to Judge Reynolds's parking. When the SUV didn't respond to his horn, the judge got out of his car to ask them to move, but instead, two men got out of the SUV and just shot him."

"I heard they wore masks," she said tentatively, her eyes cast at her hands.

"Yes, Halloween masks."

I watched her face, checking for some recognition or shift that would tell me she'd been expecting something, but I only saw more tears.

"I know this is rough, but can you think of any reason someone might want to harm the judge? Had there been any threats or any unusually hostile cases he was involved in?"

She looked up, her watery eyes full of questions. "You don't think it was a carjacking, do you?"

"If it was, it seems unusual to me," I said tentatively.

I wasn't sure how much to say. I had questions but no answers, and my journalistic speculation would simply add to her burden when there was already too much.

"How so?"

"Well, from my vantage point, it seemed planned. As if they were waiting for him. Or at least waiting for someone. And Judge Reynolds didn't fight. He offered up the vehicle the minute he saw the gun, but they fired anyway. I came here because I'm wondering if you know about anything going on in his life, personally or a tough case, even if it seems harebrained, it might lead to an answer."

"I don't know. The man is—excuse me, was—a divorce judge. I can't believe that he's gone." Her voice cracked with the words. "I've worked here for almost twenty years, eight of those for Judge Reynolds."

She paused to collect herself, the shock still staggeringly fresh.

"Ending a marriage isn't exactly happy stuff for anyone to go through," she continued. "I've been there myself, and I'd rather cut off an arm than go through that again. But normally, it's not the judge that gets the brunt of the heat. Attorneys and your ex, that's where the venom is directed. Ninety percent of these things are wrapped up outside of the courtroom, anyway. I don't see this as a pissed-off dad taking his revenge. Maybe if it were a dead attorney, I could see the argument. You should hear some of *those* stories." She grimaced. "It baffles me that anyone would voluntarily become divorce counsel. You see people at their worst, then become their closest confidant, and they hate you in the end, resenting every dime they had to spend getting through the divorce, regardless of the outcome."

She'd nailed the sentiment, and I smiled to myself.

"Was there anything in his personal life that might have been challenging for him?"

"Last year was a rough one for his family. His wife, Eileen, died. She had pancreatic cancer. Suffered for about two years before she lost the battle. They tried everything. Surgery, immunotherapy, even a bunch of really out-there alternative therapies at some clinic in Mexico. And that stuff isn't exactly covered on the government insurance plan. It was all out of pocket. God knows how much that cost. But they were determined to do everything humanly possible to treat her, and it might have given her a few more months, but ultimately, it just wasn't enough."

"He must have been devastated," I said, imagining the roller coaster of stress and fear, not only for his wife but for the complications throughout their lives. Cancer was a family disease in the same way addiction was.

"He hasn't been the same since. They didn't have kids, but it's as if a light had been turned off inside him. He went through the motions here at work, but he was flat, robotic. Just didn't seem to have any joy left in him anymore."

"Is there anything else that comes to mind?" Given what Reynolds had been through, I imagined financial concerns were likely as well.

"Well, it's pretty hard for a Black man not to have some haters. Those kooks locked back in the fifties segregation mind-set don't take kindly to an African American man in power. Most of what we've seen here in the courthouse is the subtle stuff. You know, those people who would argue to the death they're not racist and then use dismissive language in the next sentence. A Black man has to be twice as good at his job to get the same level of respect as the white guy with the same title and the same experience."

"Just like women," I added.

She chuckled. "Sad, but true. He looked past that garbage. He didn't have the mental energy or interest in trying to set someone straight about their racist tendencies. He was here to do his job, and if somebody didn't like the color of his skin or the texture of his hair, too damn bad. Their problem, not his."

"Did anyone step over the line? Perhaps threaten the judge?"

I was running through the obvious stuff, hoping for a tidbit that could direct me down one rabbit hole or another. This was how investigations worked. Gather as many bits as you could and hope some of them started a picture, but in the beginning, all you had were random puzzle pieces that may or may not belong to the story.

"It happened now and then. There'd be an occasional letter from some bozo who said he should be dead or an email talking about the awful way they wanted him to die. Of course, these are the types of fools who never have the balls to identify themselves. They're just cowards with mouths. We send those messages over to the sheriff. Standard protocol for all the judges. I don't know what else they do other than increase security now and then."

"Do you remember anything specific, or perhaps an individual who was particularly vile?"

"Every now and then, these racists come out from beneath the rocks they've been hiding under. We don't pay them much mind. The only recent one I remember is this guy who got his shorts in a bundle and kept ugly-tweeting at the Cook County Court about Judge Reynolds being corrupt. Judges aren't on social media. I'm sure you can imagine why. The court let us know as a matter of protocol. Or CYA, depending on your perspective. Why these dummies think Twitter is an appropriate legal communication tool is beyond me."

"Corrupt? Do you know what he meant by that? Do you remember the guy's handle?"

"Look, Twitter is just a place for windbags who can't handle pushback. We don't take any of that seriously. I imagine he was another one of those stupid narcissists who didn't like how his case turned out and threw out vague accusations of bribery because he lost custody of his kids. Reynolds would be the last guy to do anything even remotely illegal. I don't remember the creep's Twitter handle, but it started with something like Zippy."

8

With skyrocketing healthcare costs, medical tourism was an industry in itself, as individuals sought cheaper alternatives for plastic surgery, non-FDA-approved drugs, or anything else conventional health insurance wouldn't cover. In other words, desperation or cost drove the decision. And desperation was clearly the motive for the Reynolds family. However, flying off to some alternative clinic in Mexico for a stay wasn't cheap, nor was cancer treatment a one-and-done process. Reynolds and his wife likely made multiple trips, or she had stayed alone for an extended period. Regardless, the total expense could have easily moved into six figures.

Financial pressures were an interesting backstory. I took a seat at a cafe table under the Picasso sculpture in Daley Plaza to collect my thoughts on my conversation with the coordinator. If the judge and his wife were going as far as flying to Mexico for off-label treatment, "spend first, figure out how to pay for it later" was easy to imagine. While a judicial salary was nothing to sneeze at, it rarely supported unplanned six-figure cash expenditures, so where had the money come from? Had he mortgaged his house? Maybe a private high-risk loan?

I looked across the street at Reliance Bank, pondering other explanations for Reynolds's death. The lighted sign on the Dearborn side of the building flashed and sputtered as the letter *B* threatened to go dim, its bulb losing its juice. Not confidence inspiring. Although no attempted robbery incident had been reported, that didn't mean one hadn't been planned or aborted. I gathered my things and made my way across the traffic to the opposite side of the street and to the entrance just around the corner.

A burly man in a rent-a-cop security uniform stood on the sidewalk just east of the door, enjoying a smoke break in the pleasant September sun. With a thumb looped in his pocket and his head bobbling, he seemed more interested in the backsides of passing females than casting intimidating glares at potential wrongdoers.

I forced a smile and sidled up to the man. His radar activated, he swung his face toward mine, and I watched his bloodshot eyes slide from my face to my boobs and back up again. Subtle, this guy wasn't.

"By any chance, were you working yesterday during the shooting across the street?" I asked, trying to ignore his leery expression and wishing I'd worn a heavy oversized sweatshirt today.

"Yeah. Who wants to know?"

"I'm a journalist with Link-Media. Did you happen to see the incident?"

The spark in his eyes went flat as he realized I was not here to admire his masculine charm, but his gaze went back to my boobs anyway, out of habit, I assumed.

"Link-Media. Never heard of it. Sounds made up," he said.

I drew in a breath and reached into my bag for a business card, then handed it to him. The leery smile was back.

"So, this is you. You're Andrea? And this is your phone number?"

"Yes. Did you see what happened in the Plaza?" I asked, pretending I didn't recognize the innuendo. The delicate dance of not encouraging the guy while also not irritating him so much he wouldn't talk had begun. Maybe it was time to invest in business cards with a fake number or an answering service for emergencies such as this.

"I was out here havin' a cig. I pop out now and then if there are no customers. Gotta be seen. Make it clear to the bad guys that they'll have more than just a camera on their ass if they try something."

He puffed up his chest as he spoke, his body inflating with his bravado. Ego aside, by the look of his stomach, he wouldn't be wrestling anyone to the ground unless he fell on them. Whatever, it was his fantasy.

The screech of tires stopping short pulled my attention for a moment before I forced another smile.

"Wow. Then you had a front-row seat. You probably wanted to take those guys on, since CPD wasn't anywhere close." It made me feel a little dirty to play the flirt. I was bad at it in real life. Play-acting felt even more awkward. But guys like this seemed oblivious to the lack of authenticity, so I laid on my meager skills.

"Man, I was ready. I didn't notice right away. I was taking care of business here, ya know. But when that Lexus started laying on his horn, it got my attention."

"I bet," I said, feigning perkiness. "What did you see?"

He tossed his cigarette butt on the ground and stomped it out before responding.

"This big-ass SUV was double-parked. You know, the kind that doesn't fit right on city streets. I thought it was probably some arrogant prick from up in Lake Forest. They're always afraid of the big, bad city and can't be bothered to find a damn parking lot like everyone else. We get those types around here. Always think their business is more important than everyone else's. Blocking traffic and shit while they get their coffee or sign some document. City people know better than to drive one of those buses in the Loop."

I turned and shot my eyes across the street, checking his vantage point, noting that he would have had a good line of sight to the SUV from the passenger's side, while I'd had a view of the driver's side.

"But that's not who was in the car, right?"

"No, sure didn't look like some finance type to me. This other guy, the one who was pissed off 'cause he was blocked, goes over to tell the SUV to move his ass, and basically, the dudes in the SUV just got out and blew him away. That ain't the way the blue-suit crowd handles their grievances. I was on my way over but… can't leave the post, ya know. My priority is right here. Don't want someone thinking I'm distracted and they can get away with some bad shit while I'm occupied."

He rocked on his feet as if to show me he would have been over there in a flash under any other circumstance. He didn't look light-footed to me, but I didn't begrudge him for not throwing himself into the fray, regardless of his reasoning. The barrel of a gun would freeze most of us, as it should.

"Then what happened?"

"It was fast. One guy, down, bleeding out on the pavement, one shooter, back in the SUV zooming off, and the other jacks the dead guy's car. The whole thing was over in maybe sixty seconds."

"I assume the bank has security cameras," I said, my eyes running along the perimeter of the bank.

"Of course. We cover the doors here and in the back, and there are several inside, obviously. But nothing is angled across the street, if that's what you're wondering. We get footage as far as the corner." He jutted his chin in the direction of the Dearborn Street corner. "Not our job to monitor city buildings and all that."

So far, I wasn't learning a damn thing I didn't already know.

"Did you see the driver?"

"Nah, not really. He was kinda blocked by the car. I had a view of the passenger."

"Was there anything about the vehicle or the man you could see that seemed odd to you or anything that stood out as unusual?" This guy wasn't giving me anything, but I ran through the litany of obvious questions anyway.

"Other than he killed a guy in front of my eyes and wore a mask?" He smirked. "That big-ass SUV, well, it had a sticker on the back window. Rear passenger side. Bright red. Diamond shape, but on its side, with a white border. Couldn't read it from here, but it looked just like one I saw three or four days ago. That was a black SUV, too. The guy was parked right here, illegally." He pointed to a spot on the street in front of the bank marked *NO PARKING*. "He sat there for maybe fifteen minutes, so I go out to tell him he needs to move his ass, and he peels out as I got near the door and squeals around the corner. But I noticed that sticker. Hard to miss, being red and all. Said 'Abbiocco.' Would be really interesting if that was the same car."

9

———————

Patrons stood six deep at the reception desk as I walked into Proxi just before seven. I scanned the bar crowd, looking for Michael as I waited to check in, but he hadn't arrived yet. A young hostess in five-inch heels and perfect cat-eye eyeliner led me to our table. I ordered a bottle of sparkling water with lemon for the two of us and a glass of Nebbiolo for myself. Michael's taste in booze ran toward amber liquid served over ice, but occasionally he was in the mood for a beer, so I held off on pre-ordering his drink.

Leaning back against the upholstered bench, I relaxed into the music, the beautiful decor, and the animated crowd. After my encounter with the leery security guard, I'd returned to the office and hit the phones, hoping to find another Chicken Shack employee or the purported intentional burn victim. Someone inside had to be willing to talk about what they'd witnessed in health code violations, even if anonymously.

The data portal for the City of Chicago was a publicly available resource, and I'd spent several hours combing through it, searching by DBA, inspection dates, risk level, and looking at inspector summary notes and recommendations. Unfortunately, individual inspectors were not identified. Overall, The Chicken Shack showed a passable—but scant, for a fast-food joint—health inspection history. Their Yelp reviews told another story. Finding customers willing to talk was the easy part, but it wouldn't help me get at a broader issue if there was one. For that, I needed people who had been in the room when it happened.

Looking around at my fellow diners, I wondered if my restaurant habit was going to slow down because of this story, imagining myself checking the latest inspection report before taking a bite. Given the pricier menu in a place like this, I felt reasonably safe and resisted the urge to open my phone to check their history.

Greed and financial problems made people do drastic things, and Gaetano was no exception. Had Judge Reynolds been a desperate man? It was easy to imagine him as a man who would've done anything to save his wife, figuring it was a win as long as she made it through alive.

Tiana may have known Judge Reynolds for a number of years, but what she saw at work was not necessarily a full reflection of his personal life. There could easily be an unknown feud or a jealous lover or a former litigant whose life had spiraled down. What we thought we knew about someone was rarely the full unvarnished truth, and I wondered if Reynolds had some darkness in his past.

The sticker on the SUV. I'd almost forgotten. Grabbing my phone, I typed in *Abbiocco. The Italian expression for drowsiness that follows a big meal.* What was that supposed to mean?

I sensed him next to me before I saw him. Looking up from my phone, I saw Michael standing beside the table. A smile lit up his face, and his wavy brown hair looked as if he had just run his fingers through it. He leaned in for a kiss, and we let our mouths linger. I couldn't look at his gorgeous brown eyes without remembering his touch, the way his body felt against mine, without wanting more of him. With just a look, I could sink back into memories of rich, lusty moments together.

"Hi," I said, my voice husky. I let him pull away and slide into his chair, but my mind was already on after-dinner events.

He gave me a lopsided grin, then ordered a small-batch scotch I could never seem to remember the name of.

"You're not going to try to make me eat vegetables again, are you?" he asked, his voice playful.

"Of course I am. Man cannot live on rare beef alone. Although I know you'd like to try."

"Pommes frites are potatoes, so I think I'm covered."

I shook my head. Although he would never admit it, I knew I was loosening him up. I'd served him an arugula salad with olive oil, lemon juice, and shaved Parmesan last week and he'd eaten every bite, not complaining once about how disgusting green things were. Perhaps mounds of cheese were the answer to anti-vegetable biases.

"What did you and Janek do after I left you this morning?"

"Oh, you know, cop stuff. Fighting bad guys. Investigating crimes," he said, giving me a big grin.

I rolled my eyes and gently flipped him off.

"Ouch," he said.

"You need to be careful with that attitude. One of these days, I am going to turn the tables and start evading your questions myself."

"You know I do that just to get a rise out of you."

"There are far better ways to do *that*," I said, my mind back on pillow talk.

"And I can't wait for you to tell me all about it a little later," he said, running a finger along the side of my neck.

"Hmmm. It would be my pleasure. We'd better hurry up and order, then."

Michael laughed, and we settled on a selection of small plates to share.

"This is nice, isn't it? Us?" Michael said as we worked through burrata with sunchokes.

"Very. Eat faster."

I shot him a smile intended as provocative, but the expectant look I saw on his face told me he had something more to his question.

"When am I going to be able to convince you we should do this every night?"

"You want to eat out every night? That's a big credit card bill." I was deflecting. He wasn't referring to how often we explored Chicago's wonderful restaurants, and I knew it. I also knew I didn't want to talk about what he really meant.

He squeezed my hand again and leaned toward me. "You know what I mean. Don't pretend to be coy. You're not very good at it." He was smiling, but his eyes were deadly serious. "Aren't you ready yet to fall asleep together every night? To wake up together every day? You know I am. I've been ready for a while. I haven't changed my mind. I still want that. I want us. Are you ready for that?"

The tightness in my chest crept down to my stomach. He'd shifted the tone of the evening in a handful of words, sending my feel-good endorphins scattering.

"You've been so patient, and I appreciate that more than I can tell you," I said slowly, searching his eyes. "But I'm just not ready. I don't want to end what we have, but I can't make a commitment like that. It's not that I want to see other people. I don't. Please don't take it that way. But living together, just the thought of it, with anyone, makes me hyperventilate. I have to be truthful. This is too important of a decision. I'm scared, Michael. I wish I could tell you I just need a couple more months, but I don't know that to be true either. What we have is the best I can manage right now. I know you want more, and if at some point you feel my hesitation is getting in the way of your needs, and you need to end this, I'll be so incredibly sad, but I would understand."

I watched his body deflate as I spoke, just as it had on the two previous occasions he'd broached the subject. It pained my heart to hurt him, and the thought that he might need more than I could give was both real and uncomfortable. I didn't want to lose him, but I had good reason for my reticence, and trying to pretend it away was simply a recipe for disaster. Perhaps not immediately, but after the thrill of playing house wore off, I knew I would be back in a place of uncertainty. I couldn't do that to myself, and more importantly, I couldn't do that to Michael. It wasn't fair to either of us.

"I'm trying to remain patient. Right now I want you in my life however you can meet me. But I can't say I understand, not completely. Maybe it's because I've had more time since my own divorce. Or maybe I just don't understand the pain you've been through when it comes from a place so deep. I didn't experience betrayal, not the way you have. I'd like to understand, because then maybe I could help you believe I will never hurt you like that."

I looked at Michael, my heart full of love for him, but I had felt full of love for Erik, too, and it hadn't stopped what he'd done. Hadn't stopped how he'd hurt me. I had no simple answers for Michael. There was no instruction manual or time frame on trust. But my trust problem wasn't Michael; it was me.

How could I trust myself again when my instincts about Erik had been so wrong?

"Just continue to be patient," I said, knowing I was asking a lot of him, knowing I risked losing him. "Give me time and space and consistency."

He nodded. His smile was weak, both of us knowing the conversation was neither satisfying nor over.

We sat silently, sipping our drinks and nibbling on roasted oysters and a yellowtail and pomelo salad, letting our words and our mood readjust. But the silence was awkward and full of too many things unsaid.

"What's the current thinking on Judge Reynolds? Any leads yet?" I asked, trying to change the tone of the evening and fill the gaping hole raw emotion had left with the banality of work.

He paused mid-sip and sent me a startled look, as if I'd offended him by changing the subject, but it only lasted a split second.

"The car is long gone. Chop shops are built for speed, so I don't hold out any hope of finding the thing. We've got some security camera footage, and our team is working through it. Hopefully, we can get a shot of the guys on video, whether it's a face or a license plate."

"A headshot will not get you anywhere. Not with those masks," I said, knowing the futility of trying to trace the masks.

"True, but there might be a tattoo on the back of a neck or something else not immediately obvious. There is also the possibility of identifying the supplier of the mask. You're right that identifying the guys is tough right now, but unless they rigged the license plate, that's a reasonable target."

"Don't you find it odd that they killed him? I can see if he resisted or tried to come at them, but I'm telling you, Reynolds could not have been more willing to just let them have the damn car. It looked like a hit to me."

He took my statement in stride. We were seemingly back to our normal pattern where work was an acceptable subject to discuss, as long as we kept within the boundaries.

"And I have to agree with you. It is odd. But what's the motive if it's not the car? Look, Andrea, this is one of those situations where you need to set aside the crazy theories. Why they did it doesn't matter. Stupid, pointless shit happens all the time. What matters is that we, and I mean cops, find the shooters."

I opened my mouth to tell him about the Mexican treatment center and the Abbiocco sticker and just as quickly changed my mind as his condescension settled into my gut. Yes, trust was still an issue, even professionally. Did that say something about me or about my feelings for Michael?

10

———————

"Why do you have time for breakfast on a workday?"

Cai had sent me a text last night asking if I could meet her early this morning at Pierrot Gourmet in The Peninsula Hotel. Normally, she was running at full tilt by seven a.m., long before anyone else in her firm had tasted their first sip of coffee. In an industry known for ninety-hour workweeks, she'd blown through a gaggle of paralegals over the years who could not cope with her all-consuming work ethic before settling on two that shared her drive. Assuming something significant was up, I immediately agreed.

"If you're going to give me shit about it, I might change my mind and go back to work," she said.

In the decade that we'd known each other, we'd suffered through many of life's challenges by each other's side. We were two women who knew each other's habits and quirks intimately. The jabs, the tell-it-like-it-is honesty, and the moments when "fuck you" meant "I love you, too" were all part of our deep bond.

But underneath the words, her tone was off today. Distraction?

"Yeah, right. You're going to blow me off before you've tasted an eclair? I don't think so." I gave her a quick hug and settled into my chair on the sidewalk patio. It was early enough in the day that the patrons were mostly grab-and-go coffee and pastry types. Cai had a large mug of dark roast in front of her, half-drunk. Our server appeared, and I asked for my usual Earl Grey with lemon and honey and a must-have croissant.

"You eating? Or is caffeine your breakfast of choice today?" I asked.

"Just top me off." Cai lifted her mug. "You're annoyingly perky this morning," she said, turning to me as the server moved on. "And look at those sparkly eyes. Uh-huh, I think I know what you did last night. Or was it this morning?" Cai asked, a wicked smile on her face.

"I have no idea what you're referring to," I said, barely stifling my grin and trying to keep my mind from trailing back to last evening's sultrier moments. Michael and I had returned to my co-op after dinner and used skin-to-skin contact to chase away the tension that had been present over dinner.

I immediately reached for a sip of water, pretending I was not blushing.

"Okay, if you say so. It's your lie. Tell it any way you want to. But please, remember who you're talking to." She looked at me over the top of her mug, eyebrows raised.

"To what do I owe the honor?" I said, quickly changing the subject. I hadn't been able to read Cai on her views of my growing relationship with Michael. Although she said she was happy for me, at moments I sensed reservation, but I couldn't place its source. Jealousy? Resentment for the conflicting demands on my time? An unexpressed wish for a relationship of her own? Or did she just not like the guy? When I'd tried to probe, she insisted I was reading things into her responses that were not there. Yet, I hadn't been able to let go of the feeling that something else tempered her happiness for me.

"You have the honor of my company because I need someone with a rational mind to talk me down," she said, trying to sound flip, but I knew her too well to buy the story she was slinging.

Cai never needed talking down. She was the get-shit-done, take-no-prisoners type who always had her act together, and the role reversal was unfamiliar territory.

"What's going on?" I asked tentatively.

"Some jerk is trolling me, and I'm about ready to call in the cavalry. Rather than getting pissed off and overreacting, I thought I'd run it by someone with a clearer head. Look at some of these posts, and tell me what your gut tells you. I'm not sure what the line is between being a jackass and me having something to worry about." She tapped her phone and scrolled.

"Trolling you on social media?"

"Twitter. Home of the hidden identity and assholes with anger management problems." She attempted a laugh, but it was weak and forced. "Neither his handle nor his public name show me anything remotely real, and DMs haven't been enabled."

"You weren't thinking of contacting him, were you?" I said, more judgmentally than I should have.

"My first thought was a sternly worded message filled with scary legalese, but that idea has passed."

"Glad to hear it. That would have been immensely dumb. The first rule of dealing with jackasses is don't engage. Especially jackass cowards online. But you know that. What's this guy doing?"

"Here, take a look. It's easier if you get the full effect yourself."

She handed me the device. I read through a litany of hate-filled sound bites. Racist, sexist, egotistical. The sender was spewing all the ugliness that breeds under the mantle of secrecy when identities could be hidden online. The tweets were a rambling collection of venom directed at the world and the legal profession specifically.

God strengthens us to destroy our enemies.

These are facts only Satan incarnate would believe. I will not be deterred.

The legal profession fabricates evidence to serve their masters.

The source of his complaints wasn't clear, but he had tagged Cai in his recitation of grievances with no obvious connection to the content. His dislike for attorneys was clear, but not his reason for singling her out.

As I scrolled further, the language and tone were classic narcissistic tropes: *I'm right. I'm the expert in all things.* His belief in his own superiority was loud and the tone disturbing, but the tweets posed no specific, identifiable threat. At least not one that law enforcement would respond to. But what was his point? And why tag Cai?

I tapped on the profile. His display name was *Zipsdefender.* His bio read "Agitator. Keeper of Keys. Un saccente. Bold and beautiful." There was an aggressiveness and swagger about the posts that made me believe this was a man's account, but I couldn't be certain.

"How long has this been going on?" I asked while the clerk's reference to a Twitter handle that sounded like Zippy pinged in my brain. Coincidence?

"The first was about three months ago. It was confusing, but I didn't give it any further thought. Another about a month later, then nothing until this past week. And I've received three of these lovelies in the past five days."

"Any initial ideas on who this might be?"

I was pulling out my journalist's voice, trying to tamp down my initial fear. But the increased frequency formed a knot in my gut. What was this guy up to?

"No." She shrugged, taking a sip of her coffee. "A pissed-off client would, of course, be my first thought. You can't be an attorney without someone thinking you need to be roadkill, but it's been a while since anyone has had reason to direct that kind of rancor at me."

"No controversial cases or anyone who took a loss really badly?" Sore losers rarely kept their opinions to themselves for long, and I was running through the obvious scenarios searching for the easy and hopefully harmless explanation.

"My caseload has been boring contract law for the past nine months at least—breach of contract, a messy noncompete situation—bread-and-butter stuff. The most drama I've had is this stupid divorce situation I mentioned to you. It's got my poor client over a barrel with her franchise plans, so I know far too much about it. But that's a story we can enjoy another time when we're drinking booze and not coffee and laughing about how absurd it is."

"Has the defendant in that case tried to contact you directly? He sounds like a little off the rails." I was reaching, but the Twitter user had chosen Cai for a reason. My gut told me he had a problem with her or something she had done.

"No, of course not," she said. "I would have reported that immediately to the judge. The guy's an egotistical prick, but he is also an attorney and knows better."

"You mean he should know better. Divorce brings out the worst in everyone. People become unpredictable when they're backed into a corner." Every ugly divorce story I'd ever heard ran through my mind, and there were far too many.

"True, but this couple isn't even close to a judgment. They'll be battling for another three years if the husband has anything to do with it. Why lash out now? Anyway, my role is minor. Harassing me isn't going to accomplish much."

"Maybe not. Any DMs? And what is this 'Keeper of Keys' reference?"

Cai shrugged. "Hell if I know. He's just tagging me. No direct contact, thank God. And that keys reference, no clue. Probably some misogynistic pig stuff. Who knows what these sickos think?"

"It feels like it's about control," I said. "Keys to the Kingdom. Or the vault. Someone who decides who to let in and who not to, maybe."

"You're giving him too much credit. Since he's a creep, maybe it's keys to the chastity belt or the bondage handcuffs?" She huffed and took a swig of her coffee, trying to make the comment sound like a joke, but I knew Cai and saw the unease buried in her eyes. There were too many stories of women stalked or raped to pretend this was unimportant.

"Maybe. But those things are also about control," I reminded her. "He's not targeting you out of the blue, so we need to figure out what the connection might be. How about a romantic interest? Anyone you rejected lately?" I said, again stating the obvious.

She shot me a look.

"Correction, a rejection that was received badly..." Cai always had a contingent of male admirers swirling in the background, but I also knew her unmoderated responses to undesired attention could reduce men to quivering mounds of flesh. "I'll rephrase. Any potential suitors with a particularly frail male ego?"

She laughed. "They're all fragile underneath all that macho bravado. You know me. I like them confident, but only until the point where bare skin is involved, then I want them compliant."

"Did you have to paint that picture for me? That's way too

much information," I said, picking up my tea and wishing it were spiked with something.

"Oh, come on, you're not that different," she said. "Men sniff around you like puppies looking for a pat on the head or a treat. Most men aren't discerning until after they've gotten laid a few times. They know their priorities. If it suits my mood, I play along. If not, I tell them to bugger off. And like you, bugger off is the more frequent response. So what? Getting laid rarely means anything to them. Why should it mean anything to me? I say no and forget about the guy five minutes later."

Cai's bravado was surface level. She acted the part of not giving a damn until genuine emotions were involved, at which point she got scared and tossed men to the curb, afraid of her own vulnerability. As I watched her bluff her way through having feelings, I could not keep my thoughts from floating back to Michael's dismissiveness last night. Intended or not, the dig hurt. In a few short words, he had made me feel like I was some journalistic wannabe throwing shit theories at the wall. Is that what he thought of me?

I looked at Cai again, reading her face. Was this Twitter creep an actual threat to her? Some jilted lover or client determined to shake her emotional foundation? I didn't have an answer, but this was not to be ignored.

And the more important question: When would vitriol on a screen no longer be enough for this guy?

11

———————

Who was this Twitter creep, and was he a threat?

My mind was full of questions without answers and fears that were too easy to define. But I didn't know how to interpret the vaguely ominous language. Cai stopped abruptly on the sidewalk, swinging me into a quick sidestep, my arm bumping into her bag as we walked. We had shared a cab to Daley Plaza after breakfast, where she was on her way to an emergency hearing and I was scheduled to meet the burn victim Mateo Ortiz had told me about.

Tagging someone in an ugly tweet wasn't a cop-worthy incident—hell, that's what Twitter existed for—but it might be worthwhile to tell Michael in case things escalated. There were too many "I didn't think it was a big deal at the time" stories gone wrong. I wasn't going to take that chance.

My guilt campaign had moved Ortiz enough that he had contacted his friend Sebastian, and we'd arranged to meet before his lunch shift today. But Cai's news had my mind wrapped in knots over the jerk on Twitter instead of the jerk in The Chicken Shack.

"What is it?" I said, following Cai's gaze past a couple

arguing loudly in some Slavic language that sounded like Polish and a parked food cart hawking cafe con leche and casadielles. The scent of the fried dough tempted even me. Cai's eyes were riveted to the brown stain still holding vigil on the pavement where Judge Reynolds had lost his life. I swung my head back to her and watched her diaphragm heave and saw the tight line of her mouth hold firm.

"You okay?" I asked, touching her arm, bringing her out of her thoughts.

"I...I didn't think it would still be here." She let out a whoosh of air and gave me a weak smile. "Doesn't someone wash away the blood? I didn't think... Shit! I'm shaking all over again. It caught me off guard. I'm still trying to understand what happened."

Her eyes seemed to hold the confusion only the senselessness of an unexplained murder could provoke. The relentless *why? why? why?* uttered by centuries of people before her.

"I know," I said, my own memories of that moment gripping my gut. "You're not the only one trying to make sense of it. For now, there are no logical answers, but CPD will figure it out. Trust me. They'll find the guys that did this. Michael and Janek won't let it go."

She nodded unconvincingly. "If they'd picked off one of our own, I'd understand. Because, lawyers..." There was a false lilt in her voice as she tried too hard to make light of the stereotype.

I imagined Zipsdefender was also on her mind whether or not she admitted it. He was certainly on mine. With Judge Reynolds's murder so recent, there was a foreboding air to the tweets that I couldn't shake. It was clear the guy was a jackass, although a jackass that hadn't crossed the line between ugly free speech and threat. The bigger question was, would he?

"Well, I should probably get inside," Cai said, finally letting out another rush of air and tilting her head toward the courthouse. "I'm back in court with my spa client today, but this time for real legal work. She's counting on me to solidify her franchise contracts and, in the process, neuter the asshole she's trying to divorce before he kills her business. It isn't enough that he wants all of their marital assets. He wants to break her business and therefore her future, too."

"What's Mr. Wonderful doing now?" I asked, noting a ping on my phone and seeing a text that my burn victim was running late.

"Rae, my client, has four new franchisees ready to sign deals, and crazy ex thinks it's a fun game to piss her off and hamper her progress by threatening her potential buyers with financial complications," Cai said, her sharp lawyer voice returning as she shifted her thoughts to the work in front of her. "Naturally, the interested parties are getting cold feet, wondering if she's worth betting their futures and hard-earned money on. There are also time limits to the purchase offers that are approaching. In my opinion, the ex is trying to block her from moving forward on the deals just for spite. The motions he's filing are a complete joke. Typos. Ridiculous arguments with no standing. At best, he's a legal hack. And Rae tells me he's continuing to refuse very generous financial settlement offers that would end this madness. I think he just wants her to suffer."

"So Judge Reynolds wasn't presiding in this issue?"

"No, the contracts themselves are not under the purview of the divorce court. She can run her business as she sees fit, although the financial benefit will be part of the bigger valuation. In my opinion, the husband is hampering her business for spite. I'm pleading an emergency motion to get him off her ass before the franchisees bolt. If I can't do that, then I'll go after him for causing financial loss. That is, if my client has any money left to pay me. But you can bet the outcome will come up as they handle the settlement."

Good. Righteous anger was back. An attorney's best friend.

"Tell that son of a bitch he can get it done today, or I'll personally come over there and shove his head up his ass!"

I turned toward the sound, my eyes drilling into the man shouting into his phone as he passed us. His voice was an icy growl. Same wavy gray hair, ample stomach, and another ill-fitting suit. It was the man in the crowd who had disparaged Judge Reynolds as he lay dead in the street. He strutted toward the building entrance, his tie loose, a heavy leather briefcase in hand, as he continued to issue orders. An attorney had said such ugly things?

I turned to Cai. "You probably didn't notice, but that guy who just walked past, the one in the brown suit, he was here the other day. He was standing right behind us when CPD was processing the body. Said some ugly things about Reynolds. I don't think you saw him, but I'm certain it's the same guy."

"Wait. Cheap suit. Clompy walk? That guy?" she said, following my gaze.

"Yeah."

"That's Felix Panici, my client's husband." Her brows were drawn as she watched him cross the Plaza. "What did he say?"

"That Reynolds deserved what he got."

"I told you he was a jackass. Now I can assume a racist jackass at that."

"He saw Reynolds murdered and still said he deserved to die. That's pretty callous."

My mind tumbled with questions, wondering if there was a connection between the men or if the color of the judge's skin was the only factor in his animus. According to Cai's assessment, extreme was one of Panici's core personality traits, but wishing someone dead was beyond extreme.

"You're in court with him now, right? Mind if I sit in?" I said, stepping toward the building without waiting for her to respond.

What if his comment about Judge Reynolds deserving to die was more than racism?

Cai scrambled after me. "I don't know what you're up to, but okay? You can sit in. Just no backseat lawyering, please."

We followed Panici into the courthouse, and I watched him fumble at security, then try to muscle his way through after setting off the metal detector first with keys, then a second time with coins still in his pocket. He grumbled and joked with the guards, who simply gave him an eye roll and made him do it again, while people behind him shook their heads or looked at their watches.

We were about twenty feet back, and I watched the man as he moved through the paces. He struck me as a solo practitioner, strip-center personal injury attorney rather than a corporate heavy. There were all kinds of lawyers, but I couldn't see this guy rubbing shoulders with C-suite types.

He lumbered down the hall, briefcase half-open, buckles jingling and flapping against the squeaky leather as he walked. Stopping at room 211, he yanked open the heavy oak door with a clang.

"Here are the rules," Cai said, pausing outside and tugging her jacket into place. "Sit in the back. Say nothing. If anyone questions your presence, I intend to say you're a new attorney shadowing me today."

I smiled and mimicked a locked-lip gesture before following her inside.

Slipping into a seat that gave me a profile view of both parties, I turned my attention to Panici as he continued to paw through his ratty briefcase. He plopped a huge stack of files on the table with a loud thud, as if to imply he had lots of material to present. I smiled to myself, recognizing the fake power move of the bully attorney, and watched Rae Panici roll her eyes. She'd seen this movie before, too.

Cai leaned closer to her client, their heads just inches apart, speaking quietly until the judge entered the room, silencing everyone and signaling formalities were now underway.

Rae sat upright in her seat, carefully fluffing the teased mound of hair on top of her head. Her long, red-lacquered nails glowed against her dark strands. She had a smug arrogance about her, mirroring her husband's attitude, that I could feel from here. Images of a marriage full of fiery verbal brawls between the two flashed into my mind.

Panici was on his feet the minute Cai opened her mouth, attempting to hijack her opening summary of the issue at hand. Rae shot him a look that could have curdled milk as her estranged husband displayed his brazen disregard for both the court and her counsel.

Cai kept her cool, as she always did, protesting the breach of protocol and Panici's arrogance, which led to Panici spewing verbal diarrhea full of vague, outrageous-sounding legal claims about his estranged wife's business, forcing divorce animus into what was a business issue. Eventually, the judge, already annoyed with the legal posturing, felt the need to remind the parties they were in a courtroom, not a schoolyard.

The legal wrangling between two divorcing people who hated each other at this point was not my interest, however. Although it was huge fun to watch Cai rip into the guy, I was curious about Panici and wondering if there was anything in his history that might have inspired his animosity toward Judge Reynolds, other than the divorce proceedings. Perhaps a friend or family member had also felt his legal wrath. Or it may have had nothing at all to do with the judge's official role.

As I pondered the potential scenarios, the door behind me squeaked open and a man moved quickly up the aisle. He was thin and wiry, with a widow's peak formed by the thinning brown hair on his forehead. Panici turned toward the man mid-sentence and lifted his palms in a what-do-you-want gesture. Mumbling a weak apology to the judge, Panici stepped into the aisle and the two men leaned close in whispered conversation. After a moment, the man opened the leather portfolio he carried and handed Panici an envelope, which he stashed in his breast pocket.

The visitor moved back down the aisle as quickly as he'd come in, and I watched, curious about the exchange. What business was so urgent it required a court interruption? He wasn't an attorney, that I was sure of. Khakis, polo shirt, heavy-duty ankle-high velcroed sneakers tinged with mud that looked more like boots. He stared back at me with icy green eyes. His gaze was piercing. His jaw fixed hard. He was the kind of guy who set off a stay-the-hell-away vibe just with his eyes.

A flash of color on the black portfolio he carried drew my attention as he neared the door. It was a red diamond-shaped sticker with the word *Abbiocco*.

12

bbiocco? Just like the sticker the guard saw.

I grabbed my things and stood, preparing to scramble out of the courtroom after the man with the creepy eyes while the court was getting settled down after the interruption. Cai shot me a "What the hell?" look. I shrugged and followed the guy. I could fill her in later. He was thirty feet in front of me as he maneuvered out of the courtroom and down the marble stairs, his pace purposeful. A class of middle-schoolers touring the government building was ahead of me and clogged the staircase as I arrived, jostling and teasing, fighting the expectation of mature behavior the setting called for. I kept my eyes on the back of the man's head as he moved into the lobby and then toward the Clark Street side of the building.

Negotiating my way through the kids, I landed in the lobby and rushed toward the doors. As I exited the building into the Plaza, a beam of sunlight reflected off a neighboring glass high-rise, blinding me momentarily. I stopped, shielding my vision, and let my eyes adjust as I scanned the sidewalk. A cacophony of horns and bus engines and squeaky brakes hit my ears while I moved toward the street, my eyes searching, turning toward one corner of the intersection, then the other. Nothing. I'd either lost him in the tourist crowd, or he'd jumped into a waiting vehicle.

Abbiocco. Drowsiness after a meal. The sticker looked exactly like what the Reliance Bank security guard had described. Why was it also showing up in the Panici hearing?

And what connection did it have to Judge Reynolds's killers?

As I stood on the sidewalk furtively searching the street for the man, or a black Escalade, my phone pinged. The burn victim I'd come to the Loop to speak with was pushing back our meeting again.

Since the guy who'd interrupted the court proceeding was nowhere in sight, I headed toward a coffee shop on the south side of the Plaza to kill some time while I waited. The pungent scent of frying bacon assaulted me as I slid into a booth, and the fractured, flaking vinyl seats were just as I remembered them from my visits back during my legal days. I ordered tea, then typed *Abbiocco* into the search engine on my phone. Aside from the Italian translation I'd already seen, the results included a number of restaurants.

My eyes ran down the list—Chesterton, IN, Clarks Summit, PA—and I clicked around, testing links and scanning for something closer to home. On page three, I found a listing for Abbiocco Pizzeria in Elmwood Park, Illinois. I clicked. It was a simple one-page site featuring a pie as the money shot, glistening with pepperoni and oozing with cheese. Established in 1954, and the address was listed, hours of operation, and a now-familiar red diamond with the word Abbiocco.

A pizza joint? What could that possibly have to do with Judge Reynolds?

Chicagoans debated pizza joints as often as they debated baseball teams. Giordano's and Lou Malnati's were the big names that came to mind when you thought of "Chicago Pizza," the deep-dish concoction that could only be eaten with utensils.

These were the restaurants you always took an out-of-towner to when you wanted to give them a city experience. This was the second time Abbiocco had popped up, and if this was just about their fabulous pizza, why had I never heard of them before now?

I checked the time, then punched the name Felix Panici into the Martindale-Hubbell search bar. The site was a directory of legal professionals, their backgrounds, their specialties, and even ratings by fellow lawyers. It was a simple first pass for anyone looking to get basic information on an attorney or could serve as a referral if you didn't have a friend or neighbor willing to cough up a name. And it was also the easiest, cheapest one-stop advertising vehicle around for anyone in the legal field.

Panici's listing showed no peer reviews and no client reviews, confirming my low-rent assessment of where he stood in the legal pecking orders. I stared at the screen, looking at it again for clarity. Damn! His office was also in Elmwood Park.

I scrolled his short list of credentials, a BS in Business Management and a JD from Southern Illinois, a decent but hardly impressive program. He'd been in practice for over twenty years, and my hunch was right—he was a solo practitioner. According to the site, his areas of expertise included contracts, bankruptcy, and employment law, with a focus on small businesses, construction, real estate, and food service. Perhaps Abbiocco Pizzeria was one of his clients. The guy with the weird eyes could be the owner, but what was so urgent about restaurant work that you'd interrupt a court proceeding for it?

Nor did I see a logical connection between Reynolds, Panici, and a pizza joint.

Next, I pulled up the Circuit Court of Cook County site. It held the repository for legal records, including divorce. Typing Panici's name into the search field, I scanned the screen looking for cases where Panici was named on the off chance that he had come up against Reynolds professionally. Panici didn't list divorce as a specialty, but since he was handling his own, it was possible he'd come up against Reynolds for a client. The Panici vs. Panici divorce popped up immediately. I then quickly ran through his other filings, which gave me dates, case activity, and presiding judges. I saw no additional mention of Reynolds.

My phone rang as I started getting into the details of Panici's legal history.

"You got a minute?" Brynn said. "I found some info on that judge."

"Great. Go ahead," I said, pulling a notepad and pen out of my bag.

"You wanted to know about Judge Reynolds's financial situation. Running a hard pull credit report on the guy ain't kosher when you don't have a legitimate financial interest but, you know me, I know how to get things, shall we say. Nothing that you'd want to quote me on. If you need hard copy proof, you'll need the legitimate channels, but this should start some good questions rolling, and you can go deeper as you need to."

I cringed. There were things I didn't want to know about Brynn's methods. I just hoped there weren't too many scary things in her computer search history.

"Anyway, as you suspected, things were tight. The judge had a couple of credit cards he routinely ran up to his limit. Would pop them back down a bit each month, but never made a big dent. Car was leased. Cost him about five hundred a month. Electric bill was four months overdue and ComEd was getting antsy about it. He owned a home in Hyde Park, worth about seven hundred grand today. Had a first mortgage at around two hundred seventy-five K. Second mortgage for three hundred sixty K, which he took out eighteen months ago. So basically he had no equity there. And he owed Northwestern Hospital another hundred eighty K for his wife's medical bills."

"Ouch. That's an enormous hit every month, even on a

judge's salary. Thousands of dollars on the medical alone," I said, wondering how the added financial stress had affected him.

"His base salary was a hundred seventy-five thousand a year. Obliviously, not at all shabby, but also not enough to be sustainable. Reynolds must have had to live on ramen noodles because there couldn't have been any disposable income left after he wrote those checks each month."

Brynn paused, seeming to debate whether she wanted to say something more.

"I know this is even further out of bounds," she continued. "And I feel a little creepy prying into a dead guy's personal life, but I called a friend of mine. She works as a financial specialist in the Northern District bankruptcy court. I thought it was worth an off-the-record inquiry. Well, she tells me Judge Reynolds filed about four weeks ago. The filing isn't showing in the public system yet. They were doing what they could to slow-walk the reporting out of respect, a favor to a judge, I guess, but he was going to lose his house at some point after the lenders and the legal process got sorted out."

"Wow. That's a lot to deal with after losing your wife."

It was easy to imagine Reynolds as desperate, pulling out cash wherever he could for his wife's care, figuring he'd worry later, and then being too overwhelmed to keep track of his bookkeeping. But it was a horrible existence and unbearable stress, if my conjecture was right. But did it have anything to do with his murder?

"There is one other odd thing on the report you should know about," Brynn said. "A five-hundred-grand debt to a company called Selciatto Holdings, LLC. It's a construction company. And the really odd part is I can't find any evidence of building permits being pulled on his address. I know people try to skirt the system all the time and pretend ignorance of minor requirements like building code. Maybe it was an off-the-books reno."

"Chicago is notorious for making permits complicated. Trust me, I have first-hand experience from my reno. That is, unless you know the right people and are fully prepared to grease an expediter's palms. But with that budget, he didn't just add an unpermitted bathroom in his basement or freshen up a tired kitchen. That's major addition money or a whole-house remodeling. That also means nine months of construction dirt, noise, and pissed-off neighbors. I've done my share of renovation, and I don't know how you'd spend half a million dollars without it being damn obvious you had done so. And if he tried to do this off the books, all it takes is one neighbor pissed off because you leave your trash bins out longer than you should, who then calls the city to report you, and before you know it, there's a stop-work order on your door and a big fine. Neighbors are a blessing and a curse when it comes to remodeling."

I thanked her, and we ended the call, and then I did the quick math. All told, the judge had been on the hook for over 1.3 million dollars. Bank and hospital creditors were easy to understand. There would have been a financing plan. They had a legitimate process and an interest in keeping Reynolds solvent enough to keep paying, but what home construction and remodeling company financed their customers? And how in the world would any legitimate lender let a man in this precarious financial situation take on an additional five hundred grand of debt?

13

———————

Half a million dollars. That was build-a-home-in-the-burbs money or add-a-really-nice-second-story money. I also couldn't imagine Judge Reynolds and his wife taking on a construction project of that magnitude in the middle of her cancer treatments. Modifications to the home for her physical restrictions wouldn't cost anywhere near that much. Even if he had found someone willing to give him the loan, it made no sense.

I was walking north, snaking back through Daley Plaza for my meeting with Sebastian, the burn victim Mateo Ortiz had connected me with from The Chicken Shack, and scrolling my phone, trying to search for information on Selciatto Holdings, all while dodging tourists and hoping to avoid a pratfall off a curb. The three-block walk wasn't even close to enough time for an adequate data dive.

Sebastian worked as a prep cook at Petterino's these days, an upscale Loop tradition, nestled between the Goodman Theatre and the Nederlander Theatre, that catered to business lunch types and the theater crowd. A little bit steakhouse, a little bit Italian, and a little bit seafood. In other words, something for everyone. Its claim to fame was the framed cartoons on the walls of all the famous people, actors and politicians alike, who had dined there over the years. It was hardly an innovative design statement, but I imagined decades of tradition were hard to change.

It was just before eleven when I arrived, and the mouthwatering scent of marinara sauce was pungent. Although too early for the first lunch seating, prep was underway, and two young men in crisp white shirts and navy aprons were laying out the table settings and small bud vases filled with red carnations.

I waited on the sidewalk, shooting off a text to let Sebastian know I'd arrived, but my mind was on loans and suburban pizza joints.

It wasn't long before a man pushed through the revolving door and locked his eyes on me expectantly. I nodded, and he came toward me.

"Sebastian?"

He was tall and thin with dark, chiseled features and a pencil mustache. His high-waisted baggy jeans were cuffed and belted, and he wore a simple white pocket T-shirt that showed off his intricate sleeve tattoos. He reminded me of someone from a different era, Salvador Dalí perhaps, minus the crazy bug eyes and bandana around his neck.

"Yeah. Are you the reporter who wants to know about inspectors?"

"I'm Andrea Kellner. As Mateo told you, I'm working on a piece about your former boss, Orlando Gaetano."

A crooked smile tilted up one side of his mouth. Interesting.

"Look, I gotta make this quick, okay? Midday crowd and all." He shoved his hands in his pockets and looked at me.

"How long did you work at The Chicken Shack?" I asked. The length of time he'd been employed mattered, as the longer the stint, the more he might have seen.

"I put in almost two torturous years at that shithole. The job was crap, but it only took me ten minutes to get to work and I liked the people. Made some good friends." He shrugged. "Or maybe we just all had collective PTSD. I don't know. Feels like we alums ought to get medals once a year for breaking out of purgatory like they do in AA."

"You think of working there like an addiction?" I asked, uncertain if he was being literal or simply felt the need for a reward after putting in the time.

"Kinda. Or maybe it's more like a cult. They prey on folks who don't have options. Broke-ass poor. Illegals. Addicts needing cash for the next fix. It's the job-of-last-resort stuff. If they could get away with running a Craigslist ad that said, 'When no one else will hire you, we will!' they'd do it. Once you're in the door, you're stuck. Then they break you down, find your weak spot, remind you your status is shaky. Anything that keeps you afraid. Then they use it."

"Use it how?"

"Long hours. Low pay. A little ass grab here and there. More if they can manage it. Basically sweatshop stuff. You're trapped. You need the dough and there ain't much else, so you shut up and put up with it. 'Cause what choice is there? You gotta eat."

"But you complained." I watched his gaze turn direct.

"I'm legal. I may have had a shit-filled history when I walked in that door, but they couldn't hold an ICE raid over my head," he said, a challenging edge in his voice. "It was always an empty threat. Gaetano and his boys aren't going to be stoking the fryer all day. But real or not, the threat spooked people, and no one wanted to test them. I was dealing with some personal stuff and needed to be close to home, but after a while, ya get fed up. It ain't right to work your ass off and not get paid, right? Gaetano's makin' his. Livin' in a big-ass mansion. I had to say something 'cause no one else could."

"But that didn't go over well, did it?" I watched his face, trying to gauge his level of hostility.

He glanced behind him before continuing.

"No, but I kept at it. Every few weeks when Gaetano would show his fat ass at the restaurant, I'd corner him and remind him of the laws he was breakin'. Didn't take long before they put me on probation and told me I'd better shape the hell up and be grateful for having the job at all. Then one night after closing, Gaetano and his boys—his club, he calls them—they were hanging out, a full feast on the table, all of 'em loud and laughin' it up like they always do. I'm in the kitchen doing my thing, anxious to get the hell home. I had just turned off the fryers and was skimming the vats when the night supervisor comes over. He reaches up to get something off the shelf where I'm working, which ain't cool, anyway. Knocks a metal bowl into the hot oil. Splashes up over my arm. Burns the fuck out of me. I'm howlin'. That stuff is 450 degrees. He gives me an 'Oops, sorry about that,' all with a smile on his face. I wrap my arm in ice and head for the door, on my way to the emergency room. Gaetano looks at me and says, 'You take care, now.' I'll never forget that smirk as long as I live."

He held out his right forearm.

"Look close, under the tat. I had a partial before, but the burn mangled the hell out of it, so I went next level, got the full sleeve to cover up the scars."

I stared at the tattoo, seeing the uneven, wrinkled skin poking through the patchwork of ink, wondering about the additional pain on the new, sensitive tissue and what other atrocities had occurred under Gaetano's watch. His callous disregard for his employees disgusted me and, looking at this, health code violations might be the least of Gaetano's ugliness.

"Were you around during any of the health inspector's visits?" I asked as Sebastian pulled back his arm.

He gave me another smug look. "Why don't we get right to the point? You want to know if the inspector was on the take. Who do you think was sitting at that table with Gaetano, shoving down fried chicken as fast as he could get it in his mouth, grease dripping down his chin? Mr. Nestor Morales, of course. Health inspections are supposed to be unannounced, but we always knew. Not the exact day, but you could tell it was coming. The supervisors would start having us clean shit that never got cleaned, harp on us about how we bagged the trash. Suddenly the refrigerator had to be at the proper temp."

"How often did that happen?"

"The city assigns risk levels based on history, and we were a level-one risk based on past complaints, so that means inspections twice a year. That's the worst category. Best is three. They only get hit up every other year. But Morales, he'd come in and blow through the place in ten minutes, and half of that would be schmoozing with the supervisor. It was a joke. What I don't get is why Morales would eat the food knowing what he knows. I sure didn't."

"And Morales spent time at the restaurant socially, outside of his inspection duties. Correct?"

"Every Wednesday night, like clockwork. Gaetano and his boys. His squad. There was a revolving door of them coming and going after close, like it was the private social club in *Goodfellas*. His suburban goons snuck into the city all the time for whatever it is these guys do after the shop closes. And knowing Gaetano, I would bet that there is money involved. Probably dirty money."

14

"**C**an I buy you a chicken dinner?"

I was on the phone with Brynn and bribing her with a free meal if she'd accompany me to The Chicken Shack this evening. If Sebastian was right, the gang would be at the restaurant tonight, and their after-hours events had me curious. If Morales was taking payola from Gaetano, perhaps Morales had other restaurants on his short list with favored-client status.

Minor details were floating loosely through my mind, competing for attention as I spoke to her. Morales and his personal connection to Gaetano. Judge Reynolds was in debt for half a million dollars to a construction company, and some social media creep called *Zipsdefender* was coming after Cai.

We firmed up the details for the evening and ended the call.

I had parked myself at a cafe table inside Intelligentsia after my meeting so I could capture my notes on the meeting with Sebastian while they were still fresh in my mind and plan where I was going with this story. Sipping my Earl Grey, I considered the new information as the chatter of patrons around me melded into white noise broken by the occasional hiss of the steamer on the cappuccino machine.

Borkowski would probably be pressuring me for some new content first thing in the morning, but I didn't see a clear enough story path on either Gaetano's bribes or the judge's murder to move beyond my long list of questions and speculation, none of which I had answers to. And Cai's creep was front and center in my mind.

Tapping into Twitter, I typed in *Zipsdefender* and scrolled his posts. His avatar was innocuous, just a red circle with the word *Defender* in bold Times New Roman font. Over the past few months, his meager posts were random personal opinions, seemingly without context. *Alderman Farnsworth is demented. Only vile and compromised agents wield power. The guilty fabricate their truth.* Random drivel by all appearances, fueled by some internal grievances that weren't clear. In other words, just another day on Twitter. Farnsworth likely meant Reggie Farnsworth, commonly called Striker, of the 36th Ward.

Another Elmwood Park reference.

Un saccente. What did that mean? It was the Italian word for *opinionated,* or a know-it-all. That certainly matched the attitude of the posts.

I tapped and ran through the accounts he was following. Attorneys, local government, TV news stations, a handful of bars, and what looked to be a social club, also in Elmwood Park. It seemed like a good bet that this was his home base.

Abbiocco, Panici, and now Zipsdefender, all with connections to Elmwood Park. It didn't feel like a coincidence, but what was the connection to Judge Reynolds? Or Cai, for that matter?

An incoming text popped up on my screen. "U got something new on that judge story or is your love life interfering in your job again?" Borkowski. I'd underestimated him by at least sixteen hours. Did he have to be such an ass? I cringed, wondering if this was some blanket dig or if he knew something about Michael and me. Brynn, of course, knew about our relationship, but as far as the rest of my coworkers were concerned, it was only an unconfirmed rumor. However, the comment was a fresh reminder of every reason Michael and I should not be dating, even if our hearts and bodies said differently.

I popped the lid back on my cup of tea, tossed my phone in my bag, and headed toward the door. Like it or not, Borkowski was right. I needed something more on the judge.

Fifteen minutes later, I pulled my Audi into a strip mall parking lot on West Diversey Avenue. The low-slung brick building was a shabby, we'll-take-anybody-willing-to-sign-a-lease-and-fork-up-a-deposit six-unit affair. A bodega with hand-painted paper signs, advertising a sale on avocados and yucca, filled three spaces on the north end. A takeout-only pizza place was next door, along with a scary-looking nail salon with dust-caked signage, and a cell phone joint on the end. What was I missing? This didn't feel like any construction company site I'd ever come across.

Reynolds's debtor, Selciatto Holdings, LLC, listed a suite at this address in their Articles of Organization, but I hadn't been able to find a website associated with the business or any further description of the type of construction work they performed. Leaving my car, I opened my phone, double-checked the suite number, and began my walk down the row of businesses. The nail salon was even scarier once I could see the pedicure stations inside. Visions of fungus-riddled toenails sitting in an un-sanitized soak tub flashed in my mind. But there was still no suite 701 as I reached the end of the row.

I glanced back toward the bodega in case I'd missed something and then pulled open the glass door to the cell phone shop. A loud ding announced me to the lone employee crouched at a pegboard display of phone accessories. He seemed to be inventorying shelf stock when he heard the bell. Pulling himself up to his feet, he smiled and came toward me.

"Welcome. What are you in the market for today? We've got some great deals on the latest Samsung Galaxy, if you're ready for an upgrade," he said, working the salesman schtick with ease.

"Sorry, I'm just looking for directions. I can't find suite 701, Selciatto Holdings. Do you know where it is?"

His smile dimmed, realizing I wasn't a live lead, but he didn't let it hamper his cheery customer service sales voice.

"Oh, yeah, they're upstairs. It's hard to find. We get their mail by mistake all the time. Just go around the corner of the building, between the buildings, actually, and you'll see a red metal door. Kinda rusty. The stairs are behind that door. But I doubt anyone is there. I can usually hear people walking around when they're in. Sounds like they wear combat boots, given all the clomping around." He chuckled.

The heavy feet of upstairs neighbors would not have been amusing to me.

"And is that often? Seems like a lot of work if you want your customers to find you up there." I was having a hard time picturing a business with any kind of forward-facing customer base choosing an office location that took a roadmap to reach and required a creepy access point wedged between buildings. Perhaps they only used it for back-office functions.

"Don't I know it! The first rule of retail is location, location, location." He laughed again. "Nah, I don't think this is a walk-in traffic kind of place. Must be more of an office for them. You're the first person I've had looking for them in months."

"Do you know what kind of work they do? My boss just said

it was construction." The guy seemed willing to talk and wasn't exactly overrun with customers himself, so I dug, hoping I sounded vaguely like I'd been sent on a task I didn't understand.

"I think it's a bunch of businesses. Like they all use the space but don't work there every day. What do they call them when you just rent the desk for a few hours? Co-working spaces. But not the cool, hip kind with a coffee bar and networking parties, like they have downtown. These are blue-collar guys. The last person who came in looking for them was this big guy in a sweaty T-shirt trying to find a paving company."

"Thanks. I appreciate your help. I would have been wandering for hours."

"You bet. And come on back when you're ready to upgrade that phone."

I left the store, walked to the end of the concrete, and peered around the corner. It was even worse than my new friend had described. It was nothing more than a dark, trash-laden dirt path wedged between two concrete buildings. About thirty inches wide, the meager space was strewn with used Styrofoam cups, empty chip bags, and assorted sale flyers and ran the depth of the building. About forty feet back, the walkway opened to an alley, where I could make out the edges of a blue dumpster.

I kicked aside a pile of paper jammed against the only door, hoping I wasn't disturbing a rat family napping underneath, then stepped into a tiny landing. No signage. Cracked linoleum, dust bunnies, and dirty footprints led me up a narrow staircase lit by two wobbly fluorescent fixtures.

At the top, another landing, another door, and a simple paper sign printed on card stock taped up with black electrical tape.

Selciatto Holdings, LLC

Smooth Top Paving
Rastello-Marcetti

I noted the business names, then tested the knob. Locked. So I raised my hand and knocked loudly. Nothing. I rapped again, the thud hollow, listening for signs of life, but it remained quiet. After a moment, I trudged back down the stairs to my car. Settling into the seat, I pulled out my phone and typed *Rastello-Marcetti* into the search bar. Also a paving company. Was Selciatto simply the corporate structure for these two paving companies? If so, why would Judge Reynolds owe them half a million dollars?

As I contemplated the possibilities, a black pickup with oversized tires and dirt-caked mud flaps slid into the last parking slot. The driver, a bulky man in a T-shirt and jeans, exited and lumbered toward the walkway at the end of the building. He looked like the construction type. I tossed my phone in my pocket and stepped out of my car, fumbling in my bag and pretending I was on my way to a nail appointment.

He stopped on the sidewalk as a burgundy Cadillac pulled up to the curb beside him and turned his square head toward the vehicle. Hooking his thumbs into a belt hidden somewhere under his beast of a belly, he waited for the driver, his face scrunched in annoyance.

"What the hell is wrong with you?" he screamed as the man exited his car. "When are you gonna learn to keep your goddamn trap shut? You've got a problem! And you better take care of it before she becomes a problem someone else needs to handle."

"Don't worry about it. I've got it handled," the man said, shrugging and leaning an arm on the top of the open car door. His voice had an edge of overconfidence, but it wasn't clear if he was trying to convince his friend or himself. "Let's just sign these docs and you let me worry about her. She may run her mouth from time to time, but she don't know shit."

The driver of the truck shot an icy scowl toward the new arrival but said nothing as the Cadillac man shut the door of the car.

Squat body. Big belly. Gray wavy hair. I was looking at Felix Panici.

15

"You aren't going to sneak in a green juice or a kale salad, are you? I don't think it would help you blend in."

Brynn sat in the passenger seat of my Audi, shooting amused digs at me as I eased the car into a parking slot near enough to the front door of The Chicken Shack that I could get a read on the customers before we went in.

If Sebastian was right, Gaetano would be holding court tonight, and a certain health inspector was likely to be one of his guests. It wouldn't provide proof of wrongdoing, but as the saying went, a picture was worth a thousand words, and a photo of them together socially would add a nice bit of color to my reporting.

"This is what I get for offering to buy you dinner? Abuse? Healthy food discrimination?" I shot back, secretly wishing I'd thought to fill my travel mug with something green.

"I just can't believe I'm going to get to watch your face as you bite into a piece of crispy, salty, greasy, chicken deliciousness."

"You mean antibiotic-, hormone-, preservative-, and trans-fat-laden, chicken-like product, don't you?"

"You're just afraid you're going to like it and you won't be able to keep that joy off of your face." Brynn laughed and raised an eyebrow.

I flipped my attention back to the restaurant, hoping she wasn't right. And that I didn't go home with food poisoning.

It was just past sunset, and the ruby tinge of the western sky was fading rapidly. Fluorescent lights blazed inside the restaurant, illuminating the red vinyl benches, scuffed checkerboard floor tile, and air vents that hadn't been wiped clean of dust or cobwebs in years. Posters showing creamy, buttery mounds of mashed potatoes and baskets of perfectly golden fried chicken graced the walls. The operating-room lighting also gave me a full view of the handful of patrons inside.

Gaetano had taken up residence in a corner booth with one other man and was giving the poor gal wiping down tables nearby an intimidating stare.

"So, here's the plan," I said to Brynn. "We'll go in, place our orders, then grab a table near the two guys in the far-right corner booth. The big, bald guy is the one I'm interested in. Don't sit right next to him, but close enough that I can get a good line of sight. And if we can hear him, all the better."

"Which one is he? The owner or the inspector?"

"He's the owner, Orlando Gaetano. I don't know who the other guy is. It's getting close to closing time, so we won't have the cover of lots of other customers, but I want to see who shows up for this week's boys' club meeting."

"What do you want me to do? I brought a hat. It's not much of a disguise, but it's something." She held up her baseball hat, slipping it on with a smile. "Should we split up? I can sit in the next booth with my back to him and eavesdrop. Record the conversation if anything good comes up," Brynn said, far too enthusiastically.

"Surreptitious recording of the conversation? No. Let's stick to legal measures for now. Just sit with me and help me listen in."

"You mean help you blend in? This is so exciting. I've always wanted to go on a stakeout." Brynn was out the door before I could say anything else. I shook my head, hoping this wasn't something I'd regret.

The cloying smell of the deep fat fryer slapped me in the face as I opened the glass door. And I imagined the odor permanently imbued into the surfaces, a thin sheen of oil coating even the ceiling, and a rat-infested alleyway dumpster that had to be banged on before opening. I shot my eyes over at Gaetano as I walked toward the counter. Engrossed in his phone, he tapped away, oblivious to my gaze, ignoring his companion. Sixty-something, a round face, gray chest hair creeping up beyond the open collar of his golf shirt. His ruddy skin held the battle scars of serious acne, and a lump on his nose signaled an old break. It was a face that said, *Don't fuck with me.*

We ordered and settled into a table about fifteen feet away from Gaetano's booth. Brynn's extra-crispy, extra-large, add-the-curly-fries basket both taunted me and turned my stomach. Images of fried cockroaches wouldn't leave my head as I watched her eagerly devour her meal, licking the salt and crispy breading remnants from her fingers in between bites.

I pushed food around on my plate, pretending to eat and watching Gaetano as he took a swig of beer. Apparently, carry-in alcohol, when you didn't have a liquor license, was okay when you owned the place. He probably kept a private stock on-site somewhere in the back. As we did our play-acting, he flicked his hand at a rail-thin young man, summoning him, and began issuing instructions for the evening's feast. Chicken, cornbread, coleslaw, sweet potato fries, and baked beans. Given the quantity, he was expecting his guests to arrive with an appetite.

We poked at our food, ignoring the smattering of customers

and listening to the men's inane conversation about how hard it was to find a lawn guy who cut a perfect crosshatch and bitching about a neighbor's dog who had turned his yard into a urinal. Ten minutes before closing, two more men entered, bringing a barrage of crude boy-talk with them and heading straight to the large corner booth. As promised, Nestor Morales, the health inspector, was one of them. The men exchanged handshakes and pats on the back, then took seats. Cold bottles of beer arrived on cue, and the conversation shifted to debating the likely outcome of the upcoming Cubs game.

I had Gaetano and Morales at the same table, but their conversation needed to get far more interesting than batting averages. Raising my phone, I snuck in a quick photo of the two looking chummy.

"You ladies about done?" A pimply kid was table-side, a large trash bag in hand. "We're closing up. I can get you a to-go bag if you need it."

Staff were now removing napkin dispensers and turning chairs over on top of tables as the balance of the diners started to disburse.

"I'll take a bag," Brynn said, eyeing the chicken I hadn't touched. I happily pushed my plate toward her.

Another ding of the door pulled my eyes to a man now moving swiftly to join Gaetano and his party. His pace was faster than his body would have suggested, and his eyes drilled into Gaetano. Same square head, same watermelon belly, but now wearing a plaid flannel shirt. It was the guy who was outside of the Selciatto Holdings office this afternoon, the one who yelled at Felix Panici.

"I don't care who he is or who he knows. I'm done coddling our friend," he said, shooting his ire at Gaetano. "This bullshit needs to end. I can't clean up his messes anymore."

Who was this guy? A Selciatto customer or part of the crew?

I surreptitiously snapped several more photos as the men stared each other down, but I couldn't figure out the connection. Fast food and a paving company? And one really odd coincidence, if that's what it was. Whoever this construction type was, he wasn't in the mood to analyze fielding averages.

"Cool it, okay," Gaetano responded, tipping his head toward Brynn and me. "We'll talk about this after we eat."

The pimply kid returned to our table with a takeout box and stood hovering as Brynn and I packed up. I smiled at him and fussed with my purse, looking at anything but the table of men, hoping their conversation would continue. Brynn was taking my lead on slow-walking our exit, but the kid seemed ready to grab the Styrofoam and scoop her leftovers into the box for her just to move us along.

As Brynn and I left the restaurant, my mind jumped from Gaetano to the guy outside the Selciatto office, to Panici, to the judge. If the guy outside that office was associated with Selciatto, he seemingly had connections to both stories. Why? And had he been speaking about Panici just now?

"Not exactly scintillating conversation in there," Brynn said once we were back in the car. She rested the takeout box on the floor between her feet. "Did you at least get a good shot?"

I hadn't yet filled her in on my visit to Selciatto, so she had no way of knowing there were alarm bells slamming in my head. Turning over every wild thought that might explain how these stories could possibly be connected, I tapped open my camera roll, pausing on an image of Gaetano and the guy from Selciatto. I stared at their faces, stared at the expressions of the men around them. These guys knew each other; that was clear. But how was Reynolds connected?

As Brynn leaned over my shoulder to look at the image, a dark Cadillac pulled in and parked three spaces down. A moment later, a man exited and stepped toward the entrance. His face was lit as he pulled open the door. Felix Panici. Why in the hell was he showing up at every turn?

16

Who were these guys?

The question had kept me staring at the ceiling for far too long last night. Identity shouldn't be difficult to establish, but what kind of boys' club was this? It was more than a weird coincidence Gaetano and Morales had a relationship with Panici, the man who said Judge Reynolds deserved to die. Cai had described Panici as hot-tempered, so he may have harbored a hatred of the judge, but hiring a hit because you didn't like how your divorce was proceeding was nuts.

The venom the guy at Selciatto had directed at Panici flashed back into my mind. He was pissed about something Panici had done and a woman who was complicating life for them. "She runs her mouth." "She don't know shit." Had Panici meant his wife, Rae?

My gut said to follow the money. Always follow the money. I was parked at my desk in the Link-Media office, an hour deep into an internet search of Selciatto Holdings and I still couldn't come up with a single plausible reason Reynolds would owe a paving company half a million dollars. That was a commercial paving number, not a single-family home number, and so far I'd found nothing to suggest Reynolds was dabbling in real estate development on the side. So what was the money for, and why would they have given him a loan?

The staff was filtering in, and snips of conversation broke the silence along with the low hum of national TV news that ran continuously in the background from screens hung from the ceiling in the timber loft space.

Brynn waved as she passed, winding her way to her desk, a big smile on her face, a travel mug of coffee in hand, as always. Clearly, her iron stomach had insulated her against food poisoning, or maybe all the coffee she consumed served as an antimicrobial. I lifted my bottle of green juice in salute, eliciting an amused grimace in response.

As laughter and the morning's night-before war stories pierced the air, I stared at a tagged photo of Edmund Rastello, of Rastello-Marcetti Paving. The image was attached to an article in one of the suburban weeklies, announcing the opening of a new medical clinic. They had posed him next to a mound of gravel nearly as tall as he was, arms crossed over his ample belly, feet planted in the classic construction-guy stance. The photographer had wisely gone for a wide shot. That mug of his wasn't a selling point. I guessed the photo to be at least a few years old, given the change in his hairline, but I was certain I was staring at the same man in plaid I'd seen meeting with Orlando Gaetano last night.

The same man Panici had met outside Selciatto Holdings.

Now I had a name. According to my search, Edmund Rastello was the CEO and owner of Selciatto Holdings, LLC. And Rastello-Marcetti was a wholly owned subsidiary of the organization, concentrating on commercial paving, and Smooth Top Paving, also a subsidiary of Selciatto, handled residential projects. Now that I knew the players, it was clear that the office on Diversey was likely used just for administrative functions, like bookkeeping and receiving mail. Or perhaps Rastello lived in the city and needed a more convenient location when he wasn't out in the field. Regardless, the nuts and bolts of the heavy work and the housing of the machinery were handled out of a large warehouse just south of O'Hare Airport in Schiller Park.

So, unless I was missing something, Judge Reynolds owed half a million dollars to a paving company. Something was wrong here, way wrong. I supposed Reynolds could have had some side business investments that escaped credit reports, but this was not making sense. People tried to hide assets all the time in bankruptcy, but this was a debt he wanted to be wiped clean. The court would have demanded to know the purpose of the loan and the terms.

If the loan was question one, question two was Panici. What was his connection to the paving company? And what was the source of his animus for Reynolds? And that brought me to question three. Why did Rastello and Panici and Morales and Gaetano all know each other?

I pulled out a packet of Post-its, wrote out the names and my initial questions, then arranged the cards on the whiteboard next to my desk, as was my habit. A visual schematic of sorts. Leaning back in my chair, I stared at the wall, trying to imagine the common denominator, then reached for my phone.

Cai picked up on the second ring.

"Tell me about your client's husband, Felix Panici."

"What? You're going to have to be more specific. I didn't pencil in one of your fishing expeditions on today's calendar."

Her voice was irritated, distant. It was the tone I'd heard her use with paralegals who would not make the cut.

"I'm sorry, I'm catching you at a bad time. I'm trying to piece something together and got a little overly enthusiastic. What's a better time to talk?" I said, guilt creeping in.

"Sorry, now is fine. I'm just annoyed. It's not you. This Twitter jerk is getting to be a real pain in the ass."

"You've blocked him, right?" Apprehension crawled up the back of my neck.

"Of course, but that hasn't made it stop. He tags me on his own feed. I can't stop that."

"What's he saying?"

"He's calling me sick and demented. Weird references to satanic, lawless behavior. Says 'they're' coming for me, whoever that is. It's a bunch of crazy nonsense, but I feel like I'm sitting around waiting for the wacko to snap or show up at my door. I can't tell if he's a Twitter coward trying to mess with my head and reputation or if I should worry about my safety. And I don't know how to shut him down."

"I'm on my way over to your office now." I hung up before she objected.

Fifteen minutes later, I stood in front of the reception desk in Cai's law firm, my chest tight, images of Judge Reynolds's sprawled body in my head. I'd phoned Michael on the way over and asked him to meet us. It was impossible to know if this guy was a physical threat, but cautious optimism would not settle me down. I'd seen too many versions of the "shouldas" tear people apart with guilt after someone was hurt or dead.

As the gal at the front desk announced me, I paced the elaborate oriental carpet that graced the space. The paneled mahogany walls, smooth leather chairs, and collector-level art had been chosen to instill a feeling of confidence and permanence in the firm. Not today.

Cai arrived a few minutes later. Her clipped hair and missing jacket told me she was trying to shoulder through, but the dark circles under her eyes told another story.

"Thanks for coming, but you really didn't need to run over for this. I feel silly. The guy is probably hiding in his mom's basement, afraid of his own shadow. He's just getting under my skin, and I need to stop letting him."

Her voice was still wobbly, and a hint of sheepishness leaked through.

"Don't take chances with crazies," I said, giving her a hug. "I called Michael."

She opened her mouth to protest but closed it quickly after seeing the determination on my face.

"Let's go to a conference room."

The glass doors opened behind us, and Michael pushed his way through. His eyes lingered on me for a moment before he immediately turned his attention to Cai. We hadn't spoken since our dinner the other night, exchanging only a brief text or two. His dismissive "let the cops do this" still stung. I was holding back, processing, not sure if my fear of moving in together was causing some distance or if he had interpreted my questions as challenges. The evening had proceeded pleasantly without any additional conversation about our living arrangements, yet this tension seemed to hang between us. I could see it in his reaction to me just now, feel it in my body.

"Are you okay?" he asked, placing a hand on Cai's shoulder.

"Thanks, Michael. I'll be better when this jackass finds someone else to torture. Let's talk in the other room." She said a few words to the receptionist about a call she was expecting, then we followed her down the narrow hallway to a small room partitioned off with frosted glass.

Generic instrumental music played so low in the background as to be unrecognizable. This room was the space reserved for clients who didn't need to be impressed. I settled into a squeaky faux leather chair and looked at Cai, who was already tapping into her phone.

"Show me what he's sending," Michael said, his voice steady and reassuring.

"As I told Andrea, he's tweeting this junk at me, so it's all there for the world to see. Great reputation builder. I guess I should be grateful I'm not job hunting. Here, take a look."

She handed her phone to Michael, and I watched his eyes as he scrolled, trying to read any alarm that might pop through. He was too much of a pro to let emotion cross his face in front of Cai, but since I knew him so well, occasionally a subtle tell hinted at what he was thinking.

"Any vague thoughts about who this guy might be or what this is all about?" he asked.

"No, nothing. I've reported him to Twitter, of course, but crickets. As usual, social media fails to do anything until a massive public outcry with lots of media attention forces their hand."

My thoughts tumbled back to a story of a woman who'd been murdered the previous year in Michigan by a Twitter troll. He turned out to be a jilted lover with anger management issues, and Cai had jilted her fair share of men, so I couldn't help but go down that ugly path. The knot in my gut clamped down, and I wished I'd dug further back into Zipsdefender's history.

"So, how do we shut him down?" I asked.

Michael shot his eyes at me in surprise before turning back to Cai. "I know this is hard to hear when you're on the receiving end of this kind of shit, but I'm not seeing any specific threats of harm," he said, his voice soft. "Nothing specific enough that would ratchet the level of concern up to something I could use to force Twitter to ID the guy or even to get the account shut down."

Cai nodded, but worry etched her eyes. Michael's declaration wasn't a surprise to either of us. Freedom of speech was a strongly defended concept by all attorneys, but when someone you care about was on the receiving end of even vague threats, it was hard not to hope that by-the-book legal standards could be a little more fluid.

"Hey, I'm not washing my hands of this," Michael added. "Let me see what I can do. Give me a few days. I'll watch the account. Maybe there is something further back in his history that can give us a tip to who he is."

"I think he's based in Elmwood Park," I said, watching Cai's stricken face.

Michael looked at me quizzically.

"When you dig around in the accounts he follows, you'll see a lot of references to businesses in that area. And he's also made disparaging comments about Striker Farnsworth as well."

"Okay, that's helpful," Michael said.

Cai narrowed her eyes and looked at me. Anticipating my next comment, I assumed.

"You know who else is in Elmwood Park?" I said.

She stared at me, shaking her head. "I see where you're going, Andrea, but that's really a stretch. What would hassling me accomplish? I have no influence over his divorce. I barely have control over the activities of my own client."

I turned to Michael. "A client of Cai's has an estranged husband with a serious Napoleon complex. He's a solo attorney with an office in Elmwood Park, and Cai is kicking his ass when they have been in court. His name is Felix Panici. I'd start there."

17

———

"Michael, you have to help me find this guy."

We stood close, our bodies just a foot apart on the sidewalk outside of Cai's office building. A cold wind had picked up while we'd been inside as a weather front moved in, and a stream of pedestrians was navigating around us. But my attention was on Michael's face, needing to see reassurance in his eyes.

"We can't wait around for these vague threats to become something real," I said, my eyes locked on his, hearing the urgency in my own voice. "Cai can't get hurt because of some ridiculous interpretation of free speech buried in Twitter's official handbook by some legal tribunal only looking out for the company's financial liability."

Ugly images were filling my head whether I wanted them there or not, as my mind went to the worst possible outcome. There was no room for "I should have" or "I told you" or any of the other words of lament grieving parties railed after the worst happened.

"Hey, don't go there." Michael took me by the shoulders, his gaze confident. "He's probably just some impotent blowhard trying to make himself feel better. You know how guys like this work. All bark and no bite."

"And if he's not?"

Michael said nothing. What was he going to say? That I was overreacting. Promise me that nothing would happen to her? We both knew he couldn't. We'd seen enough in our respective careers to understand platitudes wouldn't suffice. Not this time. We knew all the ugliness human beings were capable of inflicting on each other and that my fears couldn't be swept away with promises neither one of us believed.

"I'm not going to be the person kicking herself later for not trying hard enough or not taking this seriously enough. And you can't be either, Michael. Women die every day because they weren't listened to, or they felt foolish and reactionary when they called out the jackass. Please, take this seriously."

I stared at his face, oblivious to the pedestrians streaming past us. Willing him to understand. Willing him to be as concerned as I was.

He stared back, then shook his head. "I know you're worried, but the guy hasn't broken the law. He gets to say ugly things if he wants to. It's awful, but we don't get to shut people down because we don't like their language. You know that. If he makes a specific, imminent threat, I'll be all over his ass." He paused, waiting for my reaction. "I promise I'll watch his account, but I'm not sure what else I can do right now."

His voice was soft, as if he were speaking to a child or an elderly aunt who didn't understand big words any more.

I straightened my spine, my jaw set, and looked deep into his eyes. "There are the rules of your job and the rules we follow when protecting people we care about. Don't forget the difference."

———

———

———

A DUMP TRUCK the size of a Chicago bungalow rumbled past me, nearly missing my front bumper and shooting gravel at my windshield, as I pulled into the rutted parking lot at Rastello-Marcetti. I would have expected a commercial paving company to have paved their own lot, but this was no asphalt jungle, more like a pockmarked mess now becoming a minefield of puddles. The rain had begun during my hour-long drive on the Kennedy to the western suburbs, dampening my mood even further.

Michael's response still gnawed at me. This was Cai who had a creep threatening her. My friend. And, I thought, his friend too. I knew he couldn't pull out all the cop tools, but I expected urgency and concern at a minimum, even if it was just because she was important to me.

Michael had promised eyes on the account, but it wasn't enough. I wasn't ready to leave this completely in his hands. Racking my brain for sources I could tap, connections I could suss out, my mind was on overdrive. I had to find something, anything, to get a jump on shutting this guy down before his hazy threats became action.

At the moment, Panici was the only half-assed lead I had. Panici and Elmwood Park. Oddly, or perhaps tellingly, the man was also somehow connected to Selciatto Holdings, the company Judge Reynolds owed a cool half-million dollars. Adding even more weirdness, there was Panici's friendship with the King of the Chickens, Orlando Gaetano. Like attracted like and all that, but this was one way-too-cozy coincidence for all these guys to have an association without it meaning something. I just couldn't fathom what it was.

A metal-sided vanilla box of a building sat in front of me. Functional and nondescript, the building screamed construction. Four posts marked visitor parking, and a large unlit sign hung above the unadorned utilitarian door. I slid my car in, grabbed my bag, and exited, attempting to step over the water-filled pothole but hitting clay-colored mud instead. "Damn," I said, looking down at the dirt-caked suede on my feet.

About thirty yards to the right of the office building sat two additional structures. Huge multi-bay garages with tall, open rolling doors. Inside, graders and steel-wheeled rollers, and dump trucks of all sizes and shapes dotted the bays as well as the areas on the perimeter of the structure. A road from the parking area continued past the garages and around the back of the buildings, and the oily, petrol smell of asphalt assaulted my nose, apparently too stubborn to have been washed away with the rain.

As a plane from nearby O'Hare roared overhead, I pulled open the metal door and stepped into a small reception room. Scuffed linoleum was marred by the treads of dozens of dirty steel-toed boots, and a couple of cast-off hardback chairs sat waiting. To my right, a woman was parked behind tall stacks of papers that built a wall at the edges of her sturdy wooden desk. She looked up at me over the top of her lipstick-red reading glasses.

"You lost or somethin', honey?"

I gave her a light laugh. "Is there someone I can talk to about a paving project?"

She removed her glasses and gave me the once-over stare. "We aren't normally a drop-in kinda place." She seemed to be expecting me to explain my impromptu visit. When I didn't elaborate, she shrugged and asked, "Commercial or residential?"

"A small commercial project, I guess. It's an apartment building," I said, searching my memory for the address of a small six-unit building my sister, Lane, owned, intending to use it as a ruse. It wasn't a big enough property to reach into the six-figure invoice range, but I couldn't exactly pull off a fake shopping mall project.

"More than ten units?" she asked, still giving me a suspicious look.

"Six units, in Ravenswood."

"We'd put that under residential."

I ran my eyes along the wall behind her head as she pawed through a stash of forms mounted to a wall organizer. Tacked to an oversized bulletin board was a list of clients needing follow-up, a staff vacation schedule, and a site map for a large project that appeared to be a new housing development on West Belmont Avenue.

"Here, can you fill this out?" She pulled a couple of sheets off the wall-mounted organizer, tucked them into a clipboard, and handed it to me. "I don't know if anyone is around to speak to you, but give me the basics and I'll have my estimator call you."

I smiled, still trying to play the role of an aspiring customer, then took the paperwork to a chair. The form was a list of basic questions related to the location and scope of the project, nothing that would give me any understanding of the operation of the business. As I jotted down the address of Lane's investment property, angry male voices filtered through from somewhere down the hallway, getting louder as they moved closer.

A moment later, Edmund Rastello stomped into the reception area. His pudgy face was florid above his thick neck. I dropped my head back to the clipboard instinctually and ran the evening at The Chicken Shack back through my mind. He'd seemed preoccupied with the guys in his circle last night, and I couldn't recall a moment where he might have looked closely at me and Brynn, but I couldn't be certain.

I stole a glance at the equally agitated man behind him. That block-like head and misshapen nose screamed, "I was a boxer back in the day." Alderman Reggie Farnsworth, who'd earned his nickname through brute-force knockouts, was still known for his punch, although they were typically verbal these days. The Elmwood Park connection was rearing up again.

"We had an arrangement, Striker. You told me not to worry. That I could 'take it to the bank.' Those were your words."

Rastello had his back to me as he shot his venom at Striker. I turned back to my clipboard, pretending indifference, hoping the intensity of their argument would keep me invisible while I jotted their words on the last page of the form.

"It's just a minor setback," Striker shot back, his voice indignant. "You know I can make this happen. Have I ever not come through for you? Look, I'm just as invested in this outcome as you are. Come on, I always deliver. You know that."

"You'd better figure out how to make good on that promise, because, one way or another, this is going to go my way."

"I'll make this happen. I got that fucking office park handled for you last year, didn't I? And that piece-of-shit blowhard who thought he could renegotiate and stand in your way. I handled him too. Do I need to pull out my résumé and refresh your memory on the deals we've done?"

If a beat-the-crap-out-of-anyone former boxer could look like a misbehaving puppy begging for love, Striker was there. He eyed Rastello, waiting for the man's nod of grace.

I couldn't see Rastello's face, but he was letting Striker dangle like a mouse about to be dropped into the snake tank. My gut said these men had a long history and a hell of a lot of mutual dirt between them.

Rastello leaned in, saying something I couldn't make out to

Striker, who nodded, gave the man a fist bump, then headed toward the door. I waited for a beat until Rastello was out of sight, removed the final page of the form and slipped it into my bag, then returned to the desk, handing over the clipboard with the cover page.

"The estimator can call me when he's back in the office," I said, then hustled after the alderman.

So what promise was an alderman making to a man who owned a construction company? The list of possibilities was endless. This was Chicago, after all. A zoning change or a city contract were the first options that came to mind. Zoning was less likely. That would have to originate with the individual responsible for the project, and Rastello was a service provider. Although I supposed he could be playing intermediary, using his influence with Farnsworth to ensure a contract for a business associate. Nothing new there. But I saw no logical connection to Judge Reynolds's murder or to Cai, unless there was a case in her background that she hadn't connected in her mind yet.

I scanned the lot for Farnsworth, seeing him standing next to a black pickup near one of the garage bays talking to someone on his phone. I slow-walked toward my car, watching the man and racking my brain for any recent reporting on him. Ordinary construction projects and zoning changes weren't something I typically paid much attention to unless they sparked community outrage or were attached to a known offender. Nor were the inner workings of Elmwood Park.

As I reached my car, a Suburban roared up next to the alderman, splashing muddy water on Farnsworth's feet.

"What the fuck!" he yelled. "These are eight-hundred-dollar shoes."

Engine still running, the driver stepped out of the car and barreled toward Farnsworth.

"So buy yourself a new pair. You've been paid enough to

afford a closet full of the best Italian leather. Stopping being a fucking pussy and do what you're paid to do! And this better go the way it needs to." He shoved a thick envelope into Farnsworth's hand, then walked toward the office.

I was staring at the same man who'd interrupted Cai's hearing, the one with the widow's peak.

18

Had I just witnessed an alderman being bribed?

I couldn't be certain, but that envelope had looked suspiciously like a wad of cash—and a big one. The delivery man's words—"Do what you're paid to do"—rang in my ears. If Striker Farnsworth had a side hustle, it wouldn't be a surprise, given his breed. The phrase "Chicago Alderman" was synonymous with the word *grift*, but what was Farnsworth selling? And was the guy with the widow's peak the beneficiary or simply the go-between?

I slid into my Audi and watched the pickup from my rearview mirror as it pulled out, turning right onto Mannheim Road. I pushed the ignition and put the car in gear. Striker was three cars ahead of me and moving south. I kept the pace without effort, traffic cooperating, my mind wandering through all the ways the brief exchange I'd witnessed felt odd. Layer in the discussion inside the office between Striker and Rastello and it felt like I'd just watched two minutes of a heist movie without any context. I didn't know what was going on, but it sure had all the markings of something shady.

Industrial buildings and open land slowly morphed into

entry-level suburbia as we drove further away from O'Hare. Not the gated community, high-end mall, helicopter-parent variety of suburbia; instead, the surroundings were an endless, nameless series of bland mini-strip malls tenanted by tax preparers, vacuum service centers, and cut-rate immigration attorneys. This was not the high-rent district.

We picked up a stoplight about seven miles later, and Farnsworth turned left onto Grand Avenue. I'd followed his lead for about five miles when he slid into a parking spot in front of a small mom-and-pop ice cream shop. I drove past him and eased into the next open slot. I wasn't exactly super-stealthy spy material, but I didn't imagine Striker would have noticed he had a tail. But now what?

I popped on my sunglasses and moved toward his car, intending to use the ice cream shop as my ruse. He was already out of his vehicle, cell phone in hand, having stopped to read something on his screen. I maneuvered past him and eased into a chair at one of the bistro tables on the makeshift sidewalk cafe behind a woman managing a squawking newborn and a toddler about to have a tantrum because he'd licked off all of his sprinkles and wanted more.

Striker's aldermanic office was two doors from the ice cream shop, and it was a safe bet he was headed inside. However, "man goes to work" wasn't exactly great reporting.

Rastello, and whoever this guy was with the funky hairline, expected something from Striker. A paving company and an alderman. A city contract was my first thought. Striker was certainly in a position to influence who received preferential treatment when contracts were doled out. And possibly to arrange a no-bid deal, depending on how closely the community had eyes on him. I jotted a note on my phone to look for the paving contract associated with an office park that Striker had referenced.

As I sat, contemplating the endless varieties of aldermanic greed and pretending to be engrossed in the flavor-of-the-day, a male voice yelled, "Yo, shithead!"

Striker lifted his head and turned toward the sound. "Love you too, asshole. What do you want?" he replied.

The woman with the kids clucked at the language, visibly irritated that her precious ones were hearing bad words.

Moving between the parked cars, Orlando Gaetano ambled up to Striker on the sidewalk, belly first, his complexion even worse in the light of day than it had been in the fluorescent glare of his restaurant. Striker knew Gaetano, too?

The men stood playing their little game of curse word one-upmanship, which seemed to be their version of male bonding in the same way that sports affiliations and "high school back in my glory days" were for others. I watched, bored by their boorishness, wondering if mommy was going to chastise the men or complain to shop management, and ran through the list of Chicken Shack locations, coming up with nothing that would have overlapped with Striker's span of control.

"How's our project coming?" Gaetano asked. "Or are these guys still jerkin' each other off rather than tending to business?"

"It's a process. I'll get it there, but sometimes, people need a little finessing. A little reassurance, if you know what I mean," Striker said.

Striker had puffed himself up, taking on an "I know what I'm doing" tone. I could call bullshit from here. In my experience, when a supposed tough guy had to work to make himself sound confident, he had shit. But I had no inkling what kind of project they were talking about unless Gaetano was opening a location out here and encountering problems. And this sounded strangely similar to the conversation I'd just overheard between Rastello and Striker, minus the thick envelope.

"I'm getting tired of these fucks who act like they're some big swinging dick just because they have some thousand-dollar-an-hour attorney shuffling paperwork for them and standing in the way," Gaetano said.

"Excuse me, can you *please* watch your language?" Mommy interrupted, her hands covering the toddler's ears. I chuckled to myself, wondering what new words the little one would take to daycare tomorrow.

The men gave her half-assed smiles, looked at the kids, then gave each other an eye roll.

"Trust me, okay?" Striker said. "I gotta manage this. Gotta manage the process, the people. I can't bulldoze this through without causing other problems. It's a little sticky, but you'll get what you want. As you know, I want this done as much as you do. So do our mutual friends. I deliver. I always deliver."

Striker's phone rang, and he barked at the caller. "Doesn't anyone do their fucking jobs right the first time? Give me twenty minutes. I'm on my way."

He turned back to Gaetano. "I gotta go. Look, this guy may have the suits in his pocket, but we've got our own brand of artillery. He won't outlast us. We'll talk next week."

"All right. I'll give it a little more time, but I'm ready to step in if this gets bogged down."

The men clapped each other on the back and headed for their respective cars. Zoning or permitting were the only things that made sense. The only things I could think of that Gaetano would need from Striker. And Gaetano was not a man who took no for an answer. Images of Sebastian's damaged flesh flashed back into my mind.

But what did Rastello need from him? Something bigger. Something more difficult. Something more expensive than a permit for a single restaurant.

I waited until the men had pulled away, then marched over to Striker's office. A young woman in her early twenties was at the desk. Phone in one hand, she was patiently explaining to a caller that the alderman's office could not stop roofing companies from sending her postcards despite how often they cluttered her mailbox. As she spoke, she rifled through an inbox that overflowed with mail of her own, likely full of solicitations as well, the kind that didn't involve undocumented personal favors.

I scanned the small office. Two mismatched desks in the main space. A small table piled with manila folders. File cabinets along the back wall. Campaign signage from the last two election cycles rested above, serving as a reminder of Striker's tenure. And an open door in the back connected to what I assumed was Striker's personal office. Bare-bones, garage-sale chic, and not even a potted plant to give life to the dreary space.

She was alone in the office, and I ran my eyes over her desk, taking advantage of her distraction, noticing a large roll of construction blueprints on the credenza behind her. They had unrolled about a foot, and the stack of bound documents was thick. My condo remodeling had yielded around ten pages of floor plans, electrical, and plumbing schematics. This bundle easily contained a hundred pages or more. This had to be a commercial project.

"Sorry to make you wait," she said, her smile bright.

"You have much more patience than I do," I said. "I probably would have given her the number for the post office ten seconds into the call so she would bother someone else."

"We get a lot of that." She laughed. "Elderly residents who don't know where to get help call in thinking the alderman runs everything around town, so he must be able to fix everything, too. Most of the time, they're nice. Just confused or lonely. It's just part of the job. I've only been here a few months, but I kinda like helping them out."

Her tone told me these types of calls were a common occurrence. Where had Striker found this woman willing to work for what had to be garbage pay, still showing up to work, happy to help granny with her junk mail problem? Did she make service calls to rescue lost kitties, too?

"What can I help you with?" she asked.

"I'm a reporter with Link-Media. I'm doing a story about how the construction industry is faring in the local economy," I said, keeping my pitch vague.

I'd decided to keep my storyline only a slight stretch of the truth. I sucked at lying, and since I already had Lane's fake paving project out in the world to inadvertently trip over, keeping two pieces of BS in my head was more than I could manage.

"Oh, um, how can Alderman Farnsworth help with that?"

"I have a number of sources for big statistics. Things like how the sector has increased overall, year-over-year, in the metro area, and economic contribution to the community. That big-picture stuff with so many zeros that only an economist or a finance geek would care about."

I laughed, trying to make my fake assignment sound like a treatise.

"Even my eyes start glazing over when someone starts talking local GDP. My readers care about how their lives will be made better. What employment opportunities might be coming up? What construction projects will screw up their morning commute? So, I thought one of the ways I could make the story hit a more personal tone is to speak with a few of the aldermanic offices. You guys clearly know your constituents and have insight into upcoming projects, so I was hoping you could tell me a little about projects your office is excited about."

"Gosh, I'm not sure I know what to say."

"How about if I shoot some general questions at you, just

background stuff, and we can go where the conversation takes us?"

I smiled reassuringly, and she nodded, seemingly unconcerned that her boss might not want her talking to a reporter. She was likely too new in the job to have been reprimanded for a disastrous quote or a comment that wasn't ready for prime-time release.

"I know spring is the busy construction season, and it's already September, but have you had an increase this year in permits or zoning-change requests?" I started with the easy stuff to get her comfortable with the line of questioning.

"I wasn't here yet, but Natalie, the woman that trained me, she said we had about fifty percent more permits compared to last year. I guess everyone wants to remodel their house all at once."

"That's a lot, congratulations. And very good news for the community. What about commercial projects? Anything big happening? I know the alderman loves to let the community know about new jobs coming."

Her phone rang. She held up a finger and began listening to the caller. I turned my attention to the stack of plans behind her. The cluster of text visible in the lower-left corner was too small to be readable from where I stood. My remodeling experience told me that this data would contain the history of the document, preparer, dates, revision history, etc. The pertinent data that would have clearly identified the project, the developer, and the architect was still tucked in the roll, but I could make out three letters in large font: *APR.*

"These phones are never quiet for long. Between the calls, the walk-ins, and the normal office business, we usually try to have two people in the office in the morning. These old people get up early." She laughed again.

"We were talking about commercial projects before your constituent called. Are there any big projects in the pipeline?"

She jerked her head quickly to the credenza behind her. "No, nothing," she said, turning back. Her voice had gone flat, and she absently grabbed at the first document on the top of the inbox pile and pulled it close, avoiding my eyes.

She was lying to me. Why?

19

———————

Adevelopment project was a dumb thing for an alderman's office to lie about.

Walter was meowing loud and insistently on the other side of the door to my apartment. He seemed to have an innate biological clock that told him dinner needed to be served, now. And the whoosh from the elevator shaft brought him running. I set my grocery bags on the floor and pulled my keys out of my bag. As soon as I opened the door, Walter charged into my legs, yelling and demanding a head rub and a chin scratch. I scooped him up, feeling his body go limp in my arms and his purr reverberate. If anyone wondered whether cats could smile, this was the evidence.

We traipsed to the kitchen for our nightly routine of profuse petting, followed by kibble, tuna flakes, fresh water, and later, a fur ball that seemed to forget I was around. A friend of mine described her love life the same way.

Was that my future, too? There was a new uneasiness about my relationship with Michael. I sensed he was growing tired of my inability to commit, and the more he brought up living together, the more I felt cornered by the pressure to do something so serious. But I still didn't know if my reticence was about my feelings for him or the residual damage heartbreak and betrayal had left me with from my marriage.

And I hated that a dead man still had an influence on my life.

With Walter settled, I returned to the vestibule, gathered the bags, moved everything to the kitchen, then went to my bedroom to change into jeans and a light silk sweater. I had an hour to prep dinner and clear out thoughts of my dead ex's bad behavior before Michael arrived.

I laid the branzino I had chosen for our meal in a roasting pan, then sliced lemons paper-thin and pulled sprigs of rosemary to stuff the cavity. The work was meditative. Thoughts of marital lies were pushed aside, leaving me only with the here and now.

But now other lies filled my mind. Lies told by an alderman's assistant. And not skillfully. Lies were not this woman's normal vernacular. Someone had told her not to talk about the project, but given her inexperience, she hadn't yet come up with a smooth way to say, "I can't go there" or some other version of "Nothing to see here." Politics might not be an ideal career choice for this young woman.

If her lie hadn't been so obvious when she had been presented with a simple question, I wouldn't now be convinced that the big roll of plans contained something I really wanted to know about. That reactive jerk of her head was the tell, not just to the lie but to where it lived. She was checking to see what might have accidentally been left exposed.

Aldermen didn't keep big development projects secret. Ever. They used them like catnip to build their status, their power base, and their coffers. Details of a project would sometimes be dripped years before breaking ground. Secrecy didn't fit. Which meant the project and the lie were important. And it was also a possible explanation for that envelope I'd seen. Rastello had expectations that Striker could deliver something, and so did Gaetano. Rastello made sense. A big construction project meant a big paving project and, therefore, big dollars. It would be worth it to him to slide cash under the table to get what he wanted. Gaetano, by comparison, was a small fish with an anger management problem. That roll of plans was not his.

I puttered and fussed over the food, my mind wriggling with what-ifs while I cleaned endive and shredded parmesan. Beyond the five-hundred-grand debt to Selciatto, where did Judge Reynolds fit in? It was the crucial gaping hole I didn't have an answer to. I didn't even have a hint of an answer.

There was a light rap on the door, and I smiled to myself. Michael. By this point, the front desk staff knew to send him up without an advance phone call, the rarest of privileges for those of us who chose doorman buildings because of the added security they offered.

We smiled and kissed hello at the door, a bit less enthusiastically than what was normal for us. The unease from our last conversation still hung in the air like stale smoke. Walter sat at the side of the door, eyeing him warily as he always did. He'd never taken a swipe at the man or laid his teeth into an exposed ankle, but I always had the sense that he was prepared to just in case Michael turned out to be one of the bad guys. Michael reached down to pet him, but Walter simply showed his ass and walked to the other side of the room. Typical. But Michael kept trying, regardless of how many times he was rebuffed.

"Scotch?" I asked.

He nodded and followed me to the kitchen. I handed him a glass and let him do his thing while I pulled a bottle of Vermentino out of the fridge and poured a glass for myself.

"Let me put the fish in the oven and we can sit on the terrace."

We settled into the lounge chairs, the orange glow of the setting sun to the west bouncing off the Hancock Building and lighting up its dark facade. The colors of the sky and the way they shifted and played off the structure were endlessly fascinating. Lush plantings lined the edges of my large terrace, and I relaxed into my seat, my head resting against the cushion, my heart full of gratitude, as it was every time I sat here, that this oasis was actually my home.

"Anything new on Judge Reynolds's murder?" I asked.

"Nothing more since the last time you asked me."

I looked at him hard. Had I caught him in a bad mood again, or was it that I was asking at all? Like most couples, we talked shop, where and when we could. There were things we both left unsaid. Things that were part of the muddy waters of a relationship between two people whose jobs occasionally had conflicting needs. But irritation with a simple question, the kind either one of us would ask routinely, wasn't part of our behavior. A respectful, "I can't talk about it" usually sufficed.

"You sound irritated. Have I offended you?" I asked, knowing that I wasn't being fully truthful myself. The Abbiocco sticker that I'd withheld from Michael loomed in my mind.

"I just got here, and already you're fishing for material. Don't you ever take a break?"

"You'd rather I show no interest in your work?" I shot back. A little too quickly. A little too full of attitude myself. This was a bad omen at the start of our evening.

Michael just sat in his chair scowling, lifting his drink to his mouth, and ignoring me.

"Okay. Maybe we should just enjoy our drinks for a while. But if I've done something, you should tell me, or just tell me you're in a mood right now and I shouldn't worry about it."

"I don't want to talk about work. I want to talk about us. You keep using work to avoid talking about us, and I'm getting tired of it."

His voice was clipped with annoyance, as if he'd decided to pick a fight before he'd even arrived. His jaw was set, and it seemed clear that the evening was not going to be a smooth one. I could feel myself gearing up with irritation at his accusation. The fact that I didn't want what he wanted right now didn't make it avoidance.

"So if I ask about your case, I'm not showing an interest in you, I'm avoiding? Or fishing for material, as you put it? Is that what you're saying? Because I'm confused. When did we start skipping over polite conversation about what's going on in our lives? That's what couples do."

"Couples? We're not a couple. We're apparently two people who get together now and then. I wish I could say we were a couple, but that takes commitment and setting aside your fears that I'm going to start acting like a jackass the way your ex-husband did. What more do I have to say to you to prove I'm not him? To prove I'm not a fucking cheater? What do I have to do? Just tell me and I'll do it."

I shifted in my chair, gathering my thoughts, afraid my tone or my word choice would aggravate the stuff he was processing. Any response I came up with seemed to be a minefield that could explode, creating something we couldn't come back from.

"Michael, I know you're frustrated with me. I know you are getting tired of waiting to see if my feelings about living together will change. As I've told you, my hesitation isn't about what you haven't said. I heard all the right words in my marriage, but they meant nothing."

I didn't want to flash back to the old hurts. I didn't want to assume that Michael would hurt me down the road. But I also couldn't ignore the fear and the memories that crept back in. And Michael seemed unable to understand that this ultimately was not about him or what he had or had not done or said. It was about me.

"What you're telling me through your increasing irritation is that I haven't acquiesced. And that your desire to live together is more important than my unreadiness to do so. You're sending the message that I should bend to what you want because what you want is more important than what I'm ready for. I'm not going to be strong-armed into a live-in relationship because you've decided it's time. If we aren't both ready, it's the wrong thing. I'm sorry you don't see it that way. This isn't something to be forced."

He stood, looking down at me, his eyes tense.

"I'm going home. This is a circular conversation that never changes. And I think it's just an excuse for you to hold on to your fear. I am not Erik." He paused. "Or maybe you're just using me to get information you can't get elsewhere."

20

____

I parked myself on a bench outside courtroom 302, not sure whether I'd be sitting here for fifteen minutes or three hours.

After Michael left my apartment last night, I needed a shoulder to cry on, and I phoned Cai. She cancelled her date and came right over to help me finish the branzino Michael hadn't stuck around for and to listen to my teary lament that I may have just ended my relationship. It had been a head-spinning evening as I tried to understand how I felt about what had happened. I wanted Michael in my life, but I wasn't going to be pressured into something I wasn't ready for. Ultimately, I'd need to live with the consequences, even if that meant Michael needed to move on.

Although Cai was empathetic about my emotional state, she also wasn't the girlfriend to call if I'd wanted a partner for a pity-party sob session with all the feels. She was the chick I called when I needed to be listened to thoroughly, then kicked firmly in the ass with reality.

Her advice was, "Don't give an inch on this. You'd be starting out with the power dynamics catering to his needs, rather than as partners. And the precedent would be set." It was a hard-to-hear but completely accurate truth that held even when the temptation to call him and apologize gripped me.

We'd spent the balance of the evening enjoying wine and fish and braised endive and after the consoling was done, talking about anything other than our respective romantic lives. The conversation bounced from her irritation with a new associate to a cute new boutique that had just opened in the neighborhood and my search for tile for my guest bathroom.

Thankfully, Zipsdefender had been leaving her alone and no additional tweets had found their way to her account. During the course of the evening, Cai updated me on the new domestic court judge that had been assigned to the Panici case. They were scheduled to be back in court today for one of their endless minor squabbles. The judge wasn't someone I was familiar with, but I felt sorry for him already, imagining the drudgery of reading through the drivel-filled history, let alone the animus they'd be unleashing.

Panici was somehow connected to Striker Farnsworth and to Selciatto and Abbiocco, and he had a hatred for Judge Reynolds. And I wanted to know why. So here I sat, stalking the guy and wondering about the barrage of information he and his estranged wife were likely shooting at the new judge as they jockeyed to draw first blood.

Rastello and Farnsworth were easy enough to speculate about. Rastello wanted a project to go forward that Striker could make happen, and it wasn't their first deal. A bribe was interesting in itself, but there could be more to whatever this deal was. And I didn't know how Panici fit in.

Fifty minutes later, the doors opened and Rae Panici flew out in a huff, marching toward the stairs. Her eyes were so full of anger she seemed ready to shoot fire at anyone who crossed her path, and her mouth was set into a thin, angry line. She wore a skirt so tight her panty line had panty lines. Interesting wardrobe choice for court, but I'd seen worse. Obviously, the hearing had been a shit show, and Rae was livid. Oh, to have been a fly on that wall.

A tall thin man in a cheap suit that screamed of a two-for-the-price-of-one sale, hustled down the stairs behind her, battered briefcase in hand, a look of utter confusion on his face. Clearly, this was the poor sap she'd been using as her divorce attorney, and I followed the pair down. Rae was five steps ahead of him when she spun around, having reached the lobby. Her floral-print blouse strained over her chest, threatening to expose even more of her ample cleavage.

"Why didn't you fight back?" she yelled, loud enough for half the lobby to hear. "You sat there and let him run all over these proceedings again! That was another fifteen hundred dollars in legal fees down the toilet and an hour of my time listening to that windbag ex-husband of mine pontificate on how he's smarter than everyone else. That judge didn't even try to stop him. And you didn't do any better. What the hell am I paying for? Show some fight."

"Rae, we've talked about this," the attorney said. "These games Felix is playing are wearing thin on the court. This is a new judge, and I know you're not happy about it, but he's read the history. He knows this was Felix showing more disrespect for the court and the legal process. Give the judge the benefit of the doubt. He was seeing Felix at his legal worst for himself. We're not backtracking here. Trust me. I know how to handle guys like Felix. We win by being the calm, rational party. The more balanced we are, the crazier Felix looks, and the more the court will agree that you are the one telling the truth."

He was using his inside voice, but *calm* and *rational* were not words to define Rae's current state, and quite frankly I wasn't sure they ever were. Hopefully, this attorney had other legal tricks up his sleeve, because she was having none of it. They seemed like an odd match, and it made me wonder why Rae hadn't chosen someone with more fire in his belly.

"You might know this judge and this world, but trust me, you don't know shit about how Felix operates." Her hands flew as she spoke, and she shifted her weight from foot to foot as if the effort to contain herself was too much. My guess was that this attorney had a short future with her if he didn't start pulling more punches.

The attorney's attempts at placating Rae were proving woefully ineffective. He stammered and shrugged and wrung his hands while her pressure cooker of frustration built. She was about to lose whatever semblance of composure she had left if this guy didn't come up with something better than vague assurances. She needed to vent and didn't care where she was or who heard her spew venom despite the inappropriateness of the setting. Glancing nervously at those witnessing her outrage, the attorney laid a hand on her arm and made a shushing sound. The guy was not reading the room.

"Don't patronize me! You don't know the world Felix lives in. Your world is rules and order. Felix thinks he's above all that because most of the time he is. Your idea that we sit quietly and play nice will do nothing to stop his games or get this case finalized. Don't you dare treat me like some helpless female who needs to do what she's told. You are replaceable. Just like husbands."

I stood silently off to the side, taking in every word and pretending to be engrossed in my phone. What did she mean that Felix thought he was above the rules? Above the law? Or was this just an off-handed angry comment from a wife with a narcissistic, arrogant husband? I supposed both could be true. As I watched her chastise her attorney, I also contemplated what she might have meant by "Felix's world." The men were in different stylistic camps regarding how they practiced law, that was clear, and presumably how they lived their lives, but her comment seemed to have a more corrupt undertone, as if Rae was hinting at something darker.

The clomp of heavy feet echoed, and Felix Panici strode into the lobby, a smug smile on his face. He walked right up to his estranged wife and her counsel, visibly proud of himself for his performance. And performance it clearly was. I didn't need to have been in the courtroom to know this man was gloating. I had no way of knowing if Rae's attorney was correct about the judge seeing through Felix's charade, but this man thought he had just scored.

"Hey, Rae, thanks for makin' my day. I love watching cut-rate attorneys get their asses handed to them. Where'd you find this schmuck? An ad on the back side of a toilet stall?" Felix said, standing just five feet away.

A flush of red crept up the side of the attorney's neck, but he didn't take the bait. Rae huffed and stepped toward her estranged husband, but counsel laid his hand on her arm again, slowing her down, cautioning her. She didn't respond, simply glared back at her husband.

Panici smirked and kept the taunts flowing.

"I'm running rings around this fool you hired, and you're both too stupid to see it. This guy is so outmatched I almost feel sorry for him. Nah, not really. I'm havin' too much fun. That bitch you hired for your franchise deal, at least she's got a few neurons bouncing around compared to this bozo. But you're not gonna win there either. I've got plans for you, and this moron, who thinks he can play with the grown-ups, he needs to go back to the kiddy pool. I've got tricks he hasn't even thought about.

You're going to be begging me, Rae, begging me to make it stop."

Rae hissed at him like a rattler about to strike. Her eyes narrowed, and if her attorney hadn't been holding her back, she appeared ready to throw her best right hook. The attorney looked from husband to wife to the growing audience of concerned onlookers, his mouth opening and closing as if words were eluding him.

"Face it, you're outmatched," Felix continued. His sadistic sneer was something even I felt in my gut. "You can't outsmart me. You know that, don't you? You're just some barkeeper's daughter who's never moved out of the neighborhood. Go back home and style hair. Do something useful."

"Who the fuck do you think you are!" Rae twisted away from her attorney's grip and came at her husband. They squared off, bodies close, animus oozing from each of them. It felt like a posture they had played out before.

"I'm the guy who is going to watch you grovel and spit on you when you're down thrashing in the dirt like the pig you are."

Rae moved first, her arm drawing back for the swing. Her attorney reached out a hand again, but she swatted at him like a fly, letting her anger fuel her punch. Felix opened his eyes wide as Rae's hand slammed his cheek, then the sneer slid back until she flew at him with the other hand, pummeling him left, right, left, right, face, chest, anywhere she could make contact.

Felix laughed, then let his own fists fly, hitting Rae in the eye, but she didn't go down. Her attorney did what he could to pull her back, and a man watching the melee stepped between the pair, who were now screaming obscenities at each other, while another bystander maneuvered Felix away from his wife.

"You think you can hurt me?" Rae screamed, arms flailing while her attorney strained to hold her back. Spit flew as she screamed at him, and her carefully done hair was flying into her face. "What are you going to do, send me on a long trip? You think because you're connected, you can shut me up? You think I don't have an insurance policy? If anything happens to me, you are the first person the boys in blue are going to come looking for. I know where every body is buried, don't I, Felix. And I hope that keeps you sweating for the rest of your life."

21

An insurance policy? Connected? What did Rae mean?

Rae had maneuvered past her attorney and was back in Felix's face, taunting him, her voice sharp and filled with accusation. Felix stared her down, provoking her with a condescending grin. As they faced each other, their bodies were coiled knots of rage waiting to explode.

Rae let loose, flinging her fists at her husband as he laughed at her. A tall hulk of a man in security garb rushed toward the estranged couple, easing his body in front of Felix, hands raised, as Rae's attorney pulled at her shoulders, inching her back. The security guard had forty pounds and at least six inches on Felix and, by the looks of him, could knock him flat in seconds if rational methods were ineffective. And there was also the gun on his belt, if absolutely necessary. Felix dodged, trying to side-step the guard while screaming obscene insults at his wife, but the guard matched his moves.

I recognized the court officer from my legal days and knew Felix didn't have a chance, but did Felix know that?

Observers had gathered on the fringes in small groups drawn to the noise, watching the live car crash that this marriage had become and waiting for blood to be drawn. Divorce brought out the worst in people, and these courthouse walls had seen their share of couples on the verge of blows. And often, just as quickly, the confusing 180-degree reversal and regret that only love could bring, dissolving anger into a tearful embrace. It was hard to imagine this pair back in each other's arms begging for another chance, but stranger things had happened.

"Calm it down, buddy," the guard said to Felix. "You don't want this going any further south than it has. Adding assault charges to your divorce won't play well. It ain't worth it, man. Step away so you can both cool off."

Felix shot his eyes at the guard and then his wife, working out the odds, I presumed. The attorney had managed to back Rae about ten feet away, quieting her enough that she no longer fought him, but he still held her by the shoulders as he spoke quiet words of appeasement on the off chance she had not depleted herself of rage.

"You're right," he huffed. "She ain't worth it. I got more important things to do than listen to her bitching."

Felix unflexed his hands and cracked a knuckle, then gave his wife one more scalding look before turning and heading toward an exit.

Rae was still huddled with her attorney and although not yet pacified, it didn't appear she was going to follow her husband and drag the fight into another inning. I didn't know their full story, but it sure sounded like she thought she could do some damage to Felix if she wanted. Interesting.

Wisely, the security guard was sticking around until it was obvious that both parties were under control. With Felix now out of the building, he watched Rae cautiously while hustling onlookers along and assuring them that there was nothing more to see.

I walked over. "Hey, Tommy. I was kinda hoping I'd get to see you put that guy in a headlock."

"Well, hey back at ya, Andrea. I haven't seen you in forever. You avoiding us over here?"

"No, just spending less time in front of judges." I saw no reason to elaborate. My current job status was both confusing and unnecessary at the moment. "I thought for sure someone was going to end up bruised and bloody."

"Oh, please," he said, shrugging off the suggestion. "That guy is a punk. I can't say what he'd try outside of our security cameras, but he's not stupid enough to try something here." He nodded toward his cohorts, watching from the sidelines. "I don't know about the wife, she seems like a wild cat, but Mr. Sloppy-Ass Attorney is just a thug trying to play big man. He's an idiot. I see him around all the time, pretending to be important. You know the type. You've gone up against pissant men like him. He puffs up his chest, trying to scare people into silence, and like all bullies, he's tough only because he yells louder or he's hiding behind the skirts of his protectors."

"Protectors? What do you mean?"

"Just rumors." He shrugged and let his eyes scan the lobby. "You know how people talk. Thugs don't go it alone."

Screams rang out from somewhere out in the Plaza, and I could see a gaggle of people as they began to run. I immediately looked for Rae, wondering if she and Felix had escalated their conflict, but she remained with her attorney, deep in conversation. I turned back to Tommy, but he was already on the move, listening to whoever was talking in his ear.

I sprinted after him, pausing as I exited the building to get my bearings. Seeing his large frame already at the northwest corner, I picked up my pace, heading toward him, maneuvering through the pedestrians scattering in panic.

"They shot another judge!" a man yelled as he passed me.

I stopped, looked at him, our eyes locked in shock, then swung my head around the Plaza, looking for a shooter, a cluster of cops, looking for signs of danger. I hadn't heard gunfire. Had the shooting occurred in a building? Was a silencer used? I ran toward the edge of the Plaza where I had last seen Tommy. A couple of police officers on foot were trotting north as well, while pedestrians tried to flee, fueled by rumors and raw fear.

As I neared the street, I caught sight of a black SUV double-parked on the far side, flashers blinking. Immediately I scanned the exterior, looking for a red sticker, but saw none on the driver's side that was in my view. In the midst of the growing chaos, a man walked in the middle of the street, calmly but purposefully, toward the vehicle. Caucasian, a navy unmarked baseball cap pulled low over his head, sunglasses concealing his face further, no facial hair. Although I saw no sticker, the vehicle appeared to match the one Judge Reynolds's killers had used, and I reminded myself it had been the passenger side that contained the sticker. I altered my path and went toward the man in the cap. Catching my movement, he paused long enough to turn his head toward me. The shade from his cap, as well as the distance, prevented me from seeing any identifying characteristics. He wore his long-sleeved T-shirt over jeans with no markings; in other words, he was unremarkable. Yet, that too said something.

He turned his gaze toward the vehicle, picking up his pace. About fifteen feet out, the screech of a siren and flashing lights of a police cruiser jolted us both. Immediately, the SUV sped off, leaving the man standing alone in the street. He turned and ran in the direction the cops were moving. I hesitated for only a second, then followed him. I didn't know who he was or why the driver hadn't waited for the man to walk that short distance, but I wanted to. This wasn't about a parking ticket.

As I rounded the corner, a group of officers convened.

Tommy and four cops huddled alongside a body on the ground as an ambulance maneuvered into place. I stopped abruptly, my eyes on the body, as an officer redirected me away from the scene. I wanted to stay, to know what had happened and who it had happened to, but no one was paying attention to the man in the cap. No one seemed to have noticed the SUV that sped off. I scanned the street for the man with the baseball cap, spotting the back of his head as he descended into the Pedway, and I took off, leaving the victim with those who could care for him.

Chicago's Pedway system was a series of underground tunnels and overhead bridges connecting buildings in the Loop and parts of the subway system. It meandered over forty blocks and covered roughly five miles of ground, providing Chicagoans with a way to avoid inclement weather while downtown. And this guy was hoping to get lost in the maze.

I scurried down the stairs, my eyes scanning for a man in a navy blue hat moving quickly. I caught sight of him bobbing through a group of tourists. CPD was busy at street level in the early stages of securing the scene, but I could hear the confused tones of panic starting to build in the people around me. Not knowing what had happened, just hearing the word *shooter* while trapped in a tunnel with few places to hide was starting to have an effect. I could see the confusion and panic in faces build as whispers of what had happened spread like a game of telephone. Hushed voices became loud cries of "Where do I go? Is he still here?" And that energy fed their bodies, moving people to scatter haphazardly, seeking out something that felt safe, unable to tell whether this was an active shooter situation or an isolated incident.

A scream reverberated against the ceramic tile walls from somewhere in front of me, and people began to run, unable to determine what was safe and what was not, what was true and what was not. I shimmied myself against the wall, trying to keep my eyes on the blue hat now forty feet in front of me. As I moved through the stream of bodies, pushing urgently against the tide, I lost sight of my target. Standing on my toes as the frightened visitors scattered like roaches, I peered over their heads as best I could. But I could no longer see him. Had he exited? Had he simply taken off his hat?

I was nearing an artery connecting the Pedway to the Thompson Center. I hadn't seen the man turn out of the tunnel, but I had no way of knowing that he hadn't, either, and the Pedway connected to multiple subway stops on Lake Street on the north side of the Center. I rounded the corner, debating how far to explore the connecting passageway where I was met with a group of squealing women—tourists, it seemed, unaccustomed to this weird underground network—who were now frantically rushing toward perceived safety. Paying no mind to anyone around them, they barreled forward, shopping bags and totes swinging, bumping into my back.

As I paused from the jab, a pair of hands grabbed my shoulders from behind, shoving me into the tile.

"Back off, bitch," a male voice said. I could feel him breathing hard next to me. He raised his left hand, placing his palm on the wall next to my face. "We understand each other?"

He dug the fingers of his right hand into my shoulder when I didn't respond until I flinched from the pain. "Do we understand each other?" he repeated.

As I squirmed in his grasp, his hand moved closer and wrapped around my neck, squeezing until I struggled to breathe and my vision became wavy. Then he released me, raising his palm back to the wall. I choked and gasped as my body fought the constriction. As he pulled away to leave, the sleeve of his T-shirt inched up, exposing just a bit of his pale skin.

On the inside of his wrist was a small red diamond-shaped tattoo.

22

———

"What the hell were you thinking?"

Michael stood hovering at my side while an EMT pressed an ice pack into my neck. I'd phoned in an incident report to CPD after the creep with the baseball hat choked me and slammed me into the wall, but I hadn't anticipated that Michael would be notified. I leaned against the wall of the Pedway, processing the small bits of data that were flooding my brain and watching the mixture of anger and worry that crossed Michael's face. Did my face show the same conflict?

"This is quite some damsel-in-distress network you have," I said, looking at the cops around him. "What is this, the cop version of Google alerts? You get a ping on your phone any time my name pops up on a call-in?"

I knew I sounded a little peeved, but I wasn't sure how I felt about his arrival. It was a little stalker-ish while, at the same time, sweet and loving. He didn't need to be here. Small dustups in the Pedway were not his sphere of responsibility, and I didn't like the idea that he thought me helpless, or that his fellow cops knew we had something going on. This kind of treatment was reserved for cop families, so the two beat cops who had showed up to take my assault statement would be wondering why he was involved. And they would quickly deduce a personal relationship was at the heart of it.

"Why don't we worry about what happened rather than how I got here?" Michael said. "Dispatch said this was related to the incident street-side. Something about you knowing or seeing the shooter. What the hell are you talking about?"

The incident street-side? Cops had real skill with talking around issues. The two officers had arrived prior to Michael, and we'd already gone through the details of the attack. But we hadn't discussed why I happened to be in the Pedway or my theory that the man who had attacked me somehow had a connection to the shooting moments ago or to Judge Reynolds's murder. Clearly, I couldn't withhold details that might be related to the killing, but there was no way for me to discuss what I knew or what I believed without feeling Michael's anger. And whatever was left of our relationship would be permanently damaged because I'd held back information. I'd known that was a possibility when I chose not to tell him about Abbiocco, and it was time to face that reality.

"I was in the Daley Center following a story when I heard a commotion outside. The 'street-side incident,' as you called it." Michael narrowed his eyes at the dig. "The security guard I was speaking to sprinted out, and I followed him. A guy in the Plaza told me that another judge had been shot. When I went to see what was happening, I noticed an SUV that looked remarkably like the one driven by the men who killed Judge Reynolds. The man who later attacked me was walking toward that vehicle when a police cruiser pulled up behind him, hit his siren, and scared off the SUV driver. The driver was in such a rush to get out of there that he left his companion stranded on the street.

The guy on foot ran into the Pedway, and I followed him. The rest I've already told the officers."

Michael stared at me like a cop, not my lover, and I waited for the hand slap that would remind me of how stupid it was for me to go after the guy.

"So you ran after a stranger because you thought he was about to get into a car that looked like the one another suspect drove? And put yourself in danger in the process?"

Michael's voice dripped with irritation, and the way he said it sounded ridiculous even to me, but ignoring my instincts rarely worked out. It was my job to follow hunches and vague leads and something that might become something, just as it was Michael's job to do the same.

The two cops watched the exchange, looking at me quizzically, not realizing that I was a journalist or that I had witnessed Judge Reynolds's murder and wasn't some random person who liked a foot chase just for fun. There was no reason to clarify. Their job was my assault. Michael was the one I needed to convince.

"I know that sounds a bit over-the-top," I said carefully. "I can't know for certain that the vehicles were the same, but why would he sit double-parked and then peel out, leaving his companion at the first sign of cops? And why would the guy on the street run when the car left? He wasn't running to the car to get away from whatever danger he perceived on the street. He was running from the cops."

Michael was too much of a pro to give me an eye roll in front of his colleagues, but I could read the "Are you kidding me?" in his face.

"I can think of at least fifteen reasons drivers get spooked when a cop car pulls up behind them," he said. "None of them involve murdering a judge. You are reaching again. No, actually, your imagination is taking you off on some fantasy. You want so badly to write the story that solves a crime that you're seeing things that don't exist. Stop trying to force fiction to become fact."

The red diamond tattoo again flashed in my mind. The image didn't include the word *Abbiocco*, but the Reliance Bank guard had accurately described the sideways orientation of the red diamond and the border. The two images were too close to ignore. I looked at Michael's face, debating what to tell him.

"And did this guy wear a Halloween mask too?" Michael asked.

I shook my head while Michael gave me another scathing look. The mask was a missing element, but perhaps he'd already tossed it by the time I'd seen him?

"Maybe you cops should look for it," I said. "There are plenty of trash cans and alleyways, or maybe he stuffed it inside the jacket he wore after he had done the deed."

Michael said nothing.

"Tell me about the murdered judge," I said, buying myself some time before I shared more, expecting that once he knew I'd withheld information from him about the sticker on the shooter's vehicle, this conversation would be over, and likely our relationship.

He stared at me, clenching his jaw. "You can speak with the public affairs office if you have questions, like all other journalists, or wait for an official press statement."

The two beat cops exchanged a look, now understanding one part of the dynamic.

"I see. Well, I guess that means we're done here. Thank you, gentlemen," I said to the officers. Then turning to Michael: "Here's a fact for you. The SUV driven by Judge Reynolds's killers had a sticker on the back window. A red diamond that said 'Abbiocco.' I didn't mention it at the time because I didn't see it. I interviewed a bank security guard who saw the opposite side of the car and told me about the sticker. I don't think it's a coincidence that the man who attacked me had the same red tattoo on the inside of his wrist."

Michael opened his mouth to speak, but whatever he wanted to say, he'd need to say it to the back of my head. I turned and walked into the lower level of the Thompson Center, leaving the men where they stood.

I maneuvered back toward Daley Plaza. Clark Street was completely blocked. A throng of cops, forensic teams, reporters, and the crime-curious filled the street. Something about a police incident drew a contingent of voyeuristic individuals who needed to know what was going on. Fear, blatant curiosity, thank-God-it's-not-me, I wasn't sure. My interest was always the story, and since Michael had chosen not to talk, I'd have to get what I needed the old-fashioned way.

I squeezed in as close as I could, knowing that the EMTs would have moved the body by now, but the after-stages of the investigation were still very active as the area was searched for evidence and witnesses were identified. Scanning the nearby buildings, I looked for security cameras, noting locations. With all the cameras in the Loop, hopefully, something had been caught on tape.

A journalist I had a decent relationship with was positioned near the police barricade. I inched toward the front, hoping she'd tell me what I'd missed while I had my one-on-one with my assailant and CPD.

"Hey, Amy. Looks like we're both putting in another day in the trenches together. At least it's not in the blistering heat like last time we ran into each other."

"So true. I'm tired of sweating my ass off in this concrete canyon. I keep trying to convince myself that I'd be happy working for a small local paper somewhere in rural Wisconsin, covering tractor pulls and marauding deer. Then I realize I'd have to live on cheese curds and a Friday Fish Fry if I moved, not to mention my Starbuck habit would have to go, so, instead, I'm living with the trade-offs."

"I have no romantic illusions about country life. I'm a confirmed city gal at this point." I nodded at that nearest cop. "So, have they officially announced the name of the victim yet? I had an issue that kept me occupied." I pointed at my neck but didn't elaborate. "I'm a little late to the party."

"That doesn't look like it was fun," she said, not asking for details. "Nope. No announcement. You know how they pretend it's all a big secret. Don't want the family to hear it on the news. But rumor is the vic is a judge named Doyle Atkinson. Shot in the chest point-blank, but the gunman must have had a silencer because there were no reports of a gunshot. Bold move in the middle of the street, so chances are someone saw it."

"Gunman as in gender or the generic?"

"Assumption. It always seems to be a guy, doesn't it? There are a lot of fucked-up men who need therapy, and I've dated way too many of them." She gave me a half-hearted laugh, as if I was supposed to join in and commiserate. Not today.

"Robbery attempt?"

"Don't know about that. From what I've heard, Atkinson just got shot in the chest and the killer kept walking, but that's not confirmed. Someone saw the body fall. That's all I've heard so far."

"Thanks. I owe you a coffee some time," I said, inching away.

"Make it a vodka, and you have a deal."

I nodded and moved through the crowd. Across the street, a man stood outside a tiny shoe repair shop in an apron. The yellow neon sign in the window read "Shoe Shines." This stretch of Clark Street was lined by City Hall and office towers with street-level retail. Given the heavy concentration of government buildings, retail meant Chipotle and Walgreens, banks, and various fast-food establishments catering to the nine-to-five work crowd. This shoe fixer was the smallest joint and, in my mind, therefore, most likely to have seen something.

"Not a good day for business, is it?" I said as I approached him.

"Sure ain't. Nobody who thought they wanted a shine would brave this mess. Hope they get that police tape down by tomorrow. I can't afford three days of staring at the wall with no business coming in. Rent ain't cheap down here." He shook his head, contemplating the disruption to his business instead of the victim.

"My name is Andrea. I'm a reporter with Link-Media." I handed him my card. "Can I talk to you for a minute about what you saw?"

He looked at the card, turning it over. "I don't know. I didn't see anything, really." He was short and thin, wiry like a runner, with plentiful crinkles in the dark skin around his eyes. He had a slight accent that sounded Caribbean but from way back in his past.

"Well, sometimes what seems like an unimportant detail means something when put into the context of a bigger picture. You may have seen something that you don't realize was important."

"Ah, I'm not sure I want to get involved." He shuffled at the suggestion but made no attempt to turn his eyes away from the scene across the street.

"In a way, you're already involved," I said, thinking about the ripple effects of murder number two on the neighborhood. "This incident happened across the street from your shop. Until the guy is caught, people will worry about it happening again. They don't know if it's safe to be on the street. I hate to say it, but this could affect your business for a while if the shooter isn't caught quickly."

I could see fear spread across his face as the possibility dawned on him.

"Yeah, I guess you're right," he said grudgingly. "But I really don't think I know anything."

"Maybe not, but it's better than wondering if you could have helped. What were you doing when you first realized something unusual was happening outside?"

I often brought people back to the beginning, let them start their story before they even knew there was a story to tell. Recalling the mundane brought out the important.

"No one was in the shop, so I was cleaning the window. Dust builds up on the ledge from the buffers and the street dirt, so I wipe things down and do a light window wash at least once a week. In this neighborhood, people bring in five-hundred-dollar shoes. My customers don't tolerate a sloppy shop."

"And when did you realize something was going on?" I asked.

"I heard a scream. I could tell it was a woman's voice. Looked up and saw this guy clutching his chest and leaning against the wall. Then he turned his back to the wall, he was facing me then, and there was just blood everywhere. He was a mess. His whole chest was covered. Next thing I know, he falls to the ground. The woman was standing about ten feet away. She just kept screaming and shaking her arms like she didn't know what to do."

"Did it seem like she knew him? Maybe grab his arm or something to help him?"

"Not really. It felt more like she was just shocked when she saw him and didn't know what to do."

"You didn't hear a gunshot?"

"No. And there's no way I could have missed that. This place is a sound tunnel. People are sayin' he was shot, but I thought he'd been stabbed. How do you hide that sound? One of those silencers?"

Not even the well-timed engine noise of a city bus would have obscured the sound of gunfire. I looked across the street for a doorway or alley access, anything that might have concealed the interaction, thinking the victim might have stumbled out to the sidewalk after the encounter. Nothing but a brick wall for about thirty feet. Then on the north end of the block the glass windows of a coffee joint, a sandwich place, and a small bank branch on the next corner. That meant the killer used a silencer to deliver a direct hit to the chest on the sidewalk in broad daylight. And that was as damn audacious as the killers who took out Judge Reynolds.

"Was there anyone else on the sidewalk or on the street? Maybe someone walking away from the victim?"

"The woman, she was the closest. Then I think maybe two people were together but over there near the corner. I only noticed them when they started running to her." He pointed to the southeast intersection.

"I know this is a weird question, but did you see anyone wearing a Halloween mask?"

"What?" He laughed. "I don't know what that question is about, but I can't say I did."

"And to the north? Did you see anyone on the sidewalk?" I was assuming the shooter had walked past the judge heading north, took his shot, and kept walking. A direct hit to the chest meant the judge was on the ground only moments later, so the shooter would still have been on the sidewalk trying to blend in as the judge staggered against the wall before collapsing.

"I couldn't really see much 'cause there was this big SUV moving past then. There was a little traffic, so it wasn't moving fast. I saw the guy fall, and then the car blocked my view. I was too busy trying to see what happened to the guy who got hit to notice anyone to the north."

My pulse began racing. "This SUV was north of the victim when you first saw him, and the vehicle drove past the victim and kept going south, not stopping. Correct?" He nodded. "Was there anything about the SUV that stood out to you?"

"It was one of those dark things that looks like a bunch of FBI guys are gonna jump out of. Black, dark windows, impossible to park. The only other thing I remember is there was some kind of red sticker in the back window."

"Can you recall if it was a diamond shape but lying sideways?"

"Hmm, now that you mention it, yeah, I think it was."

23

———————

I inched past the remaining observers, my mind on judges and SUVs and red stickers and Felix Panici. Steps away from the shoe repair shop, I opened my phone and searched for anything I could find about Judge Doyle Atkinson. The Twitterverse hadn't yet named the victim in the incident, and I couldn't exactly call Michael to confirm his identity under the circumstances. But my thoughts were bombarding me with what-if scenarios as I tried to understand what connected these two judges.

Cai, of course, was my next thought as a source of information. She could have given me insight on the judge's history, but she was off for a long weekend in Michigan with a guy she'd been seeing consistently for a month. In other words, it was Cai's idea of a long-term relationship, and I didn't want to do anything that would give her a reason to bail on him. She was so commitment-averse that I couldn't remember her ever taking a vacation with someone she was dating.

My quick internet search showed me that Atkinson was a circuit court judge with the law division. How could his murder be related to a judge in family court? But I was convinced these two murders were connected. And if the shoe shine guy was right about that sticker, it was more than a farfetched opinion even without the mask. Panici hated Reynolds. That seemed clear. Enough to kill him or have him killed, it seemed a stretch if this was just about a divorce. But the craziness of killers rarely followed the rules of logic.

Now, with a second judge dead, I had to wonder if Panici had had a run-in with Atkinson, too. The man was an attorney and had likely been before half the court system given his penchant for quantity over quality in his cases. The legal system seemed the obvious connection point, but it could be any number of things. The word *Abbiocco* again blazed in my mind. Something connected these two murders.

Running through the possibilities, I tried to create the movie version of how this might have played out. Unlike Judge Reynolds's murder, I couldn't imagine the shooter had jumped out of the vehicle, killed him, then gotten back in the car and driven off. Although the sidewalk wasn't terribly crowded at the time, a guy jumping out of a vehicle, firing a couple of shots, jumping back in a vehicle, and driving off would have been noticeable. And the driver would've gotten the hell out of there as quickly as possible, which also would have drawn attention. The only way I saw this going down so quietly was the shooter being on foot and the SUV driving past before getting into position to pick up the shooter at another location, so it would all look less obvious. And that SUV was likely the same one I saw double-parked. The driver would have simply needed to circle the block and wait for his companion. The timing made sense with the shooter on foot. And that could mean that the shooter was the man I saw and the man who attacked me. Although his body type didn't match Panici's, that didn't mean he wasn't behind the hit even if he hadn't been the trigger man himself.

Why was an even bigger question. I needed to figure out the connection between the murders.

Since Cai wasn't an option, I ran through a mental list of other attorneys I could pester.

Ten minutes later, I marched into Peter Retley's office, hoping I'd get lucky and find him at his desk. He wasn't a trial attorney, so the odds were in my favor that I could barge in unannounced, provided he wasn't meeting with a client.

"Hi, is Peter in today? I'm a friend of his, Andrea Kellner."

The young woman at the desk looked at me, confused. She wasn't the same receptionist, the one with the silly bun and pancake-sized earrings, who'd been at the desk the last time I'd paid Peter a visit, so I was an unfamiliar face to her. And pop-ins weren't exactly how the legal industry worked.

"Um, do you have an appointment?" she stammered. "I don't see anything on his calendar." Brows drawn, lips pursed, she clicked a few keys on her computer, trying to figure out if she had confused a date.

"No, I don't have an appointment," I said. "I was just nearby and was hoping I could have a couple of minutes with him. Could you check and see if he has time?"

Grudgingly, she picked up the phone and explained the situation to her boss. As I waited, a news alert pinged on my phone. Atkinson had been confirmed as the murder victim. I scrolled quickly through the article as I waited, but the announcement contained little detail other than he had been shot point-blank on the street by an unknown assailant. It was still too early for the how and the why. A few seconds later, Peter opened the door with a big smile on his face.

"What a nice surprise. It's been a couple of months since we last spoke, hasn't it?"

As always, Peter reminded me of a wannabe bit player in one of *The Godfather* movies. His slicked-back hair and French-cuffed shirts with their gold cuff links made him seem like he was trying too hard to tell the world he was successful. A couple of times a year he made an attempt to get me to go out with him, regardless of my marital status. I, on the other hand, had yet to feel that urge.

"Why don't you come into my office? It's a good time for a break. My eyes are glazing over on this brief I'm reviewing. And you know my work isn't exactly sexy, so if I'm getting bored, you know it's bad."

Peter dabbled mostly in real estate and contract law, usually small commercial situations and run-of-the-mill contract law. As a solo practitioner, he didn't need the fancy trappings of an impressive office, which also made his chosen attire seem all the more out of place. He was a workhorse attorney. And although there was nothing sexy about his case roster, as he fully admitted, he did an excellent job of cutting through the clutter and getting results. He wasn't the same kind of take-any-case-that-paid type of an attorney that Panici seemed to be. He took cases he thought he could win. Panici, on the other hand, seemed to care only that the client had the money to pay.

And speaking of payments, my thoughts returned to the moment in court when Panici was interrupted by the man with the Abbiocco sticker on his portfolio who handed him that fat envelope. Abbiocco kept coming up, and it sure felt like there was something more important here than a fondness for pizza.

I followed Peter into his small, cluttered office, where legal tomes and case files competed for space with White Sox paraphernalia, then slid into the seat I was offered.

Peter smiled a bit mischievously. "To what do I owe the pleasure? Have you dumped that boyfriend of yours yet?"

"No. We're still dating." I gave him a small laugh, knowing that was likely a lie, but Peter didn't need an update on my love life. "Do you know a judge by the name of Doyle Atkinson?"

"Yeah, not well, but I know him. Why do you ask?"

I opened my phone, tapping on the report. "He was just murdered." I handed him my phone.

"What? This just happened?" Peter stared at the screen, mouth open, running through the story.

"Details are still really sketchy," I said. "It's only been about an hour and a half. CPD literally just released his name. I was there. Well, I didn't see him get shot, but he was on the ground and EMTs had just arrived."

"I can't believe this. Where did this happen?"

"Try Daley Plaza. Atkinson was half a block north on Clark, and apparently, someone walked up to him on the sidewalk, shot him, and kept going, likely using a silencer, because it seems nobody heard a gunshot. I spoke to a guy right across the street, and he didn't know it had happened until he heard screaming. Obviously, they're still piecing this all together, so we don't know who or why. I came over here because I thought you might know him. Thought maybe you might've worked with him somewhere along the way, and I'm trying to get some background on the guy. By the sounds of it, to me, anyway, this was a hit, not a robbery, so there's gotta be something in the man's background."

"But that's two judges in a week. What's going on?" Peter let out a long breath and pinched the bridge of his nose.

"I don't know, but I sure want to find out. What do you know about Atkinson?" I said, watching Peter's face as he processed.

"Um, give me a minute. It's, wow, um, really hard to fathom." He reached over for his coffee mug and took a long sip. "Okay. Atkinson handled fraud cases, malpractice, and property damage, the usual stuff for the law division. If my memory is correct, he'd been on the bench for around fifteen years. I've been in his courtroom probably half a dozen times. Mostly for breach-of-contract cases."

I ran through options in my head as Peter spoke. Beyond my suspicions around Panici, it was conceivable that Reynolds and Atkinson had a common litigant but for different reasons. But something worth a well-planned murder? If that was the motivation, perhaps a significant ruling by Atkinson had affected the killer first, and then a bad ruling in divorce had set him over the edge. Sure seemed like an extreme way to handle a personal grievance.

"What did you think of him?" I asked.

"A little unpredictable. He wasn't a strict by-the-book guy. I always had the sense that I was trying to figure out his mood of the day. I could never quite get a handle on how the guy thought. There's never a guarantee of how any judge will rule, but generally, I know their proclivities. Whether they want me to get straight to the point or give them tons of background. You know how it is. You play to the audience, and a straight-up letter-of-the-law judge doesn't like surprises, so you tailor your presentation. But with Atkinson, I could never figure out the code. What worked in one case wouldn't the next. So it was always a crapshoot."

"Did you respect him?"

Peter didn't say anything. I watched his eyes, trying to figure out why this was a complicated question.

"That should be easy to answer, shouldn't it?" he said after a moment. "I'm pausing because I don't have facts. A few years back, there were allegations that Atkinson had taken a bribe on a case. Nothing was ever proven, but it makes you look at a judge differently if you think he was on the take. I guess I was never certain about him after that. And his hot-and-cold judicial style didn't help."

"Do you remember anything about the case?"

"No, I can't say I do, just that there was a construction company involved."

24

———————

The Hair Lounge. It wasn't a terribly creative or elegant name for a salon, but Rae wasn't exactly elegant herself.

Instead of hitting the Saturday morning farmers market, I had driven out to Elmwood Park and was now sitting in my car across the street from the brick building with my travel mug of Earl Grey, looking at her Elmwood Park salon. Through the large front window, I saw red velvet curtains with gold fringe edging, flocked wallpaper, and ostentatious crystal chandeliers. Rae had turned her wardrobe into a decorating theme. Although I found the decor incredibly tacky and way over-the-top, I did see the consistency of the atmosphere and suspected, like all good business people, she knew her customer intimately.

The tight branding of her business was also a sign that she had a fair amount of business acumen under her big blown-out hair. With multiple locations and franchising deals, she was smarter than her stereotypical appearance would suggest.

Could that be what made her dangerous to her estranged husband?

I'd spent last night holed up in my home office playing with sticky notes on my whiteboard, sorting through the bits and pieces of stories that seemed to have an overlap I didn't understand. Or, at the very least, people who overlapped, even if the actual incidents were not related. Two judges were dead, likely by the same killer. An alderman taking payola from a construction company. One of the judges had a huge debt to a construction company. The other had an alleged history of accepting bribes from a construction company. The Chicken Shack owner was connected to the construction people. And Felix Panici seemed to know them all, including one of the dead judges.

Panici seemed to be the key. And his estranged wife appeared to not only have important dirt on the man, but she also hated him, which was a bad combination for a divorce and an excellent combination for a journalist.

Saturdays were prime time in the salon world, so I'd driven out intending to walk into the salon the moment the door was unlocked, hoping to miss the crush of appointments.

I could see Rae checking her styling sprays at one of the front chairs as a tiny woman with short black hair hung the "Open" sign and turned the latch on the front door.

I exited my car and made my way across the street and into the salon. A soft chime alerted the women as I opened the door. Rae looked up. The smile on her face faded for a second when she saw me, as if I wasn't who she was expecting. The interior of the salon was even more grandiose in its decorating than I'd been able to see from the car. Enormous silk floral arrangements sat on pedestals in the corners. Leopard-print curtains cordoned off the shampoo station, and more hanging-crystal draped lighting dotted the back ceiling.

"I'm sorry. We don't take walk-ins on a Saturday," Rae said. "Viola can set up an appointment for you, or come back on Monday. We're slower then."

The woman who had unlocked the door was tending to a

carton of shampoo that needed unboxing and placement on the retail display shelf. She scurried over to the front desk, her heels clicking on the tile floor as she walked, ready to check her computer for me.

"Actually, Rae, I'm not here for a haircut. I was hoping we could talk. I was at court yesterday when you and your husband were leaving." I kept my language neutral, not knowing how chatty she was with her staff about her personal life. Stepping forward, I handed her my card.

"Husband? Hah! That piece of shit hasn't been my husband in two years, regardless of what the legal system has to say about it. I have plenty of words for him, and *husband* ain't one of them."

That answered my question about whether the subject was sensitive.

She looked at my card, flipping back a swath of bang that had drooped over her right eye.

"So, do you cover the ugly divorce beat or something? Wait around for couples to come to blows? Didn't know there were journalist versions of an ambulance chaser. Or is this outfit you work for a local version of *Star Magazine*? Do you have photos of us mid-scream?"

She stood, hands on her hips, defiant. Challenging my professionalism and my character. I had to smile at that. Images of the brawl in the courthouse lobby would have been perfect fodder if that was the type of organization Link-Media aspired to be.

"I don't have photographs, but they would have been terrific action shots," I said, getting a laugh in response.

She shook her head and shrugged. "Okay. What do you want? 'Cause I got appointments coming in any minute."

Three additional stylists had found their way from the back

room to their stations and were giving us curious looks as they prepped for the onslaught.

"You made some loose allegations about your husband. Something about knowing where bodies are buried. Suggesting that he might want to silence you. Can you tell me about that?"

I didn't know how much time I had before a customer would be demanding her attention, so I led with the juicy stuff. Rae grimaced slightly, glancing over toward the gals. The first customer was already at the front desk, checking in.

"Come with me," she said.

She led me out the front door onto the sidewalk while her employee Viola watched us closely from the front desk.

"Felix isn't always on the up-and-up, business-wise, is what I meant," she said. "I didn't mean *bodies* bodies. He ain't a killer. There's stuff I know that could make his life hell, and I remind him of that now and then. But he wouldn't dare come after me. He's just a narcissistic prick who thinks he can intimidate me."

Her explanation was vague, and I sensed intentionally so. "Not on the up-and-up" was not what she had screamed yesterday in the lobby. And I doubted something so bland was fueling the level of protection she thought she had.

"My understanding is that your divorce has been going on for quite some time. If you have knowledge of shady business dealings, wouldn't that help move your divorce along? Apply extra pressure?"

Something felt unsaid here. As contentious as Cai said this divorce was, why would Rae hold back information that could settle the case in her favor? That wasn't how divorce worked, not a divorce like theirs, anyway. You didn't hold back the good stuff until the last minute, playing the odds on whether you should or shouldn't put it into evidence. And Rae seemed to be holding this card close to her chest.

"You're right. This divorce has gone on so long that I've seen Felix's hairline recede two inches. The way he's playing it, he'll be needing hair plugs before we're done. He got one judge kicked off the case for a trumped-up conflict of interest, and now our second judge is dead. So the whole timeline is shit. And that's the way he wants it. Drag, drag, drag it out and he thinks he'll win."

Delay was not an unusual tactic, particularly when arrogant men were involved, but I wasn't getting the full story.

"Felix ain't exactly a choir boy. Never has been. And as they say, I've got the receipts. He just doesn't know how many of them. So, yeah, I got that in my back pocket. What they call the nuclear option. If I need to, Felix and his... Felix, he'll have to face some tough questions."

What had she stopped herself from saying? Felix and his... what? She shot her eyes over my shoulder, realizing the near miss. I watched her face, seeing a glint of emotion. Fear, perhaps? Then she turned toward the shop, and my eyes followed. Viola was still staring at us intently. Too intently.

"You claimed you had an insurance policy. That sounds like you have evidence. Is that what you mean by receipts? Documents, a paper trail, or videos, maybe, that could prove he'd had suspicious business dealings. Or were they illegal business dealings?"

For an angry ex-wife, she was blowing a lot of vague smoke, but I couldn't tell if it was bluster or self-protection. Rae was certainly hot-tempered, as was her ex, so the drama of dangling loose threats didn't surprise me. But she also didn't strike me as someone who would threaten if she didn't have the goods. That left me wondering if she was holding back because she was complicit. That would explain her "nuclear option" comment. If she released on him, she'd be releasing on herself, too.

I knew from my own marriage that a wife wasn't always enmeshed in her husband's dealings. That phrase "a wife always knows" was utter bullshit, and I was proof. Whether Felix was engaged in illegal activity or just shitty husband stuff, I couldn't assume Rae was knee-deep in whatever Felix was up to. But her silence felt like more than a divorce strategy. Who waits two years to trot out the dirt in court without a damn good reason? She was protecting herself or someone else. Why?

"Let's just say I can back up anything I say. Felix can dangle on the end of that hook, wondering what I have, for as long as I decide to toy with him. And I hope that makes his intestines cramp. I've seen his world firsthand. I know how this works. I'll get what I want eventually, one way or another. In the meantime, I'm happy to be a wild card."

She shifted her hips and tossed her hair as a smug smile crossed her face. And there it was again, a vague reference to something bigger than just Felix and their divorce.

"Felix is an attorney, correct? What kind of business dealings would he have that wouldn't be on the up-and-up, as you called it?" Of course, I had all kinds of ideas on ways attorneys could skim or manipulate filings, but Rae didn't need to know that.

"The legal stuff, the day job, he can't stray too far with that. But Felix always has a side hustle. Thinks he's smarter than everyone else. There's always some deal he's cooking up. Doesn't even keep it in the family. When his mind was still intact, my father never would have let him get tied up with that Russian. Family is everything. But Felix thinks he can play in the big leagues and control loyalties. Not outside the family, he can't. He's gonna learn the hard way."

What? Side hustles? Family? The Russian? Rae was on a roll. She was giving me clues, but I didn't have the framework to put it in perspective. I needed the decoder ring before I could make sense of this.

"What kind of deals are you talking about?" I asked.

A woman in her late fifties approached the door, her hair a

platinum-blond version of Rae's. "Good morning, Harriet. I'll be right there. Just take a seat," Rae said.

"I gotta go," Rae said, once her customer was inside. "If you want more, help me out. Be a reporter. Uncover something. Go find his secrets. He has a lot of them. Maybe you can take him down so I don't have to."

She smiled wickedly and went back inside. I watched her sashay over to her waiting customer and turn on the charm, then I returned to my car. I sat in the car for a minute, jotting down notes while they were fresh in my mind, then scrolled Twitter and email for anything that I needed to address before I moved on. Abbiocco was my next stop.

Movement at the salon door caught my attention. Viola had walked away from the desk. She shot a furtive look toward Rae, stepped to the side of the door to be out of sight, and placed a brief call.

Was she reporting to Felix, perhaps?

25
______

Abbiocco. The red sideways-diamond sign hung boldly over the canopied double-doored front entrance. Wine barrel planters loaded with red geraniums flanked the sides and smokey glass windows cut dark swaths into the red brick. It reminded me of places I'd visited during my Wisconsin childhood that, at the time, had defined fine dining but today would be considered kitschy and of another era. I imagined pine-paneled walls, Budweiser on tap, stained carpet that had been installed in the seventies, and maybe even some dead animals on the walls.

Aside from its in-town location, I could have picked it up and placed it in any rural Wisconsin town and it wouldn't have looked out of place. It was a joint, the kind my father would love, and where patrons all knew each other. A place where stories became lore and reputations were built or destroyed based on the amount of alcohol consumed. The kind of place that was far too inbred for my tastes.

An alley on the east side of the building led to a parking lot in the back, but I wanted to get my bearings on the neighborhood. The restaurant was a short fifteen-minute drive from Rae's salon and situated outside of the village's Restaurant Row. Elmwood Park was a leafy bedroom community with a population of approximately twenty-five thousand, located about ten miles from downtown. Chicago still stubbornly held onto its ethnic neighborhood history, and the village reflected that with its Italian and Polish heritage.

So, it was no surprise that an Italian pizzeria with an Italian name would exist here. The question was what role did it have in these murders? It could be a clubhouse of sorts for the various men I'd come across, I supposed.

Rae's language about her husband kept flashing into my head. *Because you're connected. The family. Send me on a long trip.* That was language right out of a fifties mob movie. Was that still a thing? I thought the old-time mafia had been replaced by gangs and drug cartels. The idea of mob involvement seemed both contrived and stereotypical as I sat across from a decades-old Italian restaurant.

I walked over to the restaurant. The waft of garlicky tomato sauce hit me as I pulled open the heavy door and stepped inside the dark restaurant. Although no dead animals graced the walls, the decor was largely as I imagined it would be. Dark paneled walls, neon beer signs, vinyl upholstered booths, red plastic carnations in a bud vase on the tables, and red plastic checkerboard tablecloths. I doubt it had looked much different in the eighties than it did today.

A sign instructed me to seat myself, so I took a booth where I could watch both the bar and the majority of the restaurant floor. A server dropped off a laminated menu, took my iced tea order, and told me that a meatball sub was the special of the day. When she returned with my drink, I added a small, thin-crust veggie pie to my order, then sat back to people-watch. The restaurant was filled to about three-quarters capacity, and the long wooden bar sat another ten. Not a bad crowd, since it was on the early side of the Saturday lunch rush. Small parties of two and four filled tables, and a couple of the larger parties contained elementary school–age boys in their soccer gear filling up on pizza after the morning game. Another Saturday in the suburbs. And nothing nefarious about it.

The pizza was damn good, but I wasn't seeing these Abbiocco stickers because of a citywide reputation for a good slice. Nor, as I sat eating, was I seeing anything or anyone that gave me a clue about the relevance of this restaurant to the murders. As near as I could tell, it was just a good neighborhood pizza joint. I finished another piece, paid my bill, and headed for the ladies' room prior to my drive back into the city. In the time-honored tradition of steakhouses that thought they were famous, the hallway was a gallery of framed photos. Patrons, local celebrities, smiling staff. The occasional official auto-graphed headshot of some C-level actor from the nineties whom I didn't know mingled with the impromptu, on-location restau-rant shots.

Slow-walking the hall, I perused the shots. The village presi-dent. Alderman Farnsworth. An annoying guy that owned half a dozen car dealerships in the burbs and plastered his face and voluminous belly on all of his commercials. A tall, dark-haired man I didn't know was at the center of many of the shots. His smile was wide, his forehead even wider. The owner, I assumed.

As I looked over the collection, familiar faces began to creep into the mix. Felix Panici with a goofy grin and highball glass in hand, next to the guy I assumed was the owner. Edmund Rastello with the same guy. Rastello and Panici and Farnsworth. Panici and Rae and Rastello with another woman, everyone's arms around each other. A dozen shots of these men in various small groups. I pulled out my phone and snapped shots of the shots as I walked the hall.

Working toward the restrooms, I came across a photo of

eight. Panici and Rae. Rastello and a woman, possibly his wife. The guy I presumed was the owner, also with a woman. And the guy from court with the widow's peak. He stood, a forced half-smile, half-sneer on his face, his arm around a woman. That woman was Rae's employee, Viola.

Quite a tight circle these people ran in. Perhaps Viola had phoned the man in the photo, her husband, and not Felix. It wasn't clear how Rae's standing in the group might have changed given the divorce. It wasn't unusual for friends to choose sides, and I wondered if Viola was choosing her employer or her employer's husband. If Felix was as "shady" as Rae indicated, having Viola snitch on Rae's activities would not be out of bounds, whether the content was for use in their divorce or to monitor whether she was a risk based on what she knew about his deeds.

My mind was rumbling through the possibilities as I got back to my car.

"You're supposed to park in the back." An elderly woman, broom in hand, stood on the sidewalk next to my vehicle, pushing dried leaves into a pile. She nodded at my box of left-over pizza. "This parking is for residents. And if you lived here, you'd know that."

"Oh, I'm sorry. I didn't see a sign," I said as I opened the passenger door and placed my box on the floor.

"You city people never do." She huffed and flicked her broom at an errant leaf. I guessed her to be around eighty, but her spine was spry and straight with pride, or perhaps stubbornness.

"I hope you have help this fall," I said. I looked at the canopy of green overhead that was about to turn color and shed. "It must be a lot of work to keep your yard so nice." Her hedges were perfectly pruned. Her coneflowers stood strong and tall. And the little bit of debris she had amassed on the sidewalk would have anyone else leaving it for another day. My knowledge of plants was limited to what I could put in a pot or what I could put in a vase. But if this woman lived across the street from Abbiocco, she likely had more information than a skim of a website and a forty-five-minute lunch could provide and was worth chatting up.

"I have a kid from the neighborhood who rakes. Can't stand those damn loud blowers everyone else seems to use. They're nothing but pollution machines for lazies."

The scowl on her face had softened. "All that noise would bother me too," I said. "Does the smell of tomato sauce start to get annoying after a while, or have you become immune to it?" I tilted my head toward the restaurant, wondering how she felt about her neighbor, other than annoyed when their customers ignored parking etiquette.

"I don't even smell it anymore. What do they call that, being nose blind? I've been in this house for forty-two years' worth of garlic and peppers. Bought this house with my husband. Raised my kids here. That was long before the kid took over the place. Not that he's changed much around the place."

"The founder's son runs the business now?" I asked.

"Not the son. A nephew, Francis. The dad, Lorenzo, he's still around, but I'm not sure he's all there anymore. Last I heard, he was drooling onto a bib at some home his daughter put him in. Back in the day, he was a hottie, though," she said, a mischievous smile on her face.

"Sounds like you had a crush on him," I said, suspecting there were some stories in her past.

"I was always soft on tall, dark-haired men," she said. "But he had a mean streak, that one. I wouldn't date him no matter how many times he asked me out. I never liked that tough-guy type. Nice to look at, but not nice in other ways, if you know what I mean. You've probably met a few in your day as well."

"Abbiocco seems like it's kind of a neighborhood hangout," I said, moving the conversation back to my area of focus.

"Yeah, always been that way. More like a men's club, though. I think some of those guys have spent more time on one of those barstools than they did in their own homes. Wasn't hard to find them that way, back before everyone had cell phones. Kids were always running in and out, telling daddy that mom wanted him to come home or to guilt him into laying off the sauce."

Again, images of childhood came back into my mind. Every local bar had a crew of faces that treated the place like a home away from home.

"Might have been a different place today if the girl had taken over," she said. "But Lorenzo and his ilk still think women belong in the kitchen, and the daughter never got the chance. The daughter, she's got more brains than the dad and the nephew combined. The nephew, he's flat-out lazy, running the business on what's left of his uncle's good will and trying to hang on to customers from the old days. Families don't stay close to home like they used to. Can't keep thinking your customers aren't going to die off and your business with it. Rumor has it that the biz is not doing so well."

"You must have spent a lot of time there yourself over the years, living so close."

"When I was first married, we did. But then Lorenzo started buddying up to my Anthony. Wanted him to hang with him and his friends. I put a stop to that. I wasn't going to be a barstool widow like every other woman around here. And they were nothing but a bunch of crooks in nice clothing, anyway."

Crooks. That was an interesting choice of words.

"What do you mean by crooks?" I asked. "That sounds juicy. What were they up to?" I was keeping my voice light, as if I were just looking for some good local gossip.

"I don't know exactly, but there were always rumors floating around. Gambling. Cash changing hands for some favor or another. That's just how those guys did things. Everything had a price."

"Is that still the case today?"

"I imagine. I think that's another reason Lorenzo passed the place on to his nephew, Francis, instead of his daughter, Rae—because she wouldn't play that game. So the men couldn't control her."

My mind was suddenly racing. "Are you talking about Rae Panici?"

"Sure am. Do you know her?"

26

"Are you rearranging your office? I know decorating is one of your favorite things, but aren't you in the middle of a couple of stories? Or is this your new way to wipe the slate clean on a Monday?"

Brynn stood in the doorway to my office, running her eyes over the stacks of documents, books, and framed art that now sat in piles on the floor.

"I needed a wall."

"And these aren't?" she said, casting her eyes around the room.

"A blank wall, smartass."

"I don't know." She laughed. "I thought maybe you were about to come in here with a sledgehammer and freshen up the place. After all that work on your apartment, you might be inspired to keep going. I don't know how this redecorating bug works. I'm just a lowly twenty-something single girl in a cheap Ukrainian Village rental. What do I know?"

"Help me out. Move this painting over to the other side of the room so I don't trip on it." Brynn's snark was one of my favorite things about her. It also served as a cover for her intelligence. And in my opinion, being underestimated was a useful quality for women in journalism. It made people more likely to talk often enough to be an important tool in the toolbox.

She set her twenty-four-ounce coffee mug on my desk and lifted the art.

"You wanna fill me in?" she said, once standing next to me again in front of my now bare wall. "Or should I just stay out of your way while you search for inspiration?"

"Here." I handed her a stack of photos and a roll of tape. "Just tape them on the wall. It's not an art project."

I'd printed out all the photos I had taken at Abbiocco while I sat in my home office over the weekend, sorting and organizing and trying to figure out what the hell was going on. Images, words, names. Visuals helped me see the story. The small bits were too hard for me to put together if they were just words on a screen. It was my version of an investigation board seen in nearly every movie scene where the detective comes up with one important unnoticed clue he hadn't seen until just the crucial moment.

We covered the wall with the photos of the men at Abbiocco, arranging, moving, placing them into associations as my instincts dictated. I added Post-its with names and question marks for those people I hadn't identified. Added photos of the two judges. Photos of locations. Then I moved to the data points. Panici's comment about Reynolds. Rae's threats. Judge Reynolds's debt to Selciatto. Note by note, I fleshed out the puzzle, leaving blank cards and wild guesses when I knew there was more information to be obtained.

An hour later, I stepped back, staring at the diagram in front of me.

"What do you see?" Brynn asked. Her instincts were still developing, needing the confidence time and setting aside doubt could bring.

"To start, that we should have laid these out in a circle, like a wagon wheel. I just don't know who to put in the center. These guys are so connected it's like they're family. Rae even used similar language when I spoke to her on Saturday. 'Keeping it in the family,' to be precise."

Brynn stepped closer to the wall, looking at the faces. "They're all Italians, right? Sorry to be stereotypical, but that close-knit family thing is big, like it is in the Hispanic community, and in the African American community. I can barely go get a coffee without one of my aunties or cousins tagging along. And dating, well, I rarely mention my dates to my mother because at least six family members would expect to weigh in before, during, and after." I cringed in sympathy. "Or did Rae mean 'the family' as in the mob?" she added.

"I wondered about that too, but there wasn't enough to the conversation to be sure. I may be adding importance to something that isn't. She could have just meant that's how her own family operated. She was commenting on her dad and her husband at the time."

I took a sip of tea and tried to isolate where my eyes were drawn most. What my own instincts were whispering.

"Speaking of the mob, did you know Baby Face Nelson is buried in Elmwood Cemetery?" Brynn said.

I laughed, amused by her ability to pull out obscure facts at the drop of a hat. "Did you go on the Gangster Tour or something? How do you always pull out these tidbits of trivia?"

"I believe I just told you that dating is challenging in my family." She laughed. "A girl has to have hobbies. Of course I went on the Gangster Tour. That's the best one. And I did a tour of the cemetery after because it was so fascinating. You know they do that at Graceland Cemetery all the time, since there are so many famous dead people there."

"And you've done that too, I'm sure." I shook my head. I was amused, but not surprised. And learning a few new details about Brynn's personal life in the process. She'd been slow to share her private life, so each new data point helped me see the complexity hidden underneath her youth.

"Is any work going on in here, or are you two spending your day...scrapbooking?" Borkowski was in my doorway staring at my office-wall-turned-pinboard with annoyance. His tortoise-shell reading glasses were perched on top of his head, white shirtsleeves rolled, boring tie worn loose. In other words, he was in his work uniform. The only time I'd seen him in anything else was at our quarterly board meetings when he added the one sport coat I suspected he owned to the ensemble.

"Good morning, Art," I said, ignoring his dig. Brynn kept her smirk contained, but I knew it was there underneath her half-smile. It wasn't that the two disliked each other; Borkowski simply didn't understand her, and she thought of him as a silly grandpa well past his journalistic prime. And I occasionally needed to play translator for both of them.

"What do you have on that chicken story you were so hot on? Is the inspector on the take with half the city or what? How about dead judges? Anything? I need content."

I opened my mouth to tell him about construction companies and pizza joints and a connection I suspected between the dead judges. Not yet. I didn't even have a solid theory. If I went down that path now, he'd be cutting me off after two sentences and I'd have poisoned the well. I'd made the mistake of making an early call on a story still in concept stage once before and learned the hard way. Waiting until I had a clean, well-formed hypothesis to share was the better tactic.

"I sent you a decent story on Saturday about the Atkinson murder. And you cut the hell out of it," I said.

"It was a good start, but there was nothing in there that every other reporter in Chicago hadn't already covered."

"Excuse me? Who else had the shoe repair guy's account? And you axed all of that copy."

"Some guy talking about how a van drove by and a woman was screaming. So what? Where's your premise?"

"He saw the victim's bloody chest. Saw him fall. And you don't think that adds to the story?"

"Only if you're going for the shock factor," he said, crossing his arms over his chest. "He didn't see the shooter. He didn't see anyone run off. He saw a car and blood. Get me more. And the chicken king? Where are you on that?"

Borkowski was only partially right. Blood alone wasn't enough. The shoe guy's account was important, and I could have added to the existing reporting, but the framework wasn't yet broad enough to make the story what I suspected it was. But I didn't want to say that.

"I've confirmed a personal relationship existed between the health inspector and the owner of The Chicken Shack, Orlando Gaetano. I have recent photos of them being chummy, and I have evidence of a hostile work environment, including an employee burned in retaliation, but I haven't made any progress on connecting the inspector to other pay-to-play situations. We're working on it."

Was it a story? Yes, just not *the* story. The murder of two judges had shifted my priorities and the urgency of where and how I spent my time. I was scattered, moving back and forth between the two stories so much that I hadn't cinched either. But unless I wanted to take on the managing editor roll, I needed to keep Borkowski happy, and the chicken story, as he called it, was further along, although lacking the sex appeal of a murder mystery that had played out before my eyes.

"How about you two stop with all the collage play, or whatever this is, and get me a story?" Borkowski said, giving both of us the stern father look that we knew well.

"We're on it, Art," I said.

He humphed and went off to slap someone else around for not developing a story faster.

"Changing your plans?" Brynn asked after he was out of earshot.

"Not yet. Let's talk this case through for a bit."

"Where's your gut pulling you?" Brynn asked. "Yours has that knack. Mine just wants more Doritos."

"Your gut instinct is better than you think. You just need confidence. However, I doubt the junk food helps." I gave her a motherly raised eyebrow.

The food gulf between us was a source of constant amusement and good-natured ribbing, often leaving us both confused. She was a grown woman with her own food decisions to make, but for the first time in my life, I had a mommy urge to lecture when I saw her choices.

"First, I want to know who this guy is," I said, pointing at the man with the widow's peak. "I've seen him with Panici, and I'm pretty certain I saw him deliver what sure looked like a bribe to Farnsworth. I suspect he was a messenger for Rastello. But I don't have proof. Second, Panici is dirty. His wife as much as said so. He's my focus. He hated Reynolds. Definitely has anger management problems. Willing to break the rules. Narcissist. I don't think he has the impulse control to have pulled off the shootings himself, and he was not the guy I ran into in the Pedway. But he seems like the kind of man who has, shall we say, unusual friends? I don't doubt he's someone willing to hire out his dirty work."

"And the wife isn't talking? That seems odd. Wouldn't that be all over their divorce? I thought that was one of the things you did. Expose the SOB and celebrate your settlement after." She shrugged and looked at me for confirmation.

"Those are my thoughts exactly. I can't figure out why she's holding back. The only explanation I can come up with is that she must have something to lose by bringing it up. So she's weighing the odds. He's an ass and a creep, but I doubt she's without some fault too."

"Or maybe she's worried about the retaliation."

"That's a good point," I said, adding another note to the board. "Maybe there's something or someone outside of the court process that she's worried about. Rae's father is the guy who founded Abbiocco, and a neighbor called him a crook. He's in assisted living now, but that could be what's holding her back. Or the cousin who now runs the restaurant could be exerting pressure."

I stared at the board again as I contemplated Rae's silence, then turned to Brynn.

"I'm going to stay on this story for now. And have you focus on The Chicken Shack. I'd like you to go a little harder on the food-inspector angle. Let's see if we can find another hint of payoffs."

"Will do. I've identified a couple of other restaurants Morales was responsible for through this gal in the Health Department, so I'll start working those leads. Maybe I can find an employee who will talk. I'll check in with you later."

She returned to her desk, and I opened a browser window on my computer, pulling up The Hair Lounge website. The About tab brought me to what I hoped I'd find, another tab for Team. Small headshots of the staff ran down the left side of the page next to each stylist's bio. The women were all done up in their best glamour looks. The hair was big, the jewelry and makeup bigger. I imagined the women all painting each other's faces, showing their prowess with curling irons and hairspray, then sitting on a studio stool, waiting their turn for the photographer.

Six photos down, there she was. Viola Laskin. It took me a

minute to connect the rather plain woman I'd seen in the shop with this dolled-up image, but her piercing green eyes gave her away. A fifteen-year veteran of the salon. Her job function was listed as manager.

Back to the browser. I typed in *Selciatto + Laskin*. Nothing on the Selciatto site identified staff, but five pages in, I got a hit. A suburban newspaper covering a Chamber of Commerce event. Clicking through, I found a photo of two men standing stiffly in dark suits. The parties were identified as Chamber President Milt Gresham and Gregori Laskin, CFO of Selciatto Holdings, LLC.

And even though the photo was a few years old, there was no mistaking Laskin's dramatic hairline.

Panici. Rastello. Farnsworth. And now this guy, Laskin. They all had connections to each other and to Abbiocco. And somehow Abbiocco was part of the thread that connected both murders. But how were the judges connected? I still had no idea why Reynolds would have had a huge debt to Selciatto.

I stared at the photos on my wall. Wait. I grabbed my phone and scrolled through my photos. Rastello. How could I have not remembered? I'd been so focused on the dead judges that I hadn't gone back to that night at The Chicken Shack.

Zooming in, I stared at Edmund Rastello's face as he lifted a beer to his mouth while sitting in a booth with Orlando Gaetano. And Panici had joined them moments later. They were connected. They were all connected.

27

Panici was the link. He was the thread that stitched these men together, knotting them into a tangled ball of greed. I didn't know what they were up to yet, but it all screamed construction. Every name I came up with had a connection, not just to Panici but to construction companies or construction projects or construction money. Now I needed to find out if Panici was also connected to Judge Atkinson.

Tiana Williams, Judge Reynolds's coordinator, was the one direct contact I had at the moment to the inside workings of the office, so I stood outside the Family Court administrative office, hoping I could get a few minutes of her time.

Feeling my phone ping, I glanced at the screen. Mateo Ortiz. Hmm. "I've got something," his text read. I stepped away from the door and dialed.

"It's Andrea Kellner. I got your text."

"Hey. I've been thinking about what you said about people getting sick," he said. "I don't want my name out there, I need to work, but I couldn't live with myself if somebody died. Can we talk without anyone knowing it was me?"

"We can talk off the record," I said.

"I saw Gaetano give Morales money. He keeps a safe in the back office. During the day, the manager pulls cash from the registers so there's never too much in any drawer. It ain't the best neighborhood, and there was a robbery about five years ago that cleaned out thousands of dollars. After, he bought these safes that only he and the manager can open. Reduces the loss if we get hit again. Anyway, I walked into the office one day looking for the manager, and I see Gaetano with this wad in his hand. He slipped it into a manila envelope when he saw me."

"And you saw Gaetano give Morales the envelope?"

"No, but I was out in the back loading trash, and about five minutes later, Morales walks out the back door. He pulls an envelope out of his jacket pocket, looks inside, and then puts the envelope back in his pocket."

An anonymous former employee saying that he saw money changing hands was a decent bit of confirmation that the bribes were happening, and I could use it, but I still thought there was more to the scheme. More people, more restaurants, more crime.

"Do you have any direct knowledge that Morales was pulling this stuff at other restaurants? I assume you have friends in the industry. Is anyone talking about this stuff where they work?"

"Not that I've heard, but Morales will be making a lot of money off of Gaetano soon. He's going to be opening five more restaurants in Chicago and wants to go nationwide. Who knows, maybe Morales will get a cushy corporate job out of this at some point."

"Thanks, Mateo. If you hear anyone talking about Morales and other restaurants, please let me know."

I phoned Brynn, sharing the information Mateo had given me about witnessing the bribe, and wondered if Gaetano's expansion plans meant anything beyond lining Morales's pockets.

Calls out of the way, I stepped inside the office, seeing a room humming with activity and markedly different from my visit just a few days earlier. Justice didn't stop for death, and court cases needed to be processed even while mourning the loss of a colleague. Several new floral arrangements graced a line of tall file cabinets along with a photo of the man, forming a makeshift altar to honor their loss.

The woman who sat at the closest desk looked up quizzically. I started to ask for Ms. Williams when Tiana saw me across the room. Smiling, she motioned me over.

"Is there some news?" she asked immediately.

"No, I'm sorry, Tiana. I don't have anything new to share about Judge Reynolds. I know CPD is doing everything they can." I hated to dash her moment of hope, but until there was new info, I had nothing to ease her pain.

Her face deflated. "Sorry, I guess I made an assumption when I saw you."

"I understand. I wish I had something to tell. Did you hear about Judge Atkinson?" I asked.

"Of course. We went on lockdown for the second time in a week. Hard not to know when fifteen members of your family start texting you all at once, terrified that you're in danger. What in the hell has happened to this world? I can't understand any of it." She shuddered and I sensed not just for herself.

"Neither can I. But I'm trying to figure it out."

"Wait, are you saying these murders are connected?" Her face went pale, and she stared opened-mouth at me.

"Let me be clear," I said. "I have no official information that these murders are connected, but there are some elements that suggest to me that might be the case. I don't want to go into those details, but I'm doing what I can to find out if that's true."

"So someone could be targeting judges? What a terrifying

situation." I saw fear in her face as she looked around at her coworkers, trying to gauge their risk by simply coming to work.

"Would you mind looking at a photograph for me?" I said, pulling out my phone. I tapped on a picture of Felix Panici and showed her my screen. "Does this man look at all familiar to you?"

She took the phone, expanding the image. "No, not to me. Who is he?"

"An attorney." I left it at that. Speculation wouldn't be helpful. I also didn't want to taint her memory by using a name she would have come across in the course of her work.

"Well, that doesn't exactly narrow it down. Can't throw a pebble in this building without hitting one of those."

A woman approached us. Her eyes were bloodshot, and strands of hair fell loose from her topknot as if she hadn't had enough time this morning to get ready.

"Tiana, I need to look at a file with you when you have a minute," she said. "I might have another override issue. I think we should walk it through together so I can figure out what I'm doing wrong."

"Of course. I'll be over in a few minutes. Wait, I should introduce you two. This is Justine. She worked in Judge Atkinson's office until about a month ago. This is Andrea Kellner. She's a reporter working on a story about the judge."

"It's nice to meet you," I said. "I'm so sorry about Judge Atkinson. Had you worked for him long?"

"I'm in shock. I worked for him for almost eleven years. How could this happen?"

I had no words for her. Nothing that could comfort. There was no explanation that would calm the disbelief or ease the hurt. Murder didn't work that way. Sudden death of any kind didn't work that way. The best we ever had was an explanation so that our logical brains could try to make sense of it somehow.

"Tell me about Judge Atkinson. What was he like to work for?" I was thinking about Peter's comment about a bribery accusation. Even if it hadn't amounted to anything, an accusation like that continued to hang around, whispered about in the hallways of law offices and the courthouse like all salacious gossip.

"He was tough. Liked things the way he liked them. Not Mr. Warm and Fuzzy by any stretch of the imagination, but you needed to know him for a while to get past that. He just didn't suffer fools, and he could smell bullshit the minute it walked into his courtroom. A lot of the new attorneys were afraid of him. But it was the attorneys who weren't afraid that should have been. Atkinson tore into those guys when they screwed up. I think he went even harder on the arrogant guys. Always seems to be guys, doesn't it, who treat the courtroom like it's a country club where they can make deals over a steak and whiskey lunch instead of arguing their case."

"Would you call Atkinson a stickler for procedure, then?" Despite his gruffness, I sensed Justine had a respect for the man.

"More of a stickler for knowing your place in the hierarchy, I would say. It was his court; therefore, he got to run it the way he wanted. Attorneys needed to get in line."

Although prickly to some, his approach wasn't unusual in the court system.

"Is this man familiar to you?" I pulled my phone back out and handed it to Justine.

She paused, looking at the photo. "Yeah, I remember him. I needed to speak with the judge about a schedule conflict that was kinda complicated, so I went over to see him in his office. When I got there, the judge was in the hallway with this guy. It was strange off the bat. I could tell he was an attorney, and that there was tension between them. I got the impression the judge was trying to shoo him away. Thought him showing up like that was inappropriate, like maybe he was trying to buttonhole the judge. It was just an impression I had, so I'm not sure. I only kept the judge's court schedule, so if there was a personal appointment, I wouldn't have known. However, it was clear the judge didn't want to talk to him."

"Do you have any idea what this guy wanted to talk about?"

"Mostly, what I heard was the judge telling this attorney he needed to leave. Other than that, I remember hearing the judge saying, 'You're out of line' and 'I'm not doing it.'"

There it was. Panici's connection to the second murder victim.

28

"I found this on my car!"

A text from Cai popped up on my phone as I reached the lobby of the Daley Center. I tapped, expanding the photo she had included so I could see what she was reacting to. The image was of a newspaper tucked under the windshield wiper of her car. The headline on the *Chicago Tribune* read "Another Chicago Judge Murdered in The Loop."

"Don't touch it! Where are you?" I sent back.

"Parking garage at work."

"I'm on my way."

Ten minutes later, I took the elevator to the fifth floor of the parking garage where her firm maintained two dozen slots assigned to senior staff. Cai paced at the back end of her Mercedes as she spoke to someone on the phone. She was in full attorney garb, a fitted skirt and matching suit jacket, paired with her signature killer heals. Her tote bag lay open on its side on the pavement behind one the wheels as if she'd dropped it. Her voice was clipped and impatient, not the steady calm she normally projected even under the worst pressure.

"I don't know when I can get there," she said. "See if you can get them to reschedule for another day." A pause. "Yes, I know it complicates things, but I can't do anything about it. Tell John I'll phone him later."

She hung up but stared down the aisle of cars, trying to settle her emotions.

"Are you okay?" I said, knowing it was a ridiculous question. Her body language told me everything I needed to know.

"Do I fucking sound okay?" She pinched the bridge of her nose. "Sorry. I was supposed to be driving out to Oak Brook for a meeting. The client isn't happy about being stood up. He's one of those super-rich guys that treats the world like we're all his personal servants. He's an asshole, and I wish he'd find another attorney to give his business to, but my partners disagree. Maybe after the huge disappointment of having to accommodate me, he'll ask to be assigned to someone else in the firm who'll do a better job of ass-kissing."

She resumed her pacing as she spoke, her voice a staccato mix of anger and indignance. Cai's rarely seen fear meter was running fast.

"Okay." I laid a hand on her arm and forced her to look at me. "Tell me what happened here."

She let out a breath and nodded. "Sorry, I'm just venting. As I said, I was supposed to drive to Oak Brook for this meeting. I got to the car. Saw something on the windshield. Thought it was junk mail. People peddle auto-detailing and transportation services all the time. They know the users of the reserved parts of the garage are professionals who often need these kinds of things. When I got close, I saw it wasn't a flyer and that the paper had been folded to emphasize that headline. That's when I texted you in a panic."

"Did you see anyone on your way to the car? Or was someone hanging out nearby, maybe watching for your reaction?" I asked. My first thought being her safety and wondering if the guy who left his message had waited around to see her receive it.

She thought for a moment. "I can't say I noticed. I was on the phone, per usual. But my car has been sitting here since Thursday night. As you know, I went to Michigan after work on Thursday, and I left the car here. The paper could have been left anytime while I was away. I turned everything off over the weekend, my phone, social, even email. I hadn't even heard about the murder until I saw this."

"And you didn't touch anything?"

"I was about to open the door when I first noticed there was something on the windshield. I touched the handle to open the door but stopped when I saw it was a newspaper. Then I stepped closer to look at it and saw the headline. I didn't touch anything after that other than my phone."

"I'm calling Michael."

She opened her mouth to object out of habit, then nodded instead. Thankfully, Michael answered and listened carefully as I explained the situation to him. We hadn't spoken since Friday in the Pedway, and I didn't know if he would want to hear from me at all, let alone be willing to rush over here to do me and my friend a favor.

"He's on his way," I said, feeling the tension in my chest release a little bit.

"Atkinson was murdered?" Cai said. "I leave town for a three-day vacation, and this is what I come back to? Another dead judge? Are these killings connected, or is some lunatic taking out his crazy on the judicial system? What the hell? I know this guy."

Her words rushed out as if she had no control of them. Fear was feeding her.

Her phone rang, and the pacing continued as she sorted out the details of her aborted meeting with her paralegal. Cai was always the calm professional, holding any anxiety inside, and I'd never seen this side of her. In court, she used her anxiety judiciously to strike at opponents when they least expected it. When they underestimated her. Seeing her agitated like this did nothing to ease my own worry.

Michael's SUV screeched to a stop a few yards from where I stood. His eyes sought mine as he walked toward me, and we looked at each other, so many things unsaid. So many things we couldn't find words for, not right now, anyway. My heart wanted me to rush into his arms. My head told me not to. Regardless, I was relieved he had set aside the tension between us to come to Cai's aid.

"How is she?" Michael asked, looking at Cai, who still could not remain in one place.

"Scared. And as you know, she doesn't scare easily."

"And how are you?" He looked at my neck, wincing lightly as he saw the bruises that had ripened over the past couple of days.

"Busy." An accurate, more fulsome answer was too complex for the moment. And I wasn't sure what I wanted him to know. It was easier to talk about Cai right now.

He nodded. Cai ended her call and joined us.

"Thanks for coming, Michael," she said. "I feel silly that I'm scared, but I am."

"Is it still on the windshield?"

He walked over and looked at the folded newsprint. Bending down, noting the way in which only this particular story had been made the focus.

"Do we know what day this story ran?" Michael asked.

"Saturday," I said. "I checked the website while you were on your way over."

"And it showed up today?" Michael asked.

"My car has been parked here since Thursday. I only noticed the paper a short time ago when I came here to drive it to a meeting. If this is a Saturday edition, it wasn't necessarily placed today," Cai said.

"Someone is sending you a message," Michael said, pulling the news article out from under the wiper, unfolding it, and running his eyes over the contents. "Any ideas on what they were trying to say?"

"That I'm next!" she said. "I was a witness in a case with Reynolds, and he's dead. I have a current case before Atkinson, and he's dead. So someone dropping this love note off on my car is a threat, pure and simple. It says, 'We're coming for you.' I don't know why someone would want me dead, but the message couldn't be clearer."

"Wait, you have a case before Atkinson?" I said. New anxiety clutched my chest. And Zipsdefender's vague threats suddenly came back into my mind. Cai had a connection to these murder victims, but I couldn't see why she was being threatened. A brick of dread pressed on me.

"A property conflict," she said. "It's been going on for months."

I looked at Michael. He met my eyes, but if he saw the fear in them, he chose to say nothing. Damn, I hated those cop eyes right now. Those eyes that refused to reveal what he was thinking, refused to show the emotions that might be pulling at him.

"Tell me about the case." My mind was racing, anticipating another point of connection, anticipating another level of fear.

"My client owns a parcel of land," Cai said. "Over the past few years, a developer has been acquiring property around him, basically trying to cut him off. They're essentially making his parcel worthless to him, and to anyone else, because he won't sell it to them. We're fighting it, but as you both know, justice doesn't always work as quickly as we want it to."

The stack of blueprints in Farnsworth's office flashed in my mind.

"Where is the land?" I asked.

"Technically, it's in the Belmont Heights neighborhood, but those boundaries are a bit fuzzy since it's Realtor speak and not a separate entity from Chicago."

That didn't fit. It wasn't Elmwood Park, but it was adjacent to the village. And although Farnsworth wouldn't have any jurisdiction, he might have influence with the neighboring community. I added the information to the list I was running through in my head as I tried to put pieces into place.

"Last we spoke, this Zipsdefender guy who was hassling you on Twitter had been pretty quiet. Has he made any new threats?" I asked. Then I looked at Michael, who was oddly quiet. Why wasn't he the one asking this question? It was an obvious and easy connection to make at this point.

"Nothing new," she said, shaking her head and just noticing that the contents of her bag had spilled out onto the pavement.

"You see this connection, don't you?" I said to Michael. "Threats from some creep on Twitter. Two judges she's worked with murdered. Now this."

He looked at me as if he was holding back something he wanted to say but wasn't sure he should. I wanted to shake him. Shake him into not being a cop right now. Shake him into letting me know he saw my fear and was going to make it go away.

"Well, are you going to file a report?" I asked, my voice rising in volume a notch. "Ask for security camera footage?" I looked around for the telltale signs of a camera. I saw one pointing toward us about forty yards away, near the entrance to the stairs. "Right there, look. It's probably on tape." I motioned in the direction of the camera.

"Look, I know you're worried," he said, turning his eyes to Cai and ignoring me, keeping his voice low. "But leaving a newspaper on a car is not a crime. While I understand you've interpreted this as a threat, and it may be one, I don't have anything direct enough to act on. If he'd written something on the paper, perhaps, even if it was your name, I'd have something to work with. Right now, someone left a newspaper on your windshield. They might have found it on the ground and thought you dropped it. I don't know, but as it stands, this is nothing I can work with."

I stared at the side of his face, my jaw clenched as I listened to him speak. My anxiety over the threat to Cai had morphed into full-blown anger, anger at him. This was Cai! How did he not see this as needing action? He stood here, patronizing her with hollow words, doing nothing other than avoiding my eyes. I turned to Cai, seeing her face fall with the realization that Michael would not do anything. Not even take a report.

"Is this about us?" The words burst from me, angry and impatient. Both of them turned toward me, confusion on their faces, unaccustomed to my raised voice.

"Andrea, don't be silly. I don't let my personal life affect my work choices. Don't you dare make those accusations when you, however, seem to be the one who can't separate the two."

"Apparently, we're on our own," I said to Cai.

As they watched me, I swallowed the tears and the anger and the utter disappointment I had in the man I thought I had shared a love with, not wanting him to see anything other than the resolve in my face.

"You can leave now," I said, my voice icy.

29

"What just happened? He wouldn't even file a police report?" Cai's voice cracked as she looked at me, her eyes full of fear.

We were still standing at the back of Cai's car in the parking garage, not having moved since I'd asked Michael to leave. My head was spinning with anger and worry and determination. Michael might have been willing to leave Cai stranded without any recourse until something awful happened. I, however, was not.

"I hope Michael didn't just make a decision based on his anger with me, but it feels like that's exactly what he did." My heart sank as I held her shoulders, and she leaned into me for a hug. "I'm so sorry. I'm going to figure this out. I promise."

I needed a plan. The connections surrounding the murder of these two men were building, but I couldn't yet understand the big picture—other than construction being at the heart of it.

Now, however, this was no longer just a story. It was personal. Now, it was urgent. Now, it wasn't just some article that I wanted my name on or an award or accolades for; it was Cai's life. Michael might be able to convince himself that there was no threat because the words "I'm going to kill you!" hadn't been written in red ink on that paper. He might be able to convince himself he was right because he stayed firmly inside the lines of police standard operating procedure. I was not going to sit by and wait for my dearest friend to be slaughtered. Damn the rules. Damn the consequences.

"Can you work from home for a while?" I asked. "It might be a good idea to stay away from Daley Plaza and your office, if you can do that."

"I'll rearrange what I can." She paused, thinking through her calendar, moving down the checklist of complications this would add to her life. "I'll have to tell Richard what's going on. He can help me decide what explanation to give the staff, clients. Shit, this is going to be complicated."

For someone whose career was as entrenched in her identity as Cai's was, the suggestion that she step back for a while would be akin to being plopped down in a foreign land with no guide and no understanding of the terrain. I hoped her fear would outweigh the career drive that was as necessary to her as breathing.

"Who is the client you were representing in Atkinson's court?"

"His name is Nathan Vogel. He inherited twenty acres from his father back when the area was mostly cornfields. He sold off all but three acres over the years. That's the parcel under dispute, or rather, the access to it. There's a ramshackle home on the property, which Vogel lives in, a shed, but nothing else. This real estate developer has been slowly buying up surrounding properties. They've approached my client numerous times, and he basically told them to go to hell. Initially he ignored them, but it has devolved into outright hostility between the parties."

"Is Vogel holding out for their 'best and final' offer?" I asked, knowing the first offer was never the highest.

"They've already passed that point and have moved on to stubborn, my-feet-are-planted-in-cement. This isn't about money for Vogel. It's principal. He wants to stay in his home for the balance of his life. He feels he's being bullied. And I agree, he is, but what a hill to die on when there's a couple million dollars on the table. That would go a long way to easing the rest of his life, but it's his choice to sell or not sell."

"Do you know what the developer wants to do with the land?" I asked.

"It's not clear. The group is called APR Holdings, LLC. It's a private company. They're keeping things close to the vest. But their bigger plans haven't really been a concern. I've been fighting their audacity to think they can muscle this guy out by cutting him off from the world."

Whoever the parties were, they were now at the "let's play hardball" stage where negotiations had basically become dares.

"Call him for me, your client. I want to talk to him. Tell him I can be there in forty-five minutes."

She nodded.

I took the newspaper from the car, gave Cai a hug, and said, "Get in a cab and go home. Right now. Don't go back to your office today. They can messenger over whatever files you need. Order takeout. Call or text me if even the tiniest thing happens or you just need to talk. I'll call you later."

She nodded, then picked up her bag off the ground. I watched her safely get into a cab, then went to recover my own car for the trip.

As I inched along the surface roads in the midday traffic, I phoned Brynn.

"I'm driving. Can you do a search on APR Holdings? I'm interested in the ownership. I'll wait while you look it up."

"Yes, boss. Anything you say, boss," she said, mocking me.

"Sorry, I barked an order at you. I'm a little on edge, it's not you. You can bark back if you want."

"Arf. Arf. Do I get a treat now?"

"Sure. Get me the name of the owner of APR Holdings and I'll buy you a box of Twinkies."

"A whole box! This must be important if you're willing to spend your hard-earned cash feeding me junk food. Challenge accepted. Let's see what I can find."

I heard the clicking of keys over my car speaker as Brynn worked her magic.

"Well, I might not be getting those Twinkies, at least not today. Ownership isn't clear. I'm going to need more time to dig. Can I call you back later?"

"Sure thing. Let me know what you find. My schedule has gotten thrown off, so I don't know if I'll make it back to the office."

Signs of construction were visible as soon as I passed the intersection of Belmont and Harlem Avenue. Industrial-sized bulldozers and graders sat in a dirt field just on the north side of Belmont. I didn't yet know the scope of the project at hand or what properties were owned by APR Holdings, but it seemed in the early stages of the project. Buildings still stood to the north and west, although vacant and moldering with neglect. It was a patchwork of empty weed-infested lots and odd structures that still held the markings of their former lives as auto repair shops and small warehouses and scary-looking former retail stores.

Siri instructed me to turn onto a narrow alley next to a defunct gas station with blacktop that was in the process of being scraped up. I proceeded until the alley ended at a gated chain-link fence with a large red *Private Property. No Tres-passing* sign. I got out of my car and walked to the gate. Six feet high, it cordoned off a huge plot of land. Large raised-bed gardens lined the west side of the property. Sunflowers and cornstalks were starting their fade into withered brown remnants. I saw tomato cages holding plants still producing fruit and structures for pole beans now wilting and losing steam. Other areas had been left to become fallow and weed infested. An old tractor and various wheel barrows were rusting in the sun.

The road continued past the locked gate to a simple two-story home with a deep front porch badly in need of paint. A shed larger than my first studio sat some distance off to the right. And more chain-link fence surrounded it all. It was a mini-farm with a city built all around it. Buildings and lots and signs of construction framed the property on the other side of the fencing. It was the oddest ramshackle farm oasis I had ever seen.

A man lumbered toward me down the driveway. His pace was swifter than the sparse white hair on his head would have suggested.

"You Ms. Farrell's friend?" he asked as he reached the gate. His spotty, bronzed skin told a story of a life under the sun. He looked at me as if I didn't match what he expected.

"Yes, Mr. Vogel. I'm Andrea Kellner. Could we speak about your property situation?"

"Situation? I guess that's one word for it. Shit show would be another." He scoffed and pulled keys out of his pocket. Turning the padlock, he slipped the lock into his Wranglers, then slid the gate out of the way.

"We can talk here if that's okay. I don't really like people in my house," he said kind of sheepishly, as if a little embarrassed.

"I don't mind. Cai tells me you've owned this property a long time."

"And my father before me. He bought the land back in the twenties when this was almost nothing but farmland. Raised five kids here, he and my mom. They're both long gone, as are my siblings, but those memories aren't. This is my home. Always has been. Always going to be. I don't care what those greedy bastards want. I ain't leaving."

"When were you first approached about selling the property?" I asked.

"About three years ago. Some lawyer sent me this letter saying to call him about my property. One of those 'Dear Homeowner' things. I threw it in a drawer and didn't give it another thought. Then about a year and a half ago, they started up again. I didn't respond, and those letters turned into phone calls, then eventually threats. They've kept trying, upping the money a little each time, but I keep saying no. I don't want to move. Where the hell would I go? And you can't force a man to give up his land just because you want it."

"In the meantime, I understand they're buying up your neighbors' property. Is that correct?"

"You got it. I don't know how much they owned before they got to me, but yeah, money talks for some. And as this lawyer buys up property, everything else around here starts to go downhill. 'Cause these guys aren't caring for the places. Don't fix 'em up or anything. They just sit and rot, which makes the neighborhood decline. You get enough of that and all of our properties lose value. So eventually the people who haven't sold, they start panic selling, thinking if they don't take the deal, the next offer will be lower instead of higher. It's part of that developers game," he said, visibly disgusted by the tactic.

"But you haven't been tempted?" I asked, wondering if he was playing the odds that as the last holdout, eventually the number would look good enough or the ordeal hard enough that he would give in and take the money.

"Never!" he said. "I'm dying in this house, even if it's this stupid shit that does me in."

That answered my "was he a holdout" question, at least for

now. His vehemence was clear. "When did the legal action start?"

"That was about a year ago. It was after that old gas station finally sold. It had been empty for a few years at that point. Costs a lot of money to modernize these little old stations. The big chains, they go for the visibility of a corner lot, so this little place wasn't something they wanted. And to turn it into another use, well, you gotta deal with the EPA and all kinds of regulation because the ground is toxic. That's serious dollars, so nobody wanted it until these guys finally worked out a deal to buy it. I don't know what they paid for it, but I suspect they saved it for the end so the owner would be nervous and take a low-ball offer."

"Being last can work in your favor, though. I imagine the offers you've received have increased over the years."

"True. I've got leverage, as they say, and they've put out damn good offers that would change my life. But I don't want my life changed. It ain't about money for me. I got no dependents to leave a bunch of money to. I just want to live here in peace. They don't understand that. So, since I wasn't a money whore, they've had to go the legal route."

"What specifically is the dispute? No one can be forced to sell a property if they don't want to."

"No, but they can make it so hard to live on the property that you get desperate. They claim that since they bought that gas station, the rights to the alley belong to them and that every time I use it I'm trespassing. Some messiness about right-of-way, something that got drawn wrong decades ago. Ms. Farrell understands all that better than I do."

"They can't win a lawsuit that denies you access to your own property," I said. I hadn't been a real estate attorney, but I knew that much. In the end, the court would force a solution on the developer if a deal couldn't be struck. What that solution looked like and how damaging it would be to their plan was debatable.

"No, they can't. Ms. Farrell said the same. They won't win a legal battle in the end. But I don't think that's the point. Not if they drag this out and bankrupt me or wait me out until I'm dead. There are other ways to get what you want if you're patient and creative. So what we got is a pissing contest. I expect they got more piss, but I got plenty of vinegar."

"Do you know what the end game is? They must have a plan for all of this land."

"They aren't telling me what it is, but the rumor mill is saying a shopping center or a housing development."

"I understand the company trying to buy your property is something called APR Holdings. Who from that company has been in contact with you?"

"No one. I've only had contact with an attorney. Here, I copied this letter for you since I knew you were coming. This is their last threat before I had to lawyer up."

He pulled a folded piece of paper out of the breast pocket of his plaid flannel shirt and handed it to me.

The letterhead read *Stephan Bruni Associates*. Who the hell was this?

30

———

Whoever APR Holdings was, they had their hands full with Nathan Vogel. It was hard to beat a client willing to fight to the death, literally. The man had nothing to lose that was important to him beyond that piece of land and not leaving his home. But APR likely had the cash to play the long game. I wouldn't take a bet on which party was more stubborn.

"Are you at home?"

I phoned Cai from the car on the painfully slow drive through city traffic back toward the Loop, worried about her emotional state and her ability to put caution before ambition.

"You'd be proud of me. I'm being a good girl, but I hate it already. I feel like a slacker on the verge of sliding toward sweats and bedroom slippers and dirty hair as my daytime attire. Please conduct an intervention if I go there." She sighed. "And Richard has been in depositions all day, so we haven't been able to talk. I actually lied to the office and told them I had a migraine so my phone wouldn't ring thirty times an hour like it normally does. I didn't want to fumble through a bullshit explanation of why I was off-site."

Cai was racing ahead, projecting both a long-term stint with work-from-home and what she assumed would be a decline into frumpery. I couldn't predict the length of her isolation, but my friend would not be ditching her mascara or buying her first pair of sweatpants.

"Richard will understand," I said. "He wants his star attorney to stay safe. The two of you just need to figure out a communication strategy."

"I can manage for a while, but I can't do this for long without my work suffering. And my sanity."

And that discomfort would lead her to take risks. "You staying safe is the most important thing. Let's concentrate on that. We'll figure this out. Take it one day at a time."

I could hear the anxiety in her voice and imagined her already bouncing off the walls, even though it had only been a few hours.

"I met with Mr. Vogel," I said. "He's quite a character. This real estate group can't be happy to have a stubborn old man to deal with. What do you know about them?"

"Not much. They've stayed in the background, using the attorney exclusively as their contact point. So far, I haven't even met him. We've handled everything via email. I don't get the impression he's a heavy hitter, but that's probably just because I've never heard of him. He certainly isn't big in the real estate mogul world, that much I know. We all know that breed. They thrive on attention."

"Did any names come up from inside APR in your dealings with the attorney?" Brynn still hadn't called with an update, so that meant she was struggling to get information.

She paused for a minute. "No, now that you ask, I don't recall any names of principals. That's odd. It's a small case for me, so I guess I overlooked that."

"Have you heard anything more from Zipsdefender?" I

asked, checking off the other threat—if it was a separate threat, that is.

"All quiet."

"Good. Stay on top of it, but let's hope it stays that way. I'll call you tonight."

I was back in the office thirty minutes later. Motioning to Brynn, I dropped my bag next to my desk and went to my wall. Adding Post-its for Vogel and APR and the attorney Bruni, I surveyed the landscape of the story.

"I'm still having trouble with that company you asked about," Brynn said as she joined me. "Private ownership. And I've yet to find a name other than this attorney who's listed as the managing agent."

"Let me guess, his name is Stephan Bruni," I said.

"Yes, it is. I guess you're ahead of me. How does this company, APR Holdings, fit into the mix on these murders?"

"What I know so far is that they had a case before Judge Atkinson that I need to know more about. I'll go into the why later," I said. "For now, APR is trying to develop some property, a decent-size project. Speculation is that the plan is for a housing development or a big retail project. I want to know what the project is. It would be easier if we knew who was behind the company versus just this front man, but we may find that out as we dig. Let's start with the scale of the project. Let's see if we can figure out the total landmass based on how many purchases they've made. That will help us narrow it down. We may also discover some names as we work through the purchases."

"I'll get my laptop," Brynn said.

I picked up mine and moved over to the corner table so Brynn and I could work. Then I printed out a parcel map of the area and grabbed more Post-its and highlighters. We plugged away on our computers, marking off parcels on the map as we discovered a sale. It was tedious work, but slowly the typography began to flesh out.

Rubbing my eyes from the strain, I plugged another parcel number into the database. When the screen filled, I blinked, looking a second time at the name in front of me.

Seller—Felix Panici.

"Do you recall seeing any parcels where the seller was Felix Panici? I know I didn't ask you to look for sellers' names, but I think I have found a new angle." Thoughts swirled in my head as I considered the possible implications of this new information.

"That name sounds familiar, but I'll have to go back through to be sure."

"Do it. And watch for Rae Panici, Edmund Rastello, Nestor Morales, Bradford Reynolds, and Orlando Gaetano on either side of property transactions." I scribbled the names on a piece of paper for her, and we got back to work. There was no need for conversation. Our fingers flew over the keys, and our eyes tired from the concentration, stopping only to take a drink or to note a new find on paper.

An hour and a half later, we had discovered four parcels sold by Panici, six by Rastello, one by Morales, and two by Gaetano out of nearly sixty lots within our target area, all sold within the last four months. Noticeably absent was Bradford Reynolds's name. This had to have been planned, as if the men knew the buyer before the deals or knew that something big was coming and intended to profit from it. What wasn't clear yet was how long ago these men had purchased those properties and how they had known a project was in the works.

We hadn't gone through parcel by parcel tracking ownership, so it wasn't completely clear how many properties were not within APR control, nor did I know if I had all the names of the parties involved, but based on what we could clearly identify as

APR owned or sympathetic to the scheme, a substantial portion was under their control.

My first thought was Farnsworth had clued them in to the development plan; the next was someone in the group knew whoever owned APR Holdings.

"What do you think is going on? Why did so many guys who know each other all own property in the same area?" Brynn asked.

"I think the most likely scenario is that these were planned, coordinated flips. The guys who knew the big picture bought what they could early. A way to prime the pump. Get in while pricing was low, I imagine, since this isn't a neighborhood on the upswing."

"Wouldn't all that sale activity have tipped someone off? Investors watch that. Neighbors talk."

"It depends on how slowly the purchases happened." I thought for a minute. "Another possibility is that the guys on the inside, and by that I mean APR, needed a guaranteed amount of land to take the project from idea to next level. Like when a housing development needs a certain number of pre-construction contracts in place to get their next level of financing. Maybe by having these owners in their back pockets, so to speak, that juiced up something else, like financing. That would explain why the sales from these guys are all recent."

"And this is all tied to Atkinson somehow?" Brynn asked.

"Whatever the plan is, right now there's a wrench in that plan. This guy Vogel. Atkinson was presiding judge in the lawsuit as APR is trying to force Vogel out."

"Where does Reynolds fit in this? We didn't find any property in his name."

I looked at her, contemplating the question.

"As we started to dig into this, I thought maybe that five-hundred-K debt might have been a loan to finance a purchase or two. The more people, the better as a way to spread the risk, but since there is nothing on the books in his name, I still don't have an answer."

I pulled over the plot map so we could see the scale.

"That's a decent chunk of land," Brynn said. "Is it a bigger area than what we found when we did that casino story?"

"Comparable, I'd say, but this location doesn't have expressway access, so whatever they're hoping to build is more intimate. And a tougher build, given the concentration of property and the different zoning involved. I'm leaning toward a residential project or a combo residential and commercial."

"What's next? You want me back on The Chicken Shack story? I'm talking to two employees on Morales's inspection beat in an hour."

"Stay on that. We just connected Gaetano and Morales to whatever this real estate deal is, so this is one complicated story, not two. I'm going to dig into the attorney who's been hitting up Vogel while you stay on the restaurant stuff. Let's touch base later."

Brynn went back to her desk, and I ran a search on Stephan Bruni. He was another solo practitioner, in the Panici vein, who dabbled in whatever legal areas struck his fancy. He also seemed an odd choice for a complex real estate development problem. The solo guys didn't have a staff of researchers and paralegals to do the background work. And often not the city government connections to get to the right people quickly. At best, he had a staff of one or two, and would call in a freelancer if something outside his wheelhouse came up. I knew the breed and knew they generally got blown away by a well-staffed corporate team. So either this attorney was just the front man for the official records and had now been brought on to run out the clock on Vogel, or he was a true insider.

I picked up my phone. "Peter, it's Andrea again. I need

another favor. You know all the development guys around town. Have you ever heard of a real estate development company called APR Holdings?"

"Never heard of them. What are they working on?"

"I don't know yet, but I think it's housing or mixed-use. There's almost nothing publicly available about them, so I thought I'd try you."

"Maybe it's newly formed. A lot of guys split off from another group to do their own thing, or small rehabbers get deluded into thinking it's easy and form a startup for one project."

"That could be. How about an attorney named Stephan Bruni?"

"Again, I got nothing."

"Thanks anyway. Now I really need to send you over a really good bottle of scotch."

"I'd settle for dinner."

I laughed it off. No, a date was not going to be the price of information.

I needed to know who was behind APR. Borkowski was too cheap to authorize a Westlaw subscription, arguing that I could use old-fashioned shoe leather. Screw that when databases were faster. I set up an account. We could fight about the expense later when I submitted the bill.

A search on APR Holdings didn't give me much more than I already had. Formed three years ago. Six employees. An address that sounded like a mailing service. No bankruptcies. Bruni was still the only contact given. Results for Bruni directly showed an eight-year legal career, always as an independent. A baby attorney as far as these things went.

However, the value of the Westlaw system was not its company structure information but its case law history, so I could dig through Bruni's legal résumé case by case.

Improper permitting of a garage, a dispute over property

lines between neighbors, some kid's vandalism charge. How did this guy get hooked up with APR? Was he someone's nephew?

And then I saw it. Four separate cases involving TCS, Inc. The Chicken Shack's corporate name. He was Gaetano's attorney, but hadn't been for the bribery case.

31

"Trouble in fantasyland?"

I gave Janek a what-the-hell look as I slid into the seat across from him at his favorite diner. My stomach was rebelling at the smell of the sizzling bacon that emanated from the back grill. Cai and I had been up way too late and had drunk way too much wine last night for the smell of grease, even though it was nearly eleven.

"Nice to see you too, Karl," I said, then fished a couple of Tylenol out of my bag and tossed them back with Janek's untouched water glass.

"Well, since you asked to meet me alone," he said, "either things are dicey between you and lover boy or you're planning a surprise for him and want my help. Given his piss-poor mood lately, I'm guessing it's the former."

Janek looked at me like a disapproving parent who was preparing to give a lecture. I hadn't been certain if Michael had spoken to him about what was going on with us or not. Apparently, the general gist of things was self-evident.

"You're right. Michael and I are working through a difference of opinion right now. So I figured I shouldn't ask him for any favors."

It was the simplest explanation I had at the moment. I also was not coming to Janek for a read on my love life and didn't want him to think he had to play mediator.

"Well, figure it out already so he can get back to working the way he's supposed to. This sad puppy dog look he's got going on is just plain embarrassing on a detective. I can't have him moping around with a broken heart when he's supposed to be strong-arming bad guys. Fix it, okay?"

"This might not be fixable, Karl." Hearing Janek's words tugged at me. If he noticed, then Michael was in a bad place, too. And it tugged on my heart, but that didn't mean there was a solution.

"Sorry to hear that," he said, this time without bluster or a lightly veiled joke. "You're good for him. I think your job conflicts are tough, but he's better with you. Happier with you. I hope you work it out."

"Thanks, Karl." That was the first time I'd heard Janek express approval of me being in Michael's life, and it both warmed me and stung. I knew it mattered to Michael that Janek gave us his blessing, but had he expressed those views to Michael, and did it even matter anymore? I'd expected this conversation to be awkward since there was no way to pretend I wasn't working around Michael, but warm-hearted Janek rooting for us was something I hadn't counted on.

"What is it that you need from me, Kellner?" he asked.

"Tell me about the mafia. Is that still a thing here in Chicago?" I said, stealing his water glass again.

He looked at me hard before responding, as if I'd caught him off guard. "Not in the old-school movie way that Hollywood romanticizes, if that's what you mean," he said. "There are vestiges of what it used to be. People who hold on to that past.

Chicago, as we all know, had its Al Capone years, and that tough guy criminal history hasn't left some circles. But I wouldn't say that's what controls criminal activity. But then we'd need to discuss the subtleties of the definition of gangs versus the mafia. Why do you ask?"

"A story I'm working on has elements that seem mob-like. Or maybe people who seem and talk mob-like." The conversation felt silly even as I was asking the questions, but Rae's talk of "the family" and bribery and some construction scheme all seemed to be overlapping into something that made the conversation necessary.

"Can you be specific?"

I wasn't sure how much to say after Michael's tepid response to my attempt at engaging him in conversation on the Reynolds case. "Well, some of the elements are men who hang together in a pack. Payoffs. Bribes. References to how important 'the family' was back in the day. And lots of secret dealings."

"That fits the basic mold, all right. What kind of bribes? Or who is being bribed?"

"The usual. Aldermen, government employees." I was still being cautious, partly because I didn't want Janek to tell me to get lost, partly because I was afraid to hear my imagination was getting away from me.

"You wanna start some straight-talking here?" Janek sat back, crossing his arms over his chest, waiting for me to stop sounding like a child. "'Cause this sounds like more than a little curiosity. Who's bribing an alderman?"

"I'm keeping this vague because I don't have proof yet, and we both know how cops react to maybes, so I think it's best if I keep this generic for now." Michael's dismissive tone came back into my mind, disappointing me all over again.

"I'm not sure I agree with your logic. Seems like the best thing you could do is bounce this off a cop."

I stared at him. "I tried that, and it didn't go well."

"Ah, so you're looking for a second opinion?" He nodded, suddenly understanding one part of Michael's recent bad mood.

"Of sorts," I said. "I actually think our friend was letting his frustrated boyfriend status overshadow what I had to say. So he couldn't hear me when I needed to discuss this."

"Then try me. I don't share that prejudice." Janek popped a forkful of runny egg into his mouth as he waited for me to respond.

"Okay, but just listen for a minute before you jump and try to give me answers. I'm speaking to you primarily as a friend who has more experience in this area than I do, not as a detective I need to report a case to."

He nodded.

"First, and most importantly, someone is threatening Cai, and I think whoever is doing so is connected to the murders of the two judges. I don't know how, or why, but I believe that to be true."

He sat up straight, his eyes full of concern.

"And Michael didn't want to hear that?" he said. "What am I missing?"

"The threats against her haven't been direct enough for his liking. Vague tweets. A newspaper left on her car with an article about Judge Atkinson's death. He has declined to do anything until there is something more obvious. Of course, we've all heard that story before, usually after the fact. I'm not going to be the one waiting for an I-told-you-so moment after my friend is dead. Two judges have been shot, out in the open in broad daylight in the middle of Daley Plaza, a place Cai frequents. So I'm working my ass off to figure out what's behind all this, with or without his help."

"Where does Cai fit in these murders?" he asked.

I could see his mind working. Questions forming. The questions Michael would have asked if he hadn't been pissed off at me.

"That's not clear yet. But she had cases with both judges, and right after Atkinson was murdered, that newspaper was left on her car. I know it's a weak association, but I have to consider it a direct message even if there is no specific threat attached. Cai sure is."

"Is she safe?" he asked. Concern filled his eyes.

"She's working at home for the near term and staying away from Daley Plaza, but we both know Cai, and it will be hard to keep her there for long."

"Where does the mafia come in?" He stirred his coffee unnecessarily as his mind worked over what I shared with him.

"The next part of this is that I think there's a connection between the two dead judges. That the same killer or group was responsible for their murders. I don't know why they were killed, exactly, and I'm stating my suspicions, not necessarily known facts. I'm stepping into your territory with that comment. And I'm not trying to get you to share details of the case, but sharing my suspicions is necessary in order to answer your question, so bear with me. Anyway, the info I have shows me there are connections between a group of shady people and these judges. The mob-like language has come from these people on the periphery of those two dead men. People who seem to operate on a pat-my-back-I'll-pat-yours system."

"Without knowing details, that fits mob-style behavior," Janek said. "I assume you're holding back a bunch of stuff, so for the sake of argument, let's assume you're correct that we're talking mafia. Can you give me any more details? I assume you're investigating the hell out of these people, so toss me some of the highlights."

"The people I'm talking about are connected via the

construction industry and a pizzeria in Elmwood Park called Abbiocco."

"So the alderman taking bribes is Striker Farnsworth. That fits. He'd sell his grandmother's dead body if the price was right."

I didn't say anything. It was better to let Janek use his well-developed cop brain to draw his own conclusions, in effect confirming mine.

"I don't know Abbiocco," he said as the server refilled his coffee and brought me a glass of water. "But if any community has held on to the mob mentality, it's those Italian oldsters in Elmwood Park. You can't throw a rock out there and not hit someone who's got mob lineage going back to the old country. These days, mob activity is mostly small stuff. They leave the drug trade to the gangs, but since you said construction, that pay-to-play shit is rampant all over that industry. It's another holdover from when the mafia controlled waste management. And even today, paying 'expediters' to get a building permit approved is basically legal bribery, so at a base level you have the right industry and the right community to be exploring this, even if I don't know enough to help you confirm it."

"And today? Are there any big players? Any recent cases you're aware of?"

"The only new rumble is that the old Italian guard is being pushed out. Like everywhere in Chicago, the ethnic neighborhoods are becoming more diverse, and that puts pressure on the community in all kinds of ways. Elmwood Park has been an Italian bastion for decades, but increasingly it's Polish and Russian. That leads to tension in the community and by extension to the mob. What's left of the Italian mob isn't happy about the Russian mob trying to exert their influence. And the Russians are far more violent. The Italians, well, they're more gentlemanly about their crime. I know it's an odd way to describe criminals, but honor and tradition and family mean something in their history. The Russians are about brute force."

Rae. Rae's words came flooding back. *That Russian.* And the exchange between Felix and Rastello followed right behind. *Before she becomes a problem someone else needs to handle.* He was talking about Rae. Was she in danger, too?

"One of my contacts referenced a Russian and not in a flattering way," I said, not knowing what was appropriate to share with Janek. I didn't have proof of anything, and speculation wasn't going to get me very far, but I also needed his help. "I didn't know what this woman meant or who she was talking about, but what you've told me about the Russian tension could be helpful."

My thoughts swung from Rae to Cai to Selciatto to whatever was going on with that land grab.

"Andrea, listen to me carefully," Janek said, pulling me out of the circles my mind was taking me in. "Don't go after this. You don't know what you're messing with. These guys are a whole new level of mean."

32

"Hey, I got that Morales guy on another payoff!"

Brynn gushed out the words almost before I'd had a chance to register that it was her calling. She sounded like a kid who'd gotten a puppy as a birthday present.

"Spill it! Who did you get?"

"So, I told you that I've gotten chummy with this gal in the Health Department, and she gave me some names of restaurants Morales had inspected. She'd been following The Chicken Shack story and is pretty disgusted with what he's done, allegedly done. Anyway, she's been suspicious of the guy for a while, but after seeing the coverage, she went back through some of his history and gave me three restaurants to check out."

"And did she report any of these to anyone?" Two people having the same story was always better than one, even if they disagreed on some of the details.

"I asked about that. She said she'd gone to her supervisor about Morales before the story broke and got a firm 'stay in your lane' warning. She's an admin, so it's not supposed to be her thing. She tried again after his behavior went public and still got her hands slapped. So she's hesitant to do any more."

Once again, the person who knew the truth had gotten slapped back because it was above their pay grade. "Can she give you any records?"

"So far, she's not willing to go there," Brynn said. "What she was willing to do is to give me names and dates. So I have three restaurants with a history of crappy ratings that suddenly improved at the same time Mr. Morales became their inspector. Since I knew the date he started those assignments, I could print the inspection history for myself. From there I've been working people. And I've found this woman who did bookkeeping for a restaurant in Chinatown as a side hustle. She says she was told to enter a bunch of cash payments as cleaning expenses after she saw the owner take a wad of cash out of the drawer, stuff it in an envelope, and hand it to Morales."

"And she's willing to go on record?"

"She is."

"I gotta say, I've never heard a bribe called 'cleaning.'" I laughed. "Excellent work, Brynn. I'm proud of you. Write it up. I'll be back in the office in half an hour. We can review it together before you get it in to Borkowski."

"Thanks, boss."

When I walked back into Link-Media, I was wishing I'd suffered through some of Janek's greasy diner food while we spoke or at the very least a tasteless fruit cup. I'd skipped breakfast, and lunch was a limp, cold prepared salad I'd picked up at the corner deli. It would need to get me through until tonight. I'd promised Cai I would bring takeout from our favorite Chinese place and keep her company again.

I pulled the plastic container out of the bag, poked at the wilted lettuce, speared a piece of cucumber that tasted sour, then tossed the container into the trash. My hunger wasn't worth risking a bout of food poisoning. I fished a packet of emergency almonds out of my tote bag and opened my computer.

Someone had to be talking about the development project underway at APR. I went back to the APR website, poring over the site inch by inch. Not a word about projects, past or present. Just some stock photos of construction equipment and brawny smiling men with hard hats. It looked like a sample Wix site with the name changed.

Switching back to a browser search on the company, I scanned each link. Surely there was a story somewhere about projects this company had done in the past or a vendor talking about future plans. Page after page, there were links that led to nothing other than yellow-page listings and similar sites that seemed to regurgitate basic data, so I switched to an image search. Company logo. Photos of heavy equipment. Photos with links to buildings that had nothing to do with APR Holdings. I stared at the screen, wondering how a company existed with such a meager digital footprint.

The equipment. A company this small would not own graders and cranes and bulldozers. They would hire a service or rent.

I was back at the construction site near Vogel's property forty-five minutes later. Two men pushed around dirt in the north corner of the first lot while a third was securing a new section of chain-link fence.

I parked alongside the man working the fence and got out of my car. He looked up when I approached, giving me an expression that said, "I don't want what you're selling."

"Hi." I smiled at him, going for the friendly neighbor approach. "I noticed the work going on here the other day. It's nice to see this bit of land being cleaned up. What's going to be built?"

"I don't know. I just hang the fence," the guy said, barely looking up from where he knelt fighting with a bolt.

"So you don't work for the company developing the land?" I asked.

"Nah. I work for the fence company."

"Do you think the other guys know what the project is?"

"Maybe. Eh, Ricardo. This lady wants to talk to you," he yelled across the lot, not to the men running the equipment but to a guy on the street standing next to an enormous pickup truck.

The guy at the truck looked at me quizzically, and I traipsed across the lot through the soft dirt, my shoes sinking in, leaving a path of footprints.

The door to the cab was open, and a stack of plans were lying on the seat. As I approached, he lifted the bandana tied around his neck and wiped the dirt and sweat off of his face.

"What can I do for you, pretty lady?" He smiled in a half-leer kind of way.

He was making my skin crawl already, but men who spoke like this usually had an overly inflated sense of themselves, making them willing to talk, particularly when there was a woman to impress. And I wasn't above a tiny bit of flirting if it helped my case.

"I've seen all the work going on here, and I was curious about what's coming. All the neighbors are speculating. I've been guessing it's a new housing development. Am I right?" I smiled sweetly, feeling the wet dirt that had sunk into my shoes and my stomach sour a little with my fakeness.

"I'm not supposed to say, but you look pretty harmless, beyond being a heartbreaker, that is."

His leery smile was back, and I had to force myself not to walk away.

"I'm just a curious citizen. Nothing to worry about from me," I said, ignoring the rest of his comment.

"You're partially right," he said, his eyes moving below my face. "It's one of those combo things. Mixed-use is the official lingo, where they incorporate shopping and housing and even a grocery store. Seems to be what some people want these days. That faux lifestyle community thing where you can walk out the door and get takeout anytime you want without having to drive. Even groceries right on the premises. It's not my thing, but lots of people like that." He was trying to impress me with his knowledge of the real estate jargon. It made me wish I'd sent my sister, Lane, over here to talk to these guys. It would have been fun to watch her school the guy in real estate lingo.

"That will be really good for this area," I said. "As long as the housing is affordable. Do you know what the target date is for completion? It looks like you're just getting started." I was trying to keep him talking, but I couldn't yet tell if he worked for APR Holdings or was one of the subs.

"This is a few years out, I'd guess. We're just clearing one lot at a time until all the official approval comes through. You know how city government is, takes forever as idiots in suits debate and ask for studies."

"One lot at a time. That must complicate your work. It sounds like a slow process," I said, wondering why any developer would choose the slow, expensive route to clearing land, unless this was an attempt to work around the bigger issues of permits and zoning.

"They pay me to take it down to bare dirt. Don't make no difference to me if it takes five days or five years. I get paid regardless. The schedule is someone else's headache."

"Oh, I thought you were the project manager or something. You don't work for the developer?" Flattery was another underestimated tool in the journalistic tool box. I didn't have to like the fakery to know it was useful.

"Hell no, I'm not a corporate guy. I'm an entrepreneur. I got two crews, and we do basic excavating. I stick to what I know, make my own schedule. That's the way I like to work. The bigger guys can take on the headaches. I don't need that."

"That's smart. Independence is the way to go. It looks like you have plans for the project," I said, nodding toward the bundle of paper on the seat. "Any chance I could take a quick look?" I smiled, hoping his ego would take over from there.

"Sure, what the hell, but it's our secret."

He stepped over to the roll of documents, and I joined him. I ran my eyes over the cover page, looking for names and a project description. Noticeably absent was the permit approval stamp. These were unapproved draft plans.

I reached over and flipped through the following pages, trying to get a sense of the scope of the project. Unrolling the stack, I saw the master plan for the site. Color-coded blocks indicated the planned use for the various structures. A U-shaped mall around a central courtyard was the core element. A handful of freestanding buildings faced the primary roadways, and a row of a dozen townhouses occupied the north end of the landmass. Each section was marked with the planned stage of the construction. The first phase was the outlots. The mall itself was divided into two phases that followed, then the townhouses.

My companion leaned in until his shoulder touched mine. "You need any help reading this? I'm a pro."

I smiled and shimmied away from his arm, then drilled into the fine print. Two familiar names popped out. The Chicken Shack and Abbiocco were both tagged on freestanding structures. No other space held a business name.

Going further into the stack, I scanned pages quickly, looking for names, dates, anything that could shed light on the complexities of the project before this guy shooed me away or pushed me into his truck. A document five sheets in showed the project boundaries as it fit into the community. Belmont Avenue was the dividing line between Belmont Heights and Elmwood Park, yet a grayed-out box extended south of Belmont Avenue into the village boundaries of Elmwood Park. It was labeled Phase Five, single-family homes.

That's why Farnsworth was being bribed.

33

I was on the phone to Peter Retley the minute I was back in my car. Two things stood out to me: work being done to clear the property prior to permitting and the annexing of land inside the village of Elmwood Park. Both were signs that the developers were willing to play fast and loose with the boundary of the law. But I needed someone who understood the process far better than I did.

"Peter, I think you've just become my go-to resource on all things real estate. I have another question. Well, maybe a bunch of questions," I said, wondering what it was going to cost me.

"I'm here for you, Andrea. Whatever you need. Throw it at me."

"As I'm sure you've figured out, there's a story I'm working on that involves a real estate development project. The developer has been acquiring properties within a defined area, attempting to amass one large parcel for future development. One of the complications is that the majority of these properties are not that large, so they need lots of individual transactions in order to have the amount of space they seem to be going for."

"You're talking about this developer you asked about, APR

Holdings, I imagine. To go at a big project piece by piece like that could bring up some interesting zoning challenges, depending on the ultimate goal with the property. RS and RT and RM residential zoning all allow single-family construction. You'd need RM to get a multi-unit dwelling larger than two units. Something mixed-use would need a planned development designation. The degree of complexity depends on what's there now, what they want to do, and who is willing to go along with it. I'm going to assume that if they're trying to acquire a significant amount of land, then the intended use is something they want to change from its current state. Is that correct?"

"I've seen a schematic that shows the future development as mixed-use. The plan is a lifestyle community, so retail, restaurant, housing all combined. However, in the scheme of these types of developments, it's not big."

"Obviously that would potentially be a zoning challenge, depending on the circumstances. And I can't say with any certainty how complicated without knowing more. Location, the alderman, how it fits into the current landscape of the area. There is a whole host of complexities to getting approval for a project like that. It's also very time-consuming even for small developments. Chicago's zoning board is notoriously slow. There would also need to be public hearings allowing the community to discuss and weigh in with their views. Traffic patterns need to be studied. Environmental impact needs to be studied. If this project displaces low-income people, accommodations would need to be made. Then there is the whole issue of possibly needing to pay people to relocate. Not everyone is excited to move."

Without knowing it, Peter had already identified one of the major obstacles, Nathan Vogel.

"From what I can tell, it's very early in the process, as far as approval and permitting and all the logistical details of involving city government. What the developer has been able to do is to acquire a good chunk the land, or if not directly, interested parties have purchased. There is one significant holdout challenging the developer. He owns a couple of acres that are critically located."

"In other words, he's the developer's worst nightmare," Peter said with a chuckle.

I imagined he had a long list of stories he could tell on that subject.

"As I said, this developer seems to be operating outside of the view of the city for now. I've seen the plans. But I don't think they have even begun to approach the city. Here's my first question. As far as I can tell, no zoning or permitting work has been done yet; the developer has been acquiring individual parcels. Small parcels where a rickety old home was demolished. Or lots that were already largely vacant. What they've started to do is to go and make a first pass at leveling the land, but one parcel at a time."

"So they are trying to build the quilt by sliding one square into place, pretending that these are individual situations, not a grand master plan. Am I understanding that correctly?"

"That's exactly what it appears they're doing. Is there anything illegal about that?"

"Wow, that's a new one." He paused, contemplating the maneuver. "It's not illegal as long as they have what they need on this individual lot, but eventually they'll need to involve the city, and that tactic will be viewed, appropriately so, as sneaky and manipulative."

"I don't know for certain, but it seems to me that clearing land in this kind of patchwork method would be far more costly than demolishing everything and clearing the land in one fell swoop. So why would they be taking the slow, expensive route?"

"And you'd be right. The only thing that makes sense to me

is that by taking these lots down to the dirt, they are gambling that when it comes time to involve the city, it's an easier sell. If you have a habitable home on a property, some will argue with that. No one likes to destroy housing, particularly if the optics include displacing people or having to address income disparities. So the calculation is, this is nothing but dirt and the extra expense is worth it if it makes the approval process smoother. Communities don't like empty lots, particularly when they're large. And this developer APR Holdings is the group you're talking about?"

"Yes, but I can't find much information about them."

"As I told you, I've never heard of them, but I can ask around."

"That would be helpful. One more issue. The bulk of the planned development falls largely within the city of Chicago, but the last phase of the development includes single-family homes within the boundaries of the Village of Elmwood Park. Since there are two overlapping government entities involved, how would that work?"

This is the part that connected Farnsworth to the project. But I didn't know what influence he could have since the bulk of the development was within Chicago city limits.

"The developer would have to parallel process both parts. Elmwood Park would deal with the question of the changed land use for the area involved. The city of Chicago would do the same on the larger parcel. What would be helpful to know is how important it is to get both parts approved. I would imagine there is no project if the larger portion can't move forward. But is the phase within the village boundaries simply icing on the cake or crucial to its success."

"I don't know if the Elmwood Park phase is crucial, but I do know it has fewer obstacles to approval, if you get my drift."

"Your drift is clear. And I'd say you have an interesting situation on your hands. Developers are not typically a warm and fuzzy bunch, so kicking a few old people out of their homes doesn't make them shed a tear. However, not getting what they want brings out the ugly side of that beast. You'll have to tell me the details when you can, because I'm suddenly very curious about what you're working on."

An hour and a half later, I stepped into Cai's elevator with a leaky brown bag and smelling of Kung Pao chicken. Her door staff knew me on sight at this point, but I was pleased to see Cai was still asking for all visitors to be announced. No sense paying for a doorman building if you weren't going to use them when you needed them.

Her condo was a gorgeous twentieth-floor unit facing the lake with a balcony that ran end to end. Normally, her door would have been unlocked and opened if she was expecting me. I rapped lightly on the solid wood, hearing the click of the deadbolt before the door swung open.

She gave me a small smile and stepped aside. Her face had lost its normal spark, as if all confidence had left her. She hadn't resorted to sweats and a ratty tee, but her hair was pulled back, her only makeup mascara, and she wore the rarest of her attire, jeans. I set the bag on the marble floor of the foyer and wrapped my arms around her shoulders. We stood there feeling each other breathe and sharing love for each other that did not need words.

"I hope that's from Lao Peng You," she said.

"Under the circumstances, would I bring anything else? And I over-ordered so you would have leftovers. Since I know there is nothing in your fridge other than lemons, bubbly water, and wine. Or have you already loaded up via Instacart?"

"You know me, I know every takeout menu in a twenty-block radius. I won't starve. I will get bored, but hungry, I will not. Come on in."

I picked up the bag, holding the bottom in case whatever was leaking inside dripped onto the floor as I made my way to the kitchen. I knew Cai's apartment as well as I knew my own, having spent countless hours here over the years. I pulled out plates while Cai opened the wine. We set up our meal on the tulip table next to the windows in her kitchen. Brown paper boxes of noodles and dumplings and rice and a full selection of entrees filled the surface. The scent of garlic and hoisin sauce filled the air, making me even more ravenous.

"I know Vermentino is not the ideal pairing with this feast," Cai said, "but you know I don't do beer."

"Well, we can drink whatever the hell we want." I looked at the label. "I remember this vineyard from another time I was here. I've been meaning to ask you what it was."

We clinked our glasses and took a sip, sitting with the silence as we both loaded an array of goodies onto our plates.

"How did you do today? Were you able to coordinate a story with Richard?"

"Yes, I finally got to talk to him around two o'clock. We decided on some story that I need focused attention on a case, so I decided to work from home. Partially true, I guess. I've been in touch with clients that can be put off for a while, saying don't worry, I just need a little reprioritizing. They haven't been forgotten. Anything urgent I'm working with my paralegals, letting them be more involved so we can tag team. And I am not taking any new clients at the moment. Again, I'll make do, but I sure hope this doesn't extend for too long. The longer it goes on, the harder it is going to be to rearrange schedules. I have two trials later this month that I really don't have an option to delay. So, get on that for me, will ya?"

"I'm working on it, I promise. Can we talk about Mr. Vogel's case?"

She nodded, and I took a pad of paper and pencil out of my bag.

"When did you start working with him?"

"Let's see, it's September now. I think he first approached me in March. The developer's attorney had been hitting him up about selling for about a year at that point. Sending over lovely letters indicating how happy they would be to give him a whole bunch of money if he would only sell his property. Vogel had largely been ignoring the outreach but still had all the letters, and each time he was contacted, the dollar amount they were offering increased. The first letter was simply, hey, I'd like to buy your property. You know the kind, where it's a basic sales blast titled *Dear Sir* and given to anybody on the mailing list the company has purchased. No different from how Realtors cruise for business by sending out Dear Resident postcards, hoping the very meager odds will land them a couple of hot leads. You and I would never respond to a solicitation like that, but it's cheap and therefore the entry-level marketing step for businesses who are lazy."

"When did the letters to Vogel start including a purchase price?"

"If my memory is correct, it was correspondence number three. They continued to reach out to him, upping the offer by about fifty grand each time. When that had no effect, Mr. Vogel started receiving voicemails. He didn't respond to those either. Not long before contacting me, the tone of the communication changed. Clearly this developer was getting frustrated and started trying to intimidate him. Well, Vogel isn't exactly a guy who puts up with bullshit, so one day he answered one of those phone calls and basically told the attorney to go fuck himself. That's when the threats of removing his road access went from vague threats to legal action, so Vogel had no choice but to engage, but clearly for very different reasons."

"It seems like a really weak legal argument. No judge is going to agree to take away man's right-of-way to his property."

"I agree. But I don't think that's the point. The property lines were drawn decades ago, and technically it's messy, but I think at this point they're just trying to wear the man down or bankrupt him. And this attorney on the APR side couldn't punch his weight out of a paper bag. Like I said, they don't have a shot of winning the case. Their only shot is Vogel giving up. And this judge situation isn't helping anything."

"I imagine it will take a little time for the case to be reassigned now that Atkinson is dead. Vogel can't be happy about that."

"Well, I'm sure opposing counsel is happy. They've been trying to get this case reassigned to another judge for the last three months."

34

Panici had gotten one judge removed in his divorce, and APR had tried to remove Atkinson. Coincidence or strategy?

I stood outside the judicial coordinator's office thinking about Cai's revelation that APR had been attempting to have Atkinson removed from the case. Cai's understanding of their argument was that Atkinson was biased. Apparently, a prior case where Atkinson had ruled against the attorney had been used as evidence. A negative ruling was hardly adequate grounds to toss a case to someone else, and the argument had been dismissed promptly by the chief judge.

The question now, as I considered the situation, was had they tried to remove Atkinson because the attorney was an idiot, or was this part of a bigger strategy that I didn't yet understand? It was quite clear that this attorney wasn't exactly Harvard Law material, but that could be because the plaintiff was cheap or it could be by design. Inept attorneys who didn't know the game, who chomped at the bit to get cases that ranked higher in prestige, deluding themselves into thinking this was their big shot. Then drowning in work well beyond their pay grade, they were used as pawns so their fumbling could serve as delay. Or, his dumb mistakes could be used as part of an appeal if the process didn't go your way. Although, it would take a client that didn't mind risk to take that chance, because the strategy could easily backfire.

In this case, the choice of wet-behind-the-ears attorney in over his head felt like a delay tactic, as did the effort to switch judges.

As I walked into the coordinator's office, Tiana Williams looked up from her computer screen and waved at me across the room, motioning me in. This was my third trip into her office, and I had already become a familiar face.

"Anything new?" she said when I reached her desk.

"There is some progress, but nothing that I can talk to you about yet. I promise I'm doing everything I can to find out who killed Judge Reynolds and why."

"I know you are. I could see the intensity in your eyes the moment we met. I just wish it would be faster. It feels like every day we don't have an answer, we get further away from finding out the truth. I know it hasn't been that long, really, but each day seems like a week. I just have to keep telling myself investigations take time and the right people are working on it. Did you have a question for me?" She looked at me expectantly, anxious to help if she could.

"Actually, I was wondering if I could speak to Justine, the woman you introduced me to, the one from Judge Atkinson's office."

"I think she's in the file room right now, so hang tight for just a minute."

Tiana stood to go retrieve Justine when the woman exited a back hallway. She smiled brightly when she saw me and walked over.

"Do you have some news?" she asked with the same hopeful tone Tiana had used.

"As I just told Tiana, there are some developments, but nothing appropriate to talk about yet. But I have some questions for you, if you wouldn't mind."

"If there's anything I can do to help figure out who killed Judge Atkinson, I'm happy to do it. What would you like to know?" She swung the stack of file folders she had in her arms to the desktop and pulled over an additional chair.

Justine and I sat on the side of Tiana's desk where framed photos of two young children carried the label *World's Best Grandma*.

"I understand there was an open case before Judge Atkinson involving a company called APR Holdings," I began. "The attorney representing APR was named Stephan Bruni, and the defendant was a Nathan Vogel. Do you recall the case? It involved a right-of-way dispute involving access to Mr. Vogel's home."

"Yes, I remember the case, largely because there was so much rescheduling. Nothing bothered Judge Atkinson more than when lawyers kept going rounds over petty legal points. Especially when he thought it was nothing more than a delay tactic."

"Did he say something to you about this attorney intentionally delaying the case?" I asked, wondering how obvious the ploy had been.

"He did. As I told you the other day, he had no patience for that kind of thing. Attorneys who came in all puffed up with bravado really irked him. The plaintiff's attorney, Bruni, he repeatedly had all kinds of mistakes in his filings. Things that he would correct and resubmit after Judge Atkinson told him to get his act together. He'd fix the problem, then a week later there would be another request to push the deadline back or reschedule the conference hearing. His motions for continuance just didn't end. Atkinson thought the guy was either trying to rack up billing hours or he was intentionally delaying. And it was particularly annoying to him because he thought their legal argument was weak. I probably shouldn't say that, but the man is dead now, so I guess it doesn't hurt."

"Had this attorney been in Judge Atkinson's court prior to this case?"

"I'd have to look that up," she said. "But it sounds familiar."

Tiana scooted out of the way, letting Justine have access to her computer.

"Here it is. That was about three years ago, and the case was also a real estate issue." She scanned the screen before continuing. "The ruling did not go in attorney Bruni's favor. Well, his client's favor would be more accurate. Judge Atkinson wasn't a patient man, and the judgment was pretty harsh. He stopped short of calling Bruni incompetent, as that would have given him cause to appeal, but that's what he said without saying it, if you know what I mean."

I knew exactly what she meant. There was little worse for an attorney than a scathing ruling in which the judge felt the need to wax poetic on the ridiculousness of your argument. It had never happened to me, but I'd had the pleasure of reading a few that blasted my opponents.

"And you said that case was a real estate situation. By any chance, was the plaintiff in that case also APR holdings?"

"Yes, as a matter of fact, it was. And now that I think about it, it was that prior ruling they used to try to have Judge Atkinson removed from this recent case, arguing that he was biased against them, given the nature of his response. It was all ridiculous, of course. Some attorneys will try anything, no matter how outrageous, if they think it helps them win."

From my own legal history, I knew the process for having a

judge reassigned involved bumping the case up to the next level. The chief judge would review and make a determination. Occasionally, if a judge thought his involvement in the case muddied the waters to such a degree that both sides wondered if anyone could be fair, the judge would step aside voluntarily. But typically that would involve a highly contentious, emotion-filled lawsuit. This wasn't in the scheme of things, so I wasn't surprised that the chief judge had denied the request. However, if Bruni wanted to make this an issue, it sounded like he was willing to scream loud enough to get some attention.

My question regarding APR's strategy was still not being answered. Yes, delay was part of the intended result, but was there something more? I was having a hard time imagining a company savvy enough to develop real estate not being savvy enough to hire an attorney that would help them win. Unless delay was the win. Or when they realized delay wasn't having the effect they wanted, that's when they moved to trying for a different judge. Perhaps a more sympathetic judge.

"Do you remember when the request to replace Judge Atkinson was made?"

"Let me think. I believe the original filing was last March, and the request to change judges happened at some point in June. It was denied almost immediately. But the plaintiff came at it again, I'd say, a month later. So, late July, early August."

My mind ran through the timeline.

"Could I get the case number on the original case?"

Justine went back to Tiana's computer again and tapped at the keys. She scribbled the number on a Post-it and handed it to me.

"If the request for a new judge had been approved, who would've been assigned to the case?"

"My guess is it would have been Judge Grishin. He has a lot

of history with real estate cases. I think he was a real estate attorney prior to becoming a judge."

I tucked the note in my bag, thanked the ladies, and told them I would call them with any big news as soon as I was able. After leaving the court building, I crossed the street and headed into City Hall, straight for the zoning department.

"Hi," I said to the gal at the desk. She looked up from her paperwork and gave me a blank stare, waiting for the ask, I assumed. "I have a question about a property in my neighborhood. It used to be a gas station. It's been vacant for at least five years, and I see that the new owner seems to be preparing for some kind of construction. I'm really worried about the chemicals. You know they store those tanks underground, so if they start tearing up that blacktop, I'm worried that there might still be gas in the tank or that gas might have leached into the dirt. If I give you the parcel number, is it possible for you to look up whether permits have been properly pulled?"

"I can search by the address," she said. "Actually, anyone can. The city of Chicago maintains a database of all building permits issued in the city. You need the address or the permit number. And then you enter a date range. Just give me a second and I can pull that up for you."

I scribbled the address on the scratch paper on the desk and slid it her way. A moment later, she looked up.

"Well, I don't see any permits in the system for that address. I broadened the search to the last five years, and there's nothing here. It sounds like you're right to be concerned, however. There are very strict guidelines regarding removal and abatement of gas and oil. Like asbestos, it requires specialized contractors for the cleanup before anything new can be built."

"And who would I contact if I start seeing someone working?"

"You can call 311 and file a report, or you can do it online on the city website."

"Can you check one more address for me while you have that screen open?" I jotted down the address of the empty lot currently being graded.

"I do find a permit on that address. The permit was issued in July to raze a garage on the lot."

"And does your system indicate who requested the permit?"

"The permit was issued to Rae Panici."

35

Rae was deep in this mess too.

I ordered an extra-large Earl Grey and parked myself at a table in Intelligentsia, then pulled my iPad out of my bag. Pulling open the Cook County Assessor's Office website, I entered the parcel number of the lot I had inquired about. The lot I had seen being cleared. Felix Panici's name was listed as property owner. Which meant Felix owned this lot as well, and Rae had pulled the permits. If she was complicit in this development project, that could explain the hesitation she'd shown in her divorce. I had a feeling neither one of them had disclosed the properties as assets to the court.

Armed with a case number for the early APR lawsuit Bruni had lost spectacularly, I typed the information into the court database and pulled up the history. Castillo Imports, LLC v. APR Holdings, LLC. The suit involved a claim over shoddy workmanship. Castillo Imports alleged APR knowingly failed to install appropriate roofing underlayment as a cost-cutting measure, resulting in leaks and damage to the interior of the warehouse and the property Castillo Imports stored in the building APR built.

The legal ping-pong on the case was a staggering display of two parties with egos the size of the Grand Canyon. Once again, attorney Bruni displayed his naïveté and ineptitude, essentially arguing that APR had no knowledge that their roofing contractor had basically installed a plastic drop cloth versus a proper waterproof membrane under the coating material. In other words, he played the blame game. Naturally, Atkinson held APR responsible for supervision of their subcontractors, stating that they were free to file suit against the roofing subcontractor if that were the case. In the meantime, the new owner suffered a loss, and APR was ordered to pay a restitution of nearly $800,000. Of course, the case was further complicated by the pass-the-buck policy built in to all insurance companies, but bad insurance company practices were a subject of a different story.

Bruni's legal filings were a jumbled mess not fitting a third-year law student. It was no surprise that Atkinson quickly lost patience with the charade. If he could've gotten away with telling Bruni to go back to law school in his ruling, he would have.

Again, why had APR hired this incompetent wet-behind-the-ears attorney?

Opening a browser, I did a quick search for Castillo Imports. The business was still located in the warehouse identified in the legal filings. They ran a wholesale outfit that distributed gift items imported from Mexico. I jotted down the address, grabbed my tea, and headed for my car.

The warehouse was situated on a stretch of North Halstead that was a spotty mix of small industrial units, residential three-flats with questionable safety standards, and empty lots openly recruiting development. Set back from the street, the brick structure's main attribute was a huge three-bay garage with rolling metal doors. A sign indicated the office was behind a beige metal door on the right past the garage area. I pulled up to the office door and parked.

As I entered, I found a woman stationed at a utilitarian metal desk likely rescued from a liquidation sale. She looked up from her phone as I walked in, but didn't say anything. A large whiteboard on the wall behind her listed dates and order numbers. A shipping schedule, I assumed. Like most warehouses, the decor was minimal, functional, and cheap. A smattering of their wares sat collecting dust on top of cabinets.

"Hi, I was wondering if Mr. Castillo was available?" I said as she ended her call.

"And who are you?" Her eyes said the next part, *And why should I care?*

It was a look I'd seen many a time before. Hell, it was a look I'd given many a time. The look reserved for people assumed to be selling something no one wanted.

"I'm a reporter with Link-Media. I'd like to speak to Mr. Castillo about a story I'm working on. Tell him it involves APR Holdings."

May as well lead with the thing that would get his attention. She picked up the phone. Then a moment later, instructed me to go through the door to our left.

A man in his fifties wearing a polo shirt embroidered with the company logo walked toward me. Rows of orange industrial shelving ran from front to back. Each shelf was stacked with dozens of small boxes, all labeled and tagged. Huge fans near the twenty-foot ceiling blew air across the space. A handful of workers with clipboards and carts pulled product for associated sales orders.

"Mr. Castillo?"

He smiled at me brightly and extended his hand. "Yes, call me Marcus. How can I help you?"

"My name is Andrea Kellner. I'm a reporter with Link-Media.

I was wondering if I could talk to you about your legal situation with APR Holdings a few years ago."

"What have they done now?" His face held a mix of sarcasm and disgust.

"I'm already getting the impression you don't trust them." There was no reason to tell the man any of my suspicions, but APR Holdings did not have an ally in this man.

"No, I don't, and for good reason," he said. "These people have lied to me from the moment we started down our path together. I don't imagine they've changed. Besides, why else would a reporter care about an old case unless it was tied to something new?"

"I've read the filings, so I'm up-to-date on the basics of what happened. First off, the judgment was in your favor. Did APR pay up?"

"Eventually, but not until I threatened to drag them back into court. And when they did pay, they shorted me four thousand dollars. It wasn't worth the legal hassle of going back into court for that amount of money. No doubt they knew that and thought they could get away with it. I could have come after them and asked to be awarded legal fees, too, but at that point, I just wanted to be done with it. I was in the middle of repairing this place and replacing my inventory. It took me months to regroup. And I lost a lot of clients. Small retailers use distributors like mine because we hold inventory, we ship fast, and the minimum orders are small. Having my attention diverted for four grand was a waste of time, although it would have been fun to win twice."

"Other than APR's attorney, who did you have contact with from APR?"

"They trotted out a guy who was the project manager for this development. And we had the roofing contractor. The project manager blamed the roofing guy. The roofing guy said he did what the manager told him to. It was a circus."

"So only the project manager, not the owner or anybody from upper management?"

"I think we deposed the owner, but it's been a few years, so I might have to look back at my files on that to be sure. When I took this place, I worked with a Realtor, not the company. It was pre-construction."

"Do you remember the name of the project manager or the owner?"

"Not off the top of my head. Like I said, I have that in my notes, but I'd have to look for it."

"If you wouldn't mind looking for that information, I'd sure appreciate it. They seem to be working hard to stay off the radar." I handed him my card. "Feel free to text me."

"Sure. If I find it, I'll send it to you. People should know what they're getting into with this company. But I think the project manager isn't with them anymore. When they weren't paying up promptly, my attorney reached out to the company and was told the guy was gone."

"I'd still be interested in his name," I said.

"I'll send it." He paused. "I'm not sure if I should say this, since we never had proof, but while we were going through all this mess, my attorney said he believed APR tried to bribe the judge. Again, I don't remember the details of why he suspected bribery. I think there was something about an email sent in error. We certainly had a conversation about it. It was at the end of the case, and whoever investigates judges for corruption was just starting to look into it. We had to decide if we wanted to continue the suit or start over with a new judge. I chose to proceed. Had I lost and the judge turned out to have been on the take, I would have been able to have the ruling dismissed and the case retried, so I went forward."

"Do you know how that allegation played out?"

"My understanding is that no one could prove anything. The APR email was argued to be misconstrued, and they found no evidence the judge received any money. My case was also long over by that point, so although it was nerve-racking, it didn't ultimately yield anything."

But it did suggest APR Holdings was willing to tip the scales on an outcome.

36

———

"Where are you?"

Cai's voice had a pleading push, as if she were desperately hoping I was in the coffee shop downstairs.

"I'm in the car on the north side, heading back toward downtown now. What's wrong?"

"He's at it again. This Twitter guy. Can you come over?"

"I'll be there in twenty minutes."

My mind racing, I turned east on Irving Park Road to get to The Drive and sprinted south as quickly as traffic allowed me, feeling my blood pressure skyrocket with each mile. Rushing into Cai's building, I paced impatiently at the desk while the doorman called upstairs.

"What happened?" I shot the question at Cai the minute she opened her door.

Her face was pale and her eyes tense with a level of worry I hadn't seen in her before. There was almost a sense about her that whatever was going to happen was something she couldn't stop.

"Come on in, I'll show you."

I followed her into her living room where a glorious blue sky and the even bluer water of Lake Michigan contrasted with the mood of the room. We sat on the sofa, and she picked up her phone, tapping the screen a few times before handing it to me.

Zipsdefender. His account page listed at least a dozen tweets over the past two hours. *Corrupt attorneys need to know their place. Nothing will end well for those who overstepped their bounds. I'm watching your every move!*

He had released another flurry of tweets, some tagging Cai, others ranting at the general unfairness of the court system. This tranche, unlike the previous, was bringing his venom directly to Cai and to the Cook County court system. Neither Elmwood Park nor Farnsworth had made the cut.

"What do I do?" Cai asked, her face searching mine. "I keep thinking about the way Reynolds was gunned down right before our eyes. I can't get those pictures out of my head."

My mind was in the same place, but I didn't dare admit that to her. She was frightened and, by the look in her eyes, already feeling trapped.

"First of all, keep doing exactly what you're doing and stay right here," I said, trying to steady my voice as my own fear clutched my chest.

"For how long? I can't live my life waiting for some random creep to come after me. What am I supposed to do, hide indefinitely? Start carrying a gun? Hire a bodyguard? I don't want to live like that. I can't work like that, Andrea. I can't hold a job like that. My clients aren't going to understand. Neither is my boss."

I didn't know what to tell her. As much as I wanted to promise that Zipsdefender was not dangerous or that I could find him or stop him before he did something awful, I'd be lying if I did. Anything I said to try to assure her she had nothing to worry about would sound like a weak attempt to placate her. And it would be.

"I promise I'm doing everything I can to figure this out," I said, choosing the only words that were appropriate, honesty. "I'm making progress, but I'm not there yet. I know it's hard to be patient when this guy is coming at you, but you're safe here."

"Safe? I'm a prisoner. I jump every time I hear someone in the hall. Every time the phone rings. I'm afraid to sleep, thinking there is someone on my balcony. It's insane, of course. No one is playing Spider-Man, trying to swing down from the top of a forty-story building to get at me. But I can't shut it off. I don't know what's happening to me."

She closed her eyes and tilted her head up to the ceiling, letting out a breath.

"Look, I still think Panici is behind this account. Can I prove it? Not yet, but I'm trying. I know you have the front desk trained to call you before anyone is allowed upstairs. I'm going to suggest that you give them a picture of Panici and ask them to call the police if he shows up."

She shook her head.

"On what grounds?" she said. "He hasn't threatened me directly. There is no restraining order. Hell, we couldn't even get Michael to look into this. Why would CPD do anything?"

Her reference to Michael stung. I hadn't even been able to convince my own boyfriend, if he was still my boyfriend, of the legitimacy of the threat. I was letting Cai down. I was letting myself down. And if anything happened, it would be on me.

"True," I said. "There is nothing on record that proves Panici is a danger to you. But CPD won't know that until after they get here. If you feel threatened, make the call, sort out the legitimacy of the threat later. It creates an obstacle, and sometime that's enough. Panici has no legitimate reason to know where you live or to show up at your home, so if he does, he's proving he's involved. It's not much consolation, but if he shows up, assume he's a threat and act accordingly."

I'd never seen her without that internal fight, the one that said, "I can do anything, just watch me."

"Screenshot those tweets and send them to me," I said. "Don't let anyone come to your door that you don't know, not even food delivery. The staff can bring it up and leave it outside your door. I'm going to go back to the office, and I'll figure this out. I'll get some big, muscley guy over here if you want him. Just say the word. Please stay put."

I could hear the pleading in my own voice. The conflict of fear and frustration weighed heavy in her, and I worried that frustration would overshadow caution.

"I'll check in later. I know it feels like nothing's happening, but there is. I promise."

I leaned over and gave her a hug. She gripped my shoulders, and we sat, both scared and uncertain and hoping to hell I could fix this.

I stood, gathered my bag, and headed for the door, holding back my tears until I heard her click the deadbolt behind me.

Damn Panici! Damn Rastello! Damn Gaetano! Damn Michael!

I flew back into my office at Link-Media, my mind blinded to anything other than trying to stop Cai from being hurt. Whatever it took, I had to make sure she was okay.

A bottle of lukewarm Pellegrino in hand, I stared at my wall, desperate for a connection I wasn't seeing, a detail I'd missed, a name, a place, anything that would break through and help me find the next piece of this puzzle. I was confident I had connected the men, all of them, and I knew they were not above bribery to get what they wanted. But would they kill to get what they wanted? That was an entirely new level of evil. And what was it they really wanted?

I stared at Panici's picture. He was mean and narcissistic and capable of revenge. But he wasn't the trigger man. Instinct told me pros had done the dirty work for him. The other missing element was motive. The APR Holdings development had made money for the early buyers when they flipped. APR would make money as the project developed, and both The Chicken Shack and Abbiocco would have an additional location, but was any of this worth killing for?

"You still working on that art project?"

Borkowski was at my door, giving me one of his "Are you doing any work?" looks. He wore his uniform of white button-down and khakis, but a dribble of old coffee trailed down alongside his tie.

"It's a story, Art. A big one. Cut the shit already. Somewhere in here is the answer to why two judges have been murdered, why my friend is being threatened by some Twitter creep who calls himself *Zipsdefender*, why a real estate developer and a construction company are trying to bribe judges and an alderman, and why a chicken joint and a pizzeria are in the center of it all."

I let loose on him, unable to hold back. My worry about Cai and my frustration over not being able to see the missing links spilled out in a torrent. I had no patience for his condescending snark today.

He stared at me for a moment, eyebrows raised. "Well, then, let's get on it. What is known? An alderman taking a bribe is a given. They all are. It's just a question of which one this time."

"I know the players, at least most of them, I think," I said. "Striker Farnsworth is the alderman in question. No surprise there, but as you say, it's just a matter or degrees. They can all be purchased. Other parties include people in the construction industry. I've got a real estate development project in the mix that is playing fast and loose with permitting, trying to alter zoning, and it all ties back to The Chicken Shack guy, too."

"All right. Those are threads worth exploring. What are the holes in the story?"

"Motive. No direct evidence. And I don't know who this Zips-defender guy is."

"Motive, in this case, is likely greed or power, so who has the most to gain from the death of some judges? The guys developing the project, I imagine. And I'm sure they are at the top of your list. The question is whether this is coordinated or an individual going off the rails."

"A number of people gain from this, so I'm thinking coordinated. Or at least condoned by others, even if they weren't complicit in the murders directly. If I had a better idea of how much money was at stake, I'd feel more comfortable with that theory."

"You have substantial holes, but I can help with one part. The tweeter guy is clearly Italian."

"How do you know that?"

"*Zips*. It's an old mobster slur. The established Italian mobsters described the new Sicilian immigrants as 'Zips' when they came into the country. They didn't understand their speech pattern and thought it zipped by. The new arrivals were thought of as hicks and looked down upon. So this Twitter guy is saying he's a defender of Sicilian hicks."

"That makes sense, given the players. This guy also uses the phrase 'keeper of the keys' in his profile. Any thoughts?"

"I'd say he thinks he's the gatekeeper. All roads lead to him."

37

Gatekeeper. The son of a bitch thought all roads led to him. Did they?

"You still with me?" Brynn said. "You look like you got lost in a train of thought. Anything you want share?"

I'd called Brynn into my office after Borkowski left. I needed objectivity that I didn't possess right now. I was too close to it. Too filled with fear that something would happen to Cai. Too filled with anger and remorse that Michael seemed to have slipped from my life because I wasn't ready to set my own needs aside for his. Too filled with the convoluted maze of men connected by real estate and greed to see who led the charge.

Borkowski had given me some context on the meaning and history of Zipsdefender, and it played in to this aura of Italian mobsters, but the whole group of them fit that bill. Who was the trigger man? Who did I need to expose to keep Cai safe?

"Sorry, I'm here. Just trying to make sense of something I'm too close to," I said. She looked at me, concern in her eyes, trying to figure out how to help.

"What do you want to talk through? Use me as a sounding board. It might help if we brainstorm."

"That's a good idea. I was thinking about the Twitter handle of the guy coming after Cai, *Zipsdefender.* Borkowski said it has meaning and suggests the guy is Italian. I'm going to take that as a given. The other phrase on his account is 'keeper of the keys.' I think it says the guy is arrogant enough to believe everything goes through him."

"That sounds like your buddy Panici. You described him as a narcissist," she said.

"I think so too. All roads lead to him. In his mind and, it seems to me, in reality. But I can't prove he is the account holder or that he is a threat to Cai."

"We have to go to what we can prove or explore the holes that exist."

"Find what you can on an attorney named Stephan Bruni. I know three things about him. He occasionally represents The Chicken Shack, although he hasn't in the food inspector case; he has represented APR Holdings; and he's not good at his job.

"I'm going to keep working my leads on APR Holdings. I need to know who owns them. Then I'm going to run over to check on Cai, bring her some lunch. She's getting antsy already from the confinement, and I'm afraid she's going to say the hell with it and go to work because she can't stand her own beautiful four walls anymore."

"Can't your friend Michael help out with finding this guy? I don't mean to pry, but he is a cop."

"I won't get into it now, but let's just say he has declined. We have to figure this out on our own."

"Sorry." She looked at me as if watching for my tears to start.

Even without me saying the words, Brynn had figured out that sympathy was something I needed. But not today. My love life would need to stay in the background. We moved to our respective desks and dug in. I started with the old case, the one Bruni had lost so badly. With my legal history and the case number, I knew how to get to the details, so I started there. Going back through the various filings I fleshed out the crazy-making details that Marcus Castillo had only alluded to.

"Hey, that guy Bruni, he's related to Orlando Gaetano." Brynn was at my door, a big smile on her face. "He's Gaetano's brother-in-law. Surprise, right? Graduated in the bottom ten percent of his Western Michigan University class. I'm sure his parents are quite proud."

"That explains a lot. Working for the family is what these people do. In my quick look into his background, it appeared he went straight into private practice out of law school. Can you confirm that?"

"Yes. Obviously I don't have access to his client list, but it wouldn't surprise me if the only clients he's ever had were friends and family. I'll keep at it and let you know if there's anything else. I thought you'd want this right away."

"Thanks, Brynn."

And I imagined her "friends and family" client list was exactly right. These guys were incestuous in their business dealings.

I had just turned back to my computer screen when a text popped up.

"Hey, Andrea! It's Marcus Castillo. I found that name for you. The guy who runs APR. I was right, we deposed him in the case. His name is Edmund Rastello."

It was all of them. Every damn one of them was part of this.

38

———————

"What the hell?" I stared at the text.

"Change of plans. No need to stop by for lunch. I've got an emergency hearing at 1:00. I'm going. I can't let these bastards control my life. Don't worry. Talk to you later."

I looked at the time stamp, all thoughts of Bruni and Rastello flying out of my mind. Forty-five minutes ago. Damn! I grabbed my bag and hit the street, flagging the first cab I saw.

Jumping out at Daley Plaza, my eyes scanned the landscape. First for black SUVs with red stickers, then for faces and suspicious body language. How could Cai have put herself on display like this? My heart pounded so loud in my chest that all I could hear was the blood throbbing in my ears. I rushed into the building and through security, stopping halfway through the lobby. What courtroom was she in? She hadn't indicated the case.

Fumbling for my phone, I dialed Cai's office.

"It's Andrea Kellner, Cai Farrell's friend. She left me a message that she had an emergency hearing this afternoon. I need to know what courtroom she's in or what case she came for. Can you put me through to one of her paralegals, please?"

I paced like a caged tiger while I waited to be transferred. I knew Cai was safe inside a courtroom. Security precautions in the building were tight. Metal detectors, cameras, guards. The vulnerability was when she left. The open plaza between the building and the street gave her no protection whatsoever.

"Shannon, do you know where she is?" I shot my question at Cai's paralegal the second I heard her voice come on the line.

"I haven't seen her today. She's been out. There is nothing on her schedule. If there was an emergency hearing, it must have just come up this morning. Is there a problem? You sound worried."

"Can you find out? Can you look at her email? It's urgent that I find her. I'm at the courthouse now. Please look."

"Oh, okay. Give me a minute." I heard the click of the keyboard on the other end of the phone. While she searched, I kept my eyes fixated on the elevator doors, debating whether to guard the elevator, hoping I'd see Cai leave, or barge into every courtroom in the building. The court's public docket database would require more information than I had—the case number, the names of the parties, or the date of the filing.

"Okay, I see the email. This is a case that was reassigned to a new judge recently. Sounds like he's trying to get caught up, and he rushed this through."

"Do you know the room her case is in?" I asked, not hiding my impatience.

"It says room 211, but this isn't her case. She's a witness in Panici v. Panici."

I zoomed upstairs, yanked open the door, and entered the room. Half a dozen heads turned at the sound. Cai was on the stand. She swung her eyes toward me, shook her head and shrugged before bringing her attention back to the court activities. Rae looked at me over her shoulder, apprehension in her eyes, then she shot her gaze at her estranged husband nervously, as if anticipating a reaction.

Again, I wondered whether Rae was at risk, too. She had inside knowledge of her husband's activities. He knew it, and his cohorts knew it. The insurance policy she mentioned might not keep her untouched.

Felix Panici had been mid-rant when I walked in. As I drew his attention, I saw a mix of confusion and mistrust on his face as he tried to assess why I had crashed his party.

"Mr. Panici. Can we get back to the task at hand?" the judge admonished. "You apparently had a lot to say before the interruption."

The judge raised his eyebrows at me, and Panici turned back to his notes. Clearing his throat and fussing with the papers on his table, he attempted to get back into the groove.

"Ms. Farrell, can you explain to the court your process for determining franchise fees?"

"As I've explained previously, to you, Mr. Panici, and to the court via my deposition, I did not personally determine the fee structure of the franchise license. That evaluation was done by a CPA experienced in the franchise market, along with current market data, and brand equity valuation. I advised Mrs. Panici on the legal matters associated with each stage of the process and the eventual franchise contracts. Perhaps your question should be directed elsewhere."

I stifled a smile as Cai made Panici look like a mail clerk who'd never even seen the inside of a law library. His rambling attempt at questions became an infinity scarf of ridiculousness proving nothing other than he had a theory in search of a law. The judge sighed noticeably on several occasions as he urged Panici to get to his point quicker.

Forty minutes later, Cai was released, and the judge called

for a ten-minute break. After stepping down from the stand, Cai huddled with Rae and her attorney for a moment. She gave her client a hug and Felix a smirk. He glared at her like a boyfriend just dumped for someone taller, cuter, and more buff. She kept her smile as she made her way down the aisle toward me.

"Thought I needed a babysitter, did you? I'm still in one piece, Mom."

"You really can be a smartass," I said. "And speaking of mom, dumb move here."

I held my chastising while we removed ourselves from the confines of the courtroom. Stepping into the hallway, I cautiously ran my eyes around the space, looking at faces, looking for someone who seemed not to belong or who seem to have too much attention focused on Cai. I couldn't shake my worry even through Cai's blasé approach to her own safety and the moment. She looked at me, waiting for the lecture like a teenager caught smoking.

"Come on, let's get this over with. I know you have a bunch of stuff to say. But in my defense, it was supposed to be a short hearing, and since you think Panici's a crook, you got a chance to watch him in action. See, I helped out."

"Yeah, and piss-poor logic. You have no idea who might be following you. Who might be waiting for you outside? Who might follow you home? All for one hour of false obligation. How could you take this risk?"

"Look, it's done, and I'm fine. Now I'll just take myself home like a good little girl, okay?"

"That's exactly where you should be."

We walked down the hallway and down the escalator without saying anything. She knew I was irritated, and I knew she was being stubborn. In other words, a typical parent-child impasse. I didn't care if she was mad at me right now; it would pass. The only thing that mattered was getting her the hell out of here and home safely so I could get back to figuring out who the hell was threatening her.

We stepped into the sunlight of Daley Plaza, still quiet, ignoring the surrounding hustle. I scanned the area, then with one hand on Cai's bicep, I pulled her toward the street, raising my arm, hoping to catch the attention of one of the taxis speeding past as we walked.

"Andrea, please. Is this really necessary? I can get myself home."

We were fifteen feet away from the curb and a yellow cab zoomed across two lanes, screeching to a halt in front of us. On my left I saw him moving toward us at a fast clip. His eyes were dark pools of nothing as he came at us. Feeling my breath catch in my throat, I tugged harder on Cai's arm, pushing her toward the cab and staring at the now familiar widow's peak.

Six feet, that was all I needed, when I saw him reach under his jacket. I grabbed Cai and dragged her forward toward the taxi.

As if in slow motion, I saw him hold the gun close to his belt, heard Cai scream, and felt her body fall against me. I went down, Cai on top of me, feeling her blood splash against my face.

Screams. People running. Cars screeching away. And I saw the shooter collapse on the ground just feet away.

"Cai! Cai!" I yelled. Grabbing her shoulders as she lay on top of me, I felt the warm stickiness of her blood as it leached from her body. She lay still, her torso draped across me, but I could feel her breathing, could feel her heart pounding. I wrapped my arms around her, holding her as if she would float away without me anchoring her. Tears blinded me as I lay there listening to people yell for an ambulance.

"Andrea, are you okay?"

I looked up through the fog of my pain to see Michael staring at me, his face a frenzy of worry.

"Are you hurt?" he said again.

"No. Is she dead?" I whimpered.

"Just unconscious. The ambulance is pulling up now. Let me move her so we can see her and see what's going on."

Two EMTs were at my side. Cautiously, they lifted her, moving her to the side and rolling her to her back on the concrete. I stayed on the ground, afraid to look, afraid to move, afraid to hear them tell me the worst, my breath coming in frantic bursts.

"Honey, tell me you are not hurt." Michael knelt next to me, his hand caressing my hair, his voice pleading for me to acknowledge.

"I'm not hurt. Just let me lie here for a while. Is Cai okay?"

"She will be. I'm right here when you're ready to move."

He stood. And I stared at the blank, dead eyes of the man with the widow's peak, Gregori Laskin, as he lay on the ground, a pool of his own blood spreading rapidly around him. His gun was still outfitted with its silencer, just inches from his hand.

39

"You really need to be drinking more water."

I set the tumbler on the coffee table. Then adjusted the pillow behind Cai's head.

"Thanks, Mom." She gave me a weak smile.

She lifted an ice pack up to the bandaged spot on her forehead, looking at me through sleepy, bloodshot eyes. Her left arm was wrapped in gauze and padding and nestled in a sling. Her feet were propped on a pillow on the coffee table, and a stash of pain meds and a blanket and tissues and anything else I could think of to make her comfortable was within easy reach.

Laskin's bullet had passed through her upper arm, nicking bone in the process, but given what could have happened to her, I was overjoyed.

I sat next to her on the sofa, fretting like a mother afraid to take her eyes off her toddler playing next to the swimming pool. Janek watched from the Barcelona chair nearby, his elbows on his knees, ready to jump into action if needed, and Michael mimicked his energy as he stood next to me, still fidgety from the adrenaline, on alert for a moment of wooziness or new danger.

"How did you know to come?" I said to Michael. "How did you know Laskin was the killer?" I looked at him, trying to fill my eyes with every ounce of the gratitude I was feeling.

"I didn't. It just turned out to be very lucky timing." He looked at Cai before continuing. "I've been watching Laskin on another matter. He's implicated in a car fire incident from last year that looks suspiciously planned. A guy burned alive inside the vehicle, and it appears he was zip-tied to the steering wheel. They're trying to pass it off as a weird suicide scenario, but since the victim is alleged to have had an affair with Laskin's wife, that story is doubtful to me."

"Viola."

Michael lifted his brows, seemingly surprised that I knew more than he thought. "We believe Laskin is Russian mafia, and they are a particularly cold-hearted bunch. Janek told me about your conversation, so I upped my surveillance on Laskin. I was following him, and when I saw you and Cai in the Plaza, it clicked and I knew what he was going to do. I just don't understand why he would want Cai dead."

"She was in the way," I said. "What I know at this point is that Laskin is connected to this real estate development company called APR Holdings. You're probably aware that he's the CFO of Selciatto Holdings. Well, the Selciatto crew are also the key players in APR. But they're hiding that underneath layers of complicated ownership structure. Anyway, they've got some major expansion plans. The first part is a project that both Cai and Judge Atkinson were involved with. Although it's the biggest project they've done so far, its real significance was that it was going to be the model for more developments. If they weren't successful with the first, all the others would be in jeopardy."

"That requires serious capital," Janek said.

"Yes, they were working on securing an investor. The

investor's condition was that they use project one as proof of concept. If it worked, then he'd cough up the dough for future developments. Atkinson was taken out because he wouldn't be bought. Apparently, Atkinson had been accused of taking a bribe in the past. He was investigated and found innocent, but it seems they thought they could influence his ruling, but he wouldn't go along with it."

"So they found another solution," Michael said.

"And the likely back-up judge was more sympathetic," I said. "Cai was just another obstacle they wanted out of the way."

"Why didn't they go after Vogel? That would solve the problem too," Cai said.

"I'm not sure. Maybe they didn't have time for the probate hassles or felt they couldn't influence the outcome. Regardless, the trail of bodies is building, so I assume that would be much harder now."

"Where does this Abbiocco come in?" Janek asked.

"Peripherally. It's their clubhouse. The guys associated with Selciatto, Panici, Gaetano, Farnsworth. They're all in on this. The owners of Abbiocco and The Chicken Shack, Orlando Gaetano, were locked in on the developments to expand their restaurant chains. Farnsworth was in to help with a zoning problem. They've all got financial skin in the game."

"They coordinated a hit list to get a real estate deal done. That's cold," Cai said.

"Well, another thing I don't know is whether Laskin acted of his own accord or if this was authorized by the group."

"Laskin going rogue would make sense to me," Michael said. "I'd bet the power struggles inside that little cabal have been intense. And from what I've learned, Laskin was making moves with a few of his Russian cronies to take on some city construction projects. They want a bigger share of that pie. It doesn't sound like Laskin's loyalties were to Selciatto. He may have been angling to edge his employer out of the way."

"What about Judge Reynolds? I don't see how he fits in with this," Janek said.

"Reynolds had a half-a-million-dollar debt to Selciatto. He was about to file for bankruptcy. This is conjecture, but I'm guessing that loan was to pay for some experimental treatments for his wife's cancer. They were visiting a clinic in Mexico. I don't know how Reynolds got connected to Selciatto, unless it was through Panici, or why they thought he needed to die."

"Maybe Laskin was doing a favor for Panici," Cai said.

"Or Laskin was creating a debt to keep Panici in line. Rae was one of the wild cards," I added. "She knows a lot, and she's peripherally involved in the development project."

"Well, I should go," Janek said. "I have a new list of people out in Elmwood Park I need to have a conversation with."

He stood. Gave Cai a light squeeze on the hand and headed toward the door.

"I should join him," Michael said. "Are you staying?"

"I'm not going anywhere until the patient here is sick of me." I smiled and tipped my head toward Cai.

Michael placed his hands on my shoulders, his eyes drilling into mine. "I'm so, so sorry I didn't take you seriously. Can we talk about it later?"

"Yes, I'd like that," I said. In that moment, I knew how much I wanted him back in my life.

He smiled. "I've missed you so much." Then he took my face in his hands and kissed me. Kissed me like he meant it.

DID YOU ENJOY THE BOOK?

Thank you so much for reading THE LIAR'S CODE. I'm truly honored that you've spent your time with me.

Reviews are the most powerful tool in an authors' arsenal for getting awareness of our books to other readers. If you've enjoyed the story, I would be very grateful if you could spend a moment leaving an honest review.

You can leave your review by visiting your retailer of choice or Goodreads.

ACKNOWLEDGMENTS

Writing a novel involves months, sometimes years, of plotting, planning, and fretting over every word, and this book was no different. It also involves the support and dedication of good friends and loyal fans.

My heartfelt thanks to the readers who have stuck with me through this wonderful journey. Your encouragement and kind words are priceless.

To my wonderful editor Kate Schomaker, thank you for your enthusiasm, for tightening my prose, and for your patience with my refusal to learn the proper placement of commas.

To my boys, Alex and Zach, I hope you live dreams of your own.

ABOUT THE AUTHOR

Dana Killion grew up in a small town in northern Wisconsin, reading Nancy Drew and dreaming of living surrounded by tall buildings. A career in the apparel industry satisfied her city living urge and Nancy Drew evolved into Cornwell, Fairstein, and Evanovich.

One day, frustrated that her favorite authors weren't writing fast enough, an insane thought crossed her mind. "Maybe I could write a novel?"

Silly, naïve, downright ludicrous. But she did it. She plotted and planned and got 80,000 words on the page. That manuscript lives permanently in the back of a closet. But the writing bug had bitten.

The Liar's Code is her fifth novel. Dana lives in Tucson with her kitty, Isabel, happily avoiding snow and awaiting her next adventure.

DanaKillion.com

OTHER BOOKS BY THE AUTHOR

GET INFORMATION ON THE NEXT ANDREA KELLNER STORY

Also by Dana Killion

Fatal Choices - a free prequel short story

Lies in High Places - Andrea Kellner Book 1

The Last Lie - Andrea Kellner Book 2

Lies of Men - Andrea Kellner Book 3

Tell Me a Lie - Andrea Kellner Book 4

The Liar's Code - Andrea Kellner Book 5

I love to hear from my readers. Did you have a favorite scene? Have an idea for who I should kill off next? Jot me a note. I occasionally send newsletters with details on the next release, special offers, and other bits of news about the series.

Sign up for my Mailing List at www.danakillion.com